KU-220-982

TWICE HEXED

JULIA TUFFS

Orion

ORION CHILDREN'S BOOKS

First published in Great Britain in 2022
by Hodder & Stoughton

1 3 5 7 9 10 8 6 4 2

Text copyright © Julia Tuffs, 2022

The moral rights of the author have been asserted.

All characters and events in this publication, other than those clearly
in the public domain, are fictitious and any resemblance to
real persons, living or dead, is purely coincidental.

In order to ... ... of real places have been
included in t... ... imaginary
... ...

N... ... reproduced, stored in
a retrieva... ... without
the prior pe... ... circulated
in any for... ... ublished
and v... ... eing

LONDON BOROUGH OF
RICHMOND UPON THAMES

DISCARDED

90710 000 519 684

FROM

Askews & Holts   01-Jul-2022

JF TEENAGE 11-14   RICHMOND UPON THAMES

RTWH

LIBRARY SERVICE

is available from the British Library.

ISBN 978 1 51010 939 1

Typeset in Adobe Caslon Pro by Jouve (UK), Milton Keynes
Printed and bound in Great Britain by Clays Ltd, Elcograf S.p.A.

The paper and board used in this book are made
from wood from responsible sources.

Orion Children's Books
An imprint of
Hachette Children's Group
Part of Hodder & Stoughton Limited
Carmelite House
50 Victoria Embankment
London EC4Y 0DZ

An Hachette UK Company

www.hachette.co.uk
www.hachettechildrens.co.uk

TWICE HEXED

90710 000 519 684

By Julia Tuffs

HEXED
TWICE HEXED

For Huxley and Cooper, the best boys I know

CHAPTER ONE

The first time I saw her was in assembly. The Year Eleven, 'Welcome Back, This Is a Big Year, Be Scared' assembly. I wasn't scared though, I was ready.

Or at least I thought I was.

Turns out I wasn't ready for her.

Five Things About This Year:
1. IT'S GCSE YEAR.
2. IT'S GCSE YEAR.
3. IT'S GCSE YEAR.
4. IT'S GCSE YEAR.
5. IT'S GCSE YEAR and the first year I have actual, real life, decent FRIENDS.

That morning it had felt strange to put the green jumper on again. The green jumper that had been stuffed at the back of my wardrobe and forgotten about for six whole weeks of summer holiday bliss. The green jumper that I'd had to magic-clean this morning (due to having forgotten about it) and which I might have accidentally shrunk slightly. I was still learning.

I'd walked down the hill, rounding the corner on to the seafront, the unusually warm September sun making the sea all gorgeous and twinkly. I had a spring in my step, for, as much as I hated the green jumper, I was actually looking forward to this year. This year which would be so different to last – no new house, no starting a new school and not knowing a soul, no trying to keep myself painfully under the radar, no legion of mean, misogynist boys making my life hell and no freaking out over unexplained powers. I wasn't a pro at the magic yet (as evidenced by the slightly shrunken jumper) but I had definitely improved from six months ago, when my magic had been entry level, to say the least.

I'd been working on my magic over summer – or rather, *we'd* been working on it. *We* being me; my older sister beauty-blogger-extraordinaire Bella; my newly hippied, returned-to-her-roots Mum; and Nonna, the bangle-wearing, aura-reading, all-round megababe Grand High Witch of the family. It was going snail-pace slowly though, with most of our sessions consisting more of health and safety briefings than much actual magic.

Mum and Nonna had decided to break it to me and Bella earlier in the year (six months ago, to be precise) that we were witches. Actually, *decided* isn't quite right; they'd had no choice but to tell us, because moving back to the Isle of Wight had kicked our powers into action. Before we knew it we were accidentally turning frogs purple and making boys' noses grow when they lied. Unsurprisingly, we'd wanted answers.

It had taken us a while to . . . adjust, but Bella and I were now grasping the basics and, very gradually, in ant-sized steps, making progress – though nowhere near as fast as I would have liked. I was aiming for something along the lines of turning water into wine and we weren't even at the turning water into squash end of the scale.

Most trainee witches only get their powers during their periods but it turns out I'm super powerful and have access to mine all the time. In a shocking twist to the tale, Bella, always the A+ student and golden child, ISN'T as powerful as me and only gets her powers when she's on. Which is actually quite annoying and another speed bump on the learning-some-kickass-magic road as Nonna insists that we learn together.

As I neared the school, I heard a booming laugh. Libby.

'Jessieeeeeeee!' she squealed, breaking away from Summer and Tabs and running towards me.

'Libbeeeeeeee!' I squealed back, nearly toppled over by her hug.

'You look different,' she said, looking me up and down.

'You've only been gone three weeks, I can't look that different.'

She squinted at me. 'You look . . . taller? Or does that jumper look smaller?'

'Libby!' Summer chided. She looked me up and down herself, her turquoise-blue eyes shining bright, her golden hair two shades lighter from a summer spent in the sunshine. 'But seriously, Jessie, maybe it's time for some new uniform? It does look a bit . . . small?'

'It shrunk in the wash. It'll stretch by the end of the day,' I said, making a mental note to magic it bigger. 'How was Spain, Libby?'

'Amazing, since you ask, and very hot – in more ways than one, if you know what I mean.' She attempted a wink.

Summer looked at her watch. 'We'd better walk and talk, lads. Don't want to be late on our first day of Year Eleven. You know what it'll be today – serious lectures and stress-inducing exam talk.'

Tabs and I smiled at each other. She was fresh-faced and eager and organised to within an inch of her life, as always. Both of us were looking forward to the challenge.

'So go on then,' I prompted Libby, as we started towards school. 'Hot Spanish love affair details please.'

'I can't do it justice on a walk,' Libby said dramatically. 'I'll tell you later when we have time to go into all the juicy details and you can fully appreciate and marvel at the passion of it all. But the basics are – Spanish boys are *thirsty* and hot and I feasted on a most delightful tapas of—'

'Chorizo?' Summer offered, sniggering.

'Patatas Bravas – spicy!' Tabs added.

'It was definitely spicy,' Libby grinned, her face looking more beautiful and flawless then ever with her perfect tan. 'Anyway, what's been going on here? What did I miss?'

'Oh let's see . . .' Summer said. 'Working in the café, looking after the kids, working in the café, looking after the kids – on a loop basically.'

'No foxy mainland girls or guys over for a summer romance?' Libby asked. 'Get it? A "*Summer*" romance?'

We all groaned.

'Sadly not,' Summer said. 'Even if there had been, I wouldn't have had time. I barely managed to fit in any surfing.'

'It sucks that the café's busiest time is over the summer holidays.' I was still disappointed at having hardly been able to see Summer.

She shrugged. 'Island life.'

4

'And how are you and Le Fredster?' Libby asked, nudging me.

We were closer to school now and entering prime green jumper territory. Clusters of students were feeding in to the main slipstream heading for the gate.

'You're obsessed,' Summer said to Libby. 'One-track mind!'

I appreciated the chance to pause before answering, because, really, I wasn't sure how Freddie and I were. We'd been hanging out a lot over the summer and we'd had some nice times. There was definitely something about having a boyfriend I enjoyed, not least all the kissing – which was a whole new thing for me. I felt sad I'd wasted so many years *not* kissing.

But . . . if I was honest with myself, as lovely as Freddie was, I felt that something had shifted halfway through the summer – like a piece of our puzzle had gone missing. Beyond kissing and watching Kardashian reruns, we didn't seem to have that much to talk about any more. There's only so much discussion that can be had about who the best Kardashian is (Khloe, obvs). And only so much kissing. Though I hadn't reached my limit on that quite yet.

Sometimes I wondered if I was with Freddie just for the kissing, which didn't seem like a great reason to be with someone. We never had any deep and meaningfuls any more – never delved into our hopes and dreams and fears, our families, never discussed our feelings, or our thoughts (beyond aforementioned Kardashian favourites). Had we used up all our deep? Did he regret opening up to me in the first place? I liked Freddie – he was kind and sweet and funny – but he felt a bit impenetrable. Like a hard rock face I couldn't chisel through – a gorgeous, very hot, hard rock face.

'We're fine,' I said, trying to sound perkier than I felt.

Libby glanced at me for a moment too long before deciding not to probe further. 'And Tabs, how's . . . uh, revision?'

In our group, Tabitha and Libby had the least in common – Tabitha being very academic-focused and Libby being very boy-focused. They made it work though.

'It's going OK. I've been working at The Quay as well as revising,' Tabs said, 'though not so many thirsty boys there, more pensioners thirsty for tea.'

Libby linked arms with her, a gleam in her eye. 'Well that sounds dreadfully dull and something we need to sort.' Tabs, quite rightly, looked slightly terrified.

'Here we go then, girls,' Summer said, stopping abruptly in front of the main gate, to groans and tuts from people behind us, who had to swerve to avoid collision. 'This is it. Year Eleven. One more year of the green jumper before the relative freedom of sixth form.'

'Are we ready?' I asked. I felt a wave of joy, standing there with my friends, soaking in the excitement of a new beginning, a fresh start. Everyone nodded. 'Then let's do this,' I said, leading my friends through the gates to our first day of Year Eleven.

***

'In you come, quietly please,' Mr Sampson, our Head of Year boomed, herding us all into the hall for assembly. No one was taking any notice of him.

I shuffled along in my form line, making small talk with Heather Dunne about summer holidays and how she'd grown out of all of her skirts from last year (she obviously saw me and my too-tight jumper as a comrade). Freddie gave me a little wave from a few rows back. He looked particularly nice, I noticed.

My form took our seats a few rows from the front, breathing in the disinfectant and furniture polish of a deep clean. I was busy tugging down my jumper and wondering where I'd gone wrong with the cleaning magic. When I looked up again, my eyes met someone else's – someone I'd pushed to the back of my mind pretty effectively all summer.

Callum Henderson.

He was staring right at me, with an expression I couldn't read. It seemed somewhere between a sneer and ... cautious interest? My chest tightened. I was determined not to look away, and held his gaze until someone next to him gave him a nudge, demanding his attention.

He turned away, but the memories had come flooding back. Callum passing notes to his mates, with scores for girls on them, Callum throwing offensive paper aeroplanes at me, Callum's smug grin caught on video as he made fun of me, that unwanted kiss, and, worst of all, his face, angry and red after I had pushed him away. I shook my head, willing the memories out.

'Good morning, Year Eleven,' came a stern voice from the stage.

The last remnants of excited whispers died down and all eyes focused to the front where Ms Pritchard, the new Headteacher, was addressing us. She was tall and serious-looking, dressed in a black suit, white shirt and sensible shoes. Her hair was short, her expression a fixed half-smile. Everything about her screamed no-nonsense, ready for action. She looked poised and ready to be called to a frontline mission somewhere. It wouldn't have surprised me if she'd had a Swiss Army knife and rations in her pockets.

'As you'll know from the introduction video that was sent out over the holidays, my name is Ms Pritchard and I am your new Headteacher. I am very happy to be here at Queen Victoria Academy.'

You might want to tell your face that, I thought.

'And I am excited to begin our journey together.' *Again with the face not matching the words.*

'There is, of course, work to be done, especially after the events of last year.' Practically the whole of Year Eleven turned in my direction at that one.

'But I truly believe that, together, we can make Queen Victoria Academy a place to be proud of, a place where you will all thrive.'

She took a sip of water, straightening out her perfectly straight jacket.

'I'm sure you are aware what an important year in your academic career this is for you all. Now is not the time to rest on your laurels. Now is the time to take all those years of working hard, of learning, of striving, and apply them – to rise to the challenge.' She gestured dramatically here. She was really leaning into the Prime-Minister-addressing-the-nation vibes.

Summer caught my eye from across the hall, barely suppressing a giggle.

'I'm not going to lie to you – it will be a challenge. But it will be worth it. You only get this chance once.'

'Unless you do retakes,' a voice said, from somewhere in my vicinity. I glanced over – ugh, Marcus. Another one of Callum's misogynist cronies who had wreaked havoc on my life last year. He made my skin crawl.

Ms Pritchard paused. Her sharp eyes fixed and narrowed on where the noise had come from. I found myself shrinking back, even though I hadn't done anything.

'I would like to take this opportunity to remind you of our five School Pillars: endeavour, responsibility—'

Just then, the front hall door swung open. One of the school secretaries walked in, closely followed by a girl who was determinedly focusing on the floor like she was wishing it would indeed swallow her up and save her from the two hundred pairs of eyes that were staring at her.

She was tall and pale. Her dark hair, which had flashes of green dye running through it, was cropped into sharp edges that sat pointy against her chin, emphasising her big, kohl-rimmed eyes. She was wearing black jeans which were more holes than jean, a faded T-shirt that had some kind of obscure band logo on it, leather boots that looked like they could kick you into next week, and a long, grey trench coat that gave her the air of a TV detective – the type with a drinking problem and a troubled past.

My skin prickled. The energy in the room shifted, the hall blowing up in barely contained excitement. A new person! Or 'fresh meat', as Callum had referred to me when I arrived last year. On an island with a population roughly half the size of Sunderland, a new person definitely counts as big news.

'That's enough, thank you!' Ms Pritchard boomed from the front. 'Settle down now.'

People rearranged themselves, facing forward but keeping an obvious side-eye on the new girl.

As the hall settled, I glanced over myself, curious. And that's when I saw the new girl was staring – unmistakably, unnervingly – straight at me.

CHAPTER TWO

'Did you *see* her though?' Libby was completely over-excited at the arrival of the new girl.

We were standing outside the gates at the end of the day, waiting for Summer and Tabitha, the green tide flowing past us in a wave of animated, first-day-back conversations: holiday romances, new teachers, timetables and Mr Anstead's snazzy new haircut (it was pretty special).

'I mean, she's styling herself on some seriously extinct 90s goth. Black lipstick? *Really*?' Libby continued. 'Clearly been watching too many Tim Burton movies.'

I was looking around, searching the sea of faces – for Summer and Tabs, but also for New Girl. I was ... intrigued. Or intimidated.

'She won't get away with it,' Libby said. 'Or the hair dye.'

'It's green,' I said. 'School colour.'

'Hey, cats,' Summer said, jumping on me from behind. 'I think I can guess who you're talking about.'

'Freak Unique,' Libby said.

'Libby!' I reprimanded. The word 'freak' made my stomach clench.

'Her name is actually Sloane Smith and she's in our form,' Tabitha said.

Libby eyes widened. 'Full report STAT, please!'

'Not much to report,' Summer said. 'She sat at the back, didn't really talk to anyone but kind of stared a lot.'

It made me feel better to hear it wasn't only me the new girl was staring at. Maybe it was just her vibe – intense eye connection.

'Do you know anything about her – like where she's moved from?' I asked.

'Nope, she didn't say. I clocked a cool tattoo on the inside of her wrist though, a kind of circle with funny symbols on the outside. We only had the twenty minutes of registration after lunch, so not exactly ample time to go all Miss Marple on her.'

'Well, she looks weird,' Libby said, like that was the matter decided.

Summer shrugged. 'I think there's something kind of cool about her.'

'If your idea of cool is try-hard emo outsider,' Libby grunted.

'I thought you said she was a goth?' Tabs asked.

'Goth, emo – both weird, same difference.'

'They're not the same though,' Tabs replied, ready to launch into a full explanation of the difference.

'Just give her a chance,' I said. 'That was me last year.'

'Without the all-black vamp vibes and death stares,' Libby said. 'Summer, your inside scoop was seriously lacking, and I have to go now.'

'You can't go yet,' I said. 'We haven't talked about our Feminist Society plans yet.'

'Fem Soc,' Libby said. 'I've told you, it sounds cooler. And I can't, sorry, golden-boy brother has an away match, which means an enforced family pilgrimage to the mainland to adore him and bathe in his light. Tomorrow lunch break?' She gave us a parting wave and started off down the hill. 'Adios! Message me if you find any intel on Beetlejuice.'

I realised the green tide had turned to a trickle, just a few groups of stragglers left outside the gates now. I glanced at my watch.

'Argh, I said I'd go and watch Freddie in the match against Sacred Heart. Anyone fancy joining?' I asked, turning my puppy-dog begging eyes on.

'Sorry, Mum asked me to cover the café,' Summer said. 'Speaking of which, I'd better go. Enjoy the girlfriend duty!'

'C'mon, Tabs, I bet you'd love a bit of aimless standing around, watching boys get over-invested in kicking a ball around, right?'

She looked reluctant, but not immovable.

'For me, pleeeeeease?' I knew I nearly had her. 'We can test each other on atomic structure?'

I'd found her Achilles heel. 'You know I can't resist revision,' she said, giving in. 'But can we do particle model of matter? I've already gone over atoms about fifty times.'

'Of course you have,' I said, linking my arm through hers and heading for the football field.

***

By the time we made it up to the pitch, the match was already in full swing. I scanned the moving maroon and green bodies to find Freddie. He was fully focused, the dark hair that was usually flopping over his eye tied back in a macho version of a hairband, knees already muddy. I tried to catch his attention to let him know I was there but he was too engaged.

13

'So we just stand here for the whole match?' Tabs asked.

'We also have to cheer and groan at appropriate times.'

'And how long is the match, exactly?'

'Uh, I don't know. Like, an hour maybe? There's a break at some point but they all huddle and talk tactics.'

Just then, something happened on the pitch that caused the people around us, mostly parents and other Year Eleven boys, to break out in a loud cheer. Tabs and I joined in, belatedly.

'What happened?' she whispered.

'No idea. Just do what they do. And if you catch Freddie's eye, give him a thumbs up.'

'Got it.'

We stood and tried to pay attention, clapping and groaning when everyone else did. When there was no cheering to be done, we ran through particle theory and changing states. We waved at Freddie at half-time. In the second half though, Tabs got into the match. She even turned me down when I suggested we do some practice questions.

'Are you actually into the football or just the players?' I asked, half watching as Freddie missed a goal.

'Surprisingly, I think a bit of both!' She grinned. 'So this is sport, hey? It's kind of fun. To watch, anyway.'

'Who are you and what have you done with Tabitha?'

'Seriously, it's quite easy to get caught up in it.'

'Um, no, it's not – it's a bunch of Neanderthal boys running off their testosterone by chasing after a ball and using it as an excuse to show each other some affection without being ridiculed.'

'Except for Freddie, obviously,' Tabs added.

'Obviously,' I added, feeling guilty for calling Freddie a Neanderthal.

'And I think you're being too harsh, by the way. It's natural if you're playing on a team to bond with your teammates – plus, it's not the boys' fault society tells them they're not allowed to show affection in other ways. It's not necessarily football that's the bad guy in your scenario – I think it's just your associations with it.' I stared at her and she shrugged. 'Sorry, just saying.'

'Well thanks, Freud. I'll give you a call next time I need to be psychoanalysed.'

'Any time.'

Freddie had the ball now and was running with it, neatly evading a few players that tried to tackle him. Callum, I noticed, was helping to keep them at bay. Freddie and Callum – my boyfriend and my enemy, the two football amigos.

Freddie kicked the ball, sending it flying through the air towards the goal, but even I could see it was way too wide. I wished he'd score – he was always down about it afterwards if he didn't.

And then, suddenly, the too-wide ball wasn't too wide any more. It unexpectedly and dramatically changed course about a metre before the goal, sailing straight past the open-mouthed goalkeeper.

Everyone went crazy.

'Oh my God!' Tabs was jumping up and down cheering. 'Did you see that? It was a miracle ball!'

'Amazing!' I said, as a coldness surged through my stomach.

I had *wished* the ball would go in. And the fact it actually did was absolutely no fluke.

My magic had been inadvertently responsible for his too-good-to-be-true miracle goal. My magic that I *thought* I had under control, my magic that hadn't done anything off-kilter like this for *ages*. This was not good.

People were looking at their watches, some shouting for the whistle, which meant it must be coming up for full time. I knew I should stay and say hi to Freddie, but I was too anxious about what had just happened. I wanted to go home and gather myself. I'd worked so hard to get to my new normal, and these too-familiar feelings of being out of control were not welcome.

'You all right?' Tabs asked. 'You're doing a weird jiggling thing.'

'Just excitement,' I said, forcing a grin. 'Yay, Freddie!'

'Oh look, there's Sloane.' Tabs pointed to a dark figure standing alone across the pitch from us. 'Should we go and say hi?'

I was surprised to see her; Sloane didn't seem like the sport-supporting type. But I guess, neither did I. The thought of having to deal with more small talk didn't thrill me.

Luckily, just then the final whistle blew. By the time I'd looked over again, Sloane had disappeared. After much high-fiving and back-slapping and general post-match high jinks, Freddie made his way over to us.

'You came!' he said, flashing that gorgeous smile of his. 'Thanks, guys.'

'I said I would.'

'You didn't have to, I know it's not your thing.' *Could've told me that before*, I thought. 'But thanks. Nice to have some cheerleaders.'

'Let's not go too far, hey?'

He put his arm around me, and kissed the top of my head, the smell of earth and sweat and Freddie-ness all musky and familiar.

'It was brilliant!' Tabs squawked. 'Such a good match! And your goal was . . .'

'Unexpected,' Freddie finished. 'I don't know what happened there, but I'll take it.'

The coldness squeezed at me again. As we walked off the pitch, Freddie and Tabs chatted on about the match. I added the occasional 'yeah' and 'totally', but my mind was elsewhere. *Surely what had happened on the pitch was no big deal*, I told myself. A one-off, nothing to worry about.

The problem was, it didn't feel like nothing.

Just then my phone beeped. A message from Mum, reminding me not to be late for the special family dinner tonight – which, in fact, I had totally forgotten about. The official Meeting of the Kids. Her boyfriend (it pained me to use the word) Handy Andy was bringing his round for the first time. I think the idea was that we would all have a wonderful, bonding time and instantly feel the Disney-level love.

I hadn't been thrilled about the idea at the time – it would eat into our sacred magic-lesson time, which was scarce enough as it was owing to the fact we had to plan it around Nonna's darts, Bella's Very Important Blogging and Mum's new clothes-making business – but I was even less keen on it now. Making small talk and fake smiling all night was the last thing I felt like doing when I needed to talk to Mum and Nonna about the witchy weirdness that had just happened. I chuckled to myself, thinking about what a difference a year makes – this time a year ago I hadn't even known I was a witch and when I did find out, the last thing I'd wanted to do was to discuss it with them.

'Everything all right, Jessie?' Freddie asked.

'Kind of. I totally forgot I've got this big dinner thing on this evening – Andy's introducing us to his kids. I know I said I'd help you with your Physics . . .'

'No worries, I'm sure I can find some crib guides online or something.'

'I can help,' Tabs offered. 'Dad's working late tonight and I'm always up for extra Physics. We could go to The Quay – I get free coffees.'

'That's the Tabs we know and love!' I said. 'Good to see you're over your sporting phase!'

'Ah thanks but I don't want to put you out,' said Freddie.

'You won't be,' I replied, on Tabitha's behalf. 'Studying is her idea of fun. It's like her version of football.'

Tabs nodded.

'Well, if you're sure . . . that would be great!' Freddie said.

'She's sure!' I was pleased to be off the hook for deserting him and I knew Tabitha was always up for studying. 'Good luck, enjoy!'

'Good luck to you.' He gave me a kiss. 'Andy's great, I'm sure his kids are too – and what's not to love about you?' Another kiss.

'Hmm,' I muttered. There was quite a lot not to love about me; Freddie just didn't know about any of it yet.

CHAPTER THREE

'You're late,' Mum said, as I rushed into the kitchen, red and panting.

'They're not here yet, are they?' I glanced around. There were dirty bowls and plates, piles of chopped food and smudges of flour and sauce on all the counter tops, but no evidence of actual people.

Dave and Chicken cowered in the corner, squeezed tight together, trying to blend in to the kitchen detritus. Dave, my needy (female) cat and Chicken, who I accidentally magicked to life as a chick when I was still getting a grip on my powers. We actually thought Dave had eaten Chicky at one point, but a few weeks later, adult Chicken clucked her way into the kitchen like she belonged there and they've been friends ever since ... once Dave realised Chicken wasn't for dinner.

'No, but I wanted you to help me get ready.'

Mum was peering worriedly at whatever was in the oven.

'I thought we decided it was best if you didn't cook tonight,' I ventured.

'*We* didn't decide that. You and Bella and Nonna *suggested* it. But I want this to be lovely and homely and welcoming.'

'Which is why you shouldn't cook,' I said, going for a joke and getting a glare in response. Mum looked hot and flustered – and not in the mood to be teased. I wanted to talk to her about the magic at the football, about why she thought it was happening again and, more importantly, what I could do to stop it, but I was wise enough to appreciate the timing wasn't exactly right.

'Look, why don't we just magic up dinner? Then you can go and get ready, I can tidy up and set the table. You're getting yourself all worked up when it's totally avoidable.'

'We are not using magic today!' Mum said, turning on me with a decidedly worrying glint in her eye. 'This is the first time Andy's kids are meeting us. We are going to be normal and non-threatening and normal and welcoming and—'

'Normal,' I finished. 'OK, I got it. No magic. But you know what Nonna would say.'

'She'd say you're being an idiot.' A calm voice came from the doorway, where Nonna, frizzy-haired and heavily bangled, was standing. 'If this relationship is to go anywhere then you have to be your true self and you may as well do that now, otherwise what's the point?'

'Hi, Nonna,' I said, grinning. Nonna was not one to mince her words.

'Hi, love,' she said, turning from Mum to me.

'I understand what you're saying,' Mum sighed. 'But I don't want to tell Andy about … everything, not just yet. It might not even go anywhere. Let's just see how tonight goes first. I want to be welcoming and … normal.'

'Hmmm.' Nonna wasn't convinved. 'Fine, but for God's sake let me take over here please – there's nothing normal and welcoming about your cooking.'

'Nonna!' I said, trying to suppress a laugh. Poor Mum.

'I do need to go and get ready,' said Mum, glancing at her watch. 'OK, the lamb's in the oven, and everything's just cooking – it doesn't need anything doing except a bit of checking and stirring. And *no magic!*'

'No magic,' Nonna confirmed, taking the spoon from Mum. 'No magic my arse,' she added, once Mum had left the room, grinning in that mischievous Nonna way that makes my heart sing.

***

I didn't get the chance to talk to Nonna, Mum or Bella about my random football magic before dinner. There was too much going on – helping Nonna salvage the meal, a what-to-wear emergency with Mum and a late arrival by Bella. By the time Handy Andy and his crew arrived I was still angst-ridden and not at my small talk best.

'Hello hello, come on in,' I heard Mum say from the hallway. Nonna, Bella and I were waiting in the dining room like we were ready to receive the Queen.

Mum and Handy Andy came through, both with nervous smiles, followed by two teenagers, both tall and imposing. The girl had a wholesome-but-elegant look to her – a kind face, long blonde hair. She was wearing a simple grey jumper and jeans, but they looked expensive and classy. The overall effect was like a cross between a younger Gigi Hadid and a younger Taylor Swift. Chic and effortless and about as opposite from me and my wardrobe of holey hoodies as was possible. She handed Mum some flowers.

'Oh, you really shouldn't have, Neve, but thank you, they're lovely,' Mum said.

The boy, taller still, handed over a bottle of wine. He was what I would call well-groomed – neat hair, a shirt and jeans, wide eyes and a genuine-looking smile. As if he had mistaken this forced family dinner for something fun.

'Neve, Jake,' Mum said. 'This is Bella and Jessie and my mum, Edith.'

We all smiled and did those awkward mini waves you do when you first meet people and don't know them well enough to hug. Except Nonna, who gave each of them a huge bear hug – with added aura sniff, just to make the whole thing a slice more awkward.

'She's a hugger,' I said, trying to offer some kind of explanation.

'Sit down, sit down.' Mum jollied everyone along. 'Food's nearly ready.'

'Smells delicious,' Andy said, stroking Mum's back affectionately. 'I thought you said you were cooking?'

'Cheeky!' Mum gave him a playful nudge.

'Daniel's sorry not to make it,' Andy said. 'He's gone up to Exeter ahead of the semester to start work on the university paper. He's back in a few weeks though. We'll get together again then.'

I did a silent thank you for the absence of one more new person to make awkward conversation with.

We were eating in the dining room, which added an extra layer of formality and awkwardness to the whole event. Usually we all piled around the kitchen table.

Mum and Andy squeezed together at the top of the table, Nonna sat at the bottom and the four of us kids ended up in a potential-step-sibling sandwich in the middle.

'So,' Mum said, going to take the lid off one of the dishes, 'we have slowly braised lamb with a redcurrant reduction and a—'

Nonna coughed, loudly. 'That was the other night, love, you joker,' she said.

'It was?' said Mum, blinking.

'You decided to go for something a bit simpler. I think you cooked the chicken pasta tray bake with roast veg tonight, didn't you?'

Mum quickly adjusted her face, big smile back in place, and took the lid off. It smelled really good.

'Oooh, and I'm really looking forward to that warm chocolate brownie and ice cream for pudding,' Nonna added.

'Yes, me too,' Mum said, glaring at her.

Everyone served up and tucked in, making appreciative noises for what was actually tasty food. Even Mum seemed satisfied.

'The house is looking lovely, Allegra,' Jake said, sounding all official dinner-party guest and approximately two decades older than his age.

Mum grinned and blushed, looking like she might explode with the happiness of someone taking an interest in the house renovations. 'Well thanks, Jake – it's all down to your brilliant dad. I'll give you the tour later.'

'Brilliant?' Neve laughed. 'Have you brainwashed her, Dad?'

'Oi! It's nice that someone round here appreciates my talents,' Andy said.

Mum gave him a little leg stroke and affectionate gaze. I quickly forced in a mouthful of chicken so I wouldn't gag.

'Talking of brilliant, we've heard all about you, Jessie,' Jake said. I nearly choked on my chicken. 'Dad told us you made headline news last year with that video exposé about the sexism at your school. I remember hearing about it at the time, but I hadn't realised that was you.'

'I thought it was amazing,' Neve said, leaning in.

'Here we go, celebrity Jessie,' Bella laughed.

My mouth was still full, so I had to do the painful rigmarole of animatedly chewing and pointing to my mouth by way of explaining why I couldn't respond while basically the whole table stared at me.

Nonna took pity on me. 'Yes, she did! Showed that pathetic little—'

'It was a very insightful documentary about some unacceptable behaviour that was happening,' Mum interjected. 'Jessie's actually been invited to an event being held by Bob Henderson off the back of it, which I think is kind of special.'

I couldn't help giving a muffled groan at the mention of Bob's name. Local MP, good-for-nothing, only interested in the trappings of power and – worst of all – Callum Henderson's dad. Double-douche-whammy.

'Really?' Jake asked, looking suddenly interested. 'You're going to meet Bob Henderson?'

'It's just some charity thing he's hosting at his house with the newspaper,' I explained, finally swallowing my food.

'You're too modest, Jessie!' Mum butted in. 'They've invited local celebrities *and* regular citizens who have made a difference on the Island. It's an honour to be invited.'

It was no such thing – it was an attempt to smooth over Bob's reputation ahead of an election year, a reputation which had been tarnished by his son's disgusting behaviour. And there was no way I was going.

'It's an attempt to get some good press and a photo of Jessie standing next to Callum to show the world he's seen the error of his ways and reformed,' Nonna said, voicing my thoughts exactly. To my surprise, Jake was nodding vigorously. 'No one wants to be building any bridges with that piece of—'

'Anyone for seconds?' Mum practically shouted.

'Do you know him?' I asked Jake.

'Callum? Yeah, through football,' Jake said, his eyes darkening. 'Not a fan.'

Interesting. I was very much a fan of anyone who was 'not a fan' of Callum's. The enemy of my enemy, and all that.

'Me neither,' I said, warming to the subject now. 'In fact—'

'So,' Mum cut in before I could say anything else, trying to keep the vibe upbeat and wholesome. 'Jessie and Neve – you're both doing GCSEs this year, aren't you? How are you feeling about it, Neve? I know that Jessie is struggling to find the revision time . . .'

Way to go with the party talk, Mum. I knew she was aiming for a bosom-buddies scenario and was desperate for some common ground – but I wasn't sure talking about our impending GCSEs was going to do the trick. I played along though, exchanging bland revision talk with Neve. It felt like we were on an awkward speed date (complete with an audience) rather than like we were forming a genuine bond though.

The rest of the evening went the same way – Mum prodding the conversation on, trying too hard for an instant bond between us all. She got Bella talking about her beauty blogging, trying to force a connection with Neve by virtue of the fact Neve very occasionally wears mascara. Every now and again Nonna came

25

out with something slightly inappropriate which Mum tried to speak over.

And then there was the magic. Just small stuff – lights coming on by themselves, a glass correcting itself as it was about to fall. Nothing that couldn't be explained away by luck. Once, when the bottle of wine spun around and miraculously stopped just before it was about to fall off the edge of the table, Mum laughed nervously and said we had a poltergeist – 'but a friendly one!'

By the time we eventually said our goodbyes – which were as politely awkward as our hellos – it felt like the evening had been going on for months.

The minute the door closed behind them, the smile dropped from Mum's face. 'That was a bloody disaster!' she said.

'It was fine,' Bella said. 'They seemed nice.'

'*They* were nice, it was us who were a disaster.' Mum poured herself a whisky, slumped in the chair and glared at Nonna. 'I told you – *begged* you – no magic!'

'Don't be ridiculous – it was nothing.' Nonna shrugged her off, clearing dishes away.

'It was more than nothing – magicking lights on? Saving a bottle from smashing? How are we supposed to explain that away?'

'The way that we did explain it away,' Nonna said. 'An electrical fault and a bit of luck. They didn't even notice it.'

I made myself small, joining Bella in helping with the clearing away, not wanting to get in the middle of anything.

'And how about magicking up an entirely different meal to the one I actually cooked?' Mum said, downing her whisky a bit too quickly. 'It made me look stupid!'

I felt awful for Mum. We'd meant to tell her we'd had to scrap her food and magic something else up – her lamb dish had tasted like a mouthful of burnt tree and we weren't even sure what she'd been attempting for pudding as it was unrecognisable – but it had all been such a rush, we'd forgotten.

Nonna paused her bustling and turned around to face Mum.

'The only thing that's making you look stupid is not being yourself. No one is getting to know you if they're not getting to know the *real* you, Allegra. And slow-braised lamb with a poncy whatnot reduction – honestly, do you think you're on *MasterChef* or something? That's not you. As is the not doing magic.'

'She was making an effort, Nonna,' Bella said.

'I'm not having this conversation again,' Mum said flatly. She topped up her drink and walked out of the kitchen.

I didn't want the evening to go like this. I had important things to talk to them about! I needed them to make up.

'Thanks for dinner,' I called after Mum, before realising that was a pretty stupid comment. Bella rolled her eyes at me and Dave wound round my legs, seeking solace from the tension.

I knew what Nonna meant, but I also felt for Mum. How are you supposed to tell the person who likes you that actually, there's this kind of massive, important, and slightly (OK, very) strange thing they should know about you? Freddie's face flashed into my mind. There was no way I was telling *him* any time soon. Things were finally normal. I was happy. I wasn't about to blow that up quite yet. And like Mum had said, what's the point if you don't know where it's going?

CHAPTER FOUR

'Here we go then.' Nonna waddled into the living room holding a tray. She placed it on the coffee table and started handing out teacups. I suppressed a groan. I wanted a magic lesson, not a cup of tea.

Bella had managed to work her magic – not proper magic, just her usual Bella persuasive charm – on Mum, convincing her to come down again and do some magic practice with us. Though judging by the daggers Mum was shooting in Nonna's direction, she hadn't fully thawed.

Nonna was either completely oblivious or choosing to ignore her. Either way, the tension in the room was off the chart. Dave and Chicken were cuddled up together at the end of the sofa, Dave's paw resting on Chicken's beak, both totally unaware of the unease in the room.

'There you go, love,' Nonna said, handing me a teacup.

'I'm fine thanks,' I said, impatiently waving it away. 'I just want to get going with the lesson.'

'Well then you'll be needing the teacup.'

I looked at her questioningly.

'We're doing scrying today, petal,' she explained.

'Oooh, reading tea leaves!' Bella said, grinning.

'Seriously?' I asked. 'Because that sounds dull. Is that even real magic?'

'Excuse me!' Nonna said, straightening up and putting her hand on her hip. 'Scrying is not in the least bit dull – it's an extremely old magical practice and can be very useful.'

'For what? Working out what the weather will be on Saturday and whether to move the sheep to the upper field? We've got an app for that nowadays. This is baby magic. We've been plodding our way through this boring old rubbish for ages now. I want to get on to the real stuff – the good stuff.'

'And what exactly would the "good stuff" be?' Nonna asked sharply.

'Well I don't know, do I? Because you haven't told me! But it sure as hell isn't this tea leaves crap.'

Mum sniggered from the armchair, enjoying the show. Nonna's smile was beginning to slip.

'Don't act like a toddler,' Bella said, holding her teacup like it was the Crown Jewels. 'Nonna's already explained this, in, like, every single lesson. We're going slowly, building up the foundations. We can't expect to suddenly be manifesting rainbows and true loves.'

'*You* can't,' I muttered.

'Oh, here we go.' Bella suddenly turned acidic. 'Now we're getting to the crux of it. Me and my period-dependent powers are holding Miss Rare Superwitch back from realising her true magical potential. Poor Rare Superwitch.'

'That's not what I meant,' I said, though it was almost exactly what I meant.

Nonna waved her arms in the air like some kind of air traffic controller. 'Come on now, you two. This kind of bickering isn't helpful to anyone. For the record, Jessie, whether Bella had full-time powers or not, this is the speed we would be going at. We've spoken about this before – at length. I know it's exciting and it's great that you're keen, but witchcraft is complicated. We're going at a pace that is safe and responsible. We're building up the foundations *properly*.'

'Looking at tea leaves is not a foundation that we need to build up,' I huffed.

Bella glared at me. 'And you know that do you, Grand High Witch of all things Witch?'

I didn't often see Bella this riled up – she was usually the cool, calm, collected and mature one. But then she was used to being smarter and more talented than me. It must've killed her to see me taking that role. I kind of liked it.

'Now listen.' Nonna plonked herself next to me on the sofa. She put her hands over mine – her wrinkled hands that are always surprisingly cotton-wool soft. 'Think of it like learning to drive, my love. I know you want to be out there, on the open road, feeling the wind in your hair and relishing your freedom. But if you don't learn how to unlock the car, or reverse park, or change gears or—'

'I understand the driving analogy,' I snapped.

'If you don't know how to do those basics,' Nonna went on pointedly, 'then really, you don't how to drive at all. You could have a terrible accident – putting yourself, and others, in danger.'

'What would a terrible witching accident look like, exactly?' I asked and then instantly wished I hadn't. I knew exactly what a magical accident could look like – a few months ago my misplaced magic made Nonna very, very ill.

I grudgingly took the teacup. The sooner we got the lesson over with, the sooner we could, eventually, move on to more exciting stuff. And so Nonna bored on about tea leaves, while Bella soaked it up with an excited smile on her face, Mum sipped her whisky in the corner, shooting Nonna dirty looks and I nodded my way through it all, playing along like a good little witch, dreaming of excitement and bigger magic.

My tea leaves predicted it would rain – which it did. Although my weather app could've told me that too.

CHAPTER FIVE

'I'm pretty sure it's cottage pie,' Summer said.

We were on our way to lunch, trying to work out what the particular aroma in the air was – which is hard as all the kitchen smells at Queen Vic give off a similarly generic overcooked-stodge waft. Except for Fish Friday, which is a whole other smell experience entirely and really should never be mentioned.

'I think you're right, smells like cottage pie.' Libby sniffed the air.

'The less well-received second Nirvana album,' Summer said, laughing at her own joke.

'It's Thursday, week one on the timetable,' Tabitha said authoritatively. 'So she *is* right. Cottage pie.'

'Can you all please stop saying *cottage pie*!' I wailed. 'I hate it enough as it is.' The thought of the pungent watery mush was fast dampening my hunger.

'Cottage pie, cottage pie, cottage pie,' Libby shouted, the others joining in. I put my hands over my ears.

Revision Facts – Density of Matter (Physics)
1. All matter contains particles. The difference between the different states of matter is how the particles are arranged.
2. In a gas, particles are spread out and move randomly.

3. In a liquid, particles are tightly packed but free to move past each other.
4. In a solid, particles are tightly packed in a regular structure.
5. In Queen Vic's cottage pie, particles defy the law of physics and are packed in some kinda way that no one understands to form something completely inedible.

'I wish it was pizza,' I said, my mouth watering at the thought of it – even though school pizza was a long way off a normal pizza standard.

'You always wish it was pizza, Jessie,' said Summer. 'Strap a shell on your back and call yourself a ninja turtle.'

Libby laughed. 'Summer, the nineties called and they want their cultural references back.'

'Little brothers,' Summer offered, by way of explanation.

'Seriously, we may need to move our Feminist Society meeting – sorry, *Fem Soc* meeting,' I corrected myself, seeing Libby's glare, 'out of the canteen. I'm not sure I can stand the smell.'

'You're such a wuss,' Libby said, joining the queue. We'd been explaining to her how it's not kind to queue-jump past Year Sevens so it was nice to see it was actually sinking in.

'Freddie texted to say the revision was really helpful,' I said to Tabitha, realising I hadn't thanked her for the night before. 'I hope it wasn't too painful – Physics isn't his forte.'

'Never apologise for bonus revision opportunities,' Tabs said. 'We got the Physics done and then ended up just talking for ages.'

'Oh my God I'm so sorry!' I said. 'Did you hear all about goals and stats and line-ups?'

'We actually ended up reading some of each other's writing,' Tabs said.

'His *writing*?' I asked, shocked. 'I didn't know Freddie wrote!'

'I think he only mentioned it because he knows I write too. He was wanting a second opinion on some stuff,' Tabs said. 'It was just some short stories, nothing much.'

'Oh, yeah,' I said, acting like it sounded familiar to me. Why hadn't Freddie ever told me he'd been writing? Had I just not asked? 'Well, thanks for doing it. I'd totally forgot I had that dinner.'

'How did it go?' Summer asked. 'The big Merging of the Families dinner, right?'

'Ugh, yeah. Mainly it was just awkward and forced. They both seem decent – the girl, Neve, she's our year over at the Academy, and is really into surfing.' Summer grinned at that. 'And apparently the boy, Jake, doesn't like Callum, so you know, that's instant bonus points. But still, it was a bit . . . uncomfortable and not how I would've chosen to spend my evening.' I chose not to mention all the magic and the fallout between Mum and Nonna afterwards.

'Well, that all sounds great to me,' Summer said, ever the optimist. 'Anyone who's into surfing is a winner in my books and anyone who doesn't like Callum works for you so I reckon it's a win-win.'

'So when are you all moving in together and sharing rooms like a proper Brady Bunch?' Libby asked. 'Will you call him Daddy or Handy Daddy? Oh God no, that actually sounds very wrong!' She chuckled, finding the whole thing way more amusing than I was.

'Don't,' I said.

But the idea wormed itself into my head. A family. A big, melded, forced together with relative strangers, too-many-people family. That would never happen. We'd only just got used to being a family of four. Surely Mum wasn't going to jeopardise that for the sake of getting some action from a sweet, pot-bellied, *Buffy*-ignorant wearer of naff T-shirts.

I sighed and edged closer. *All of this would be bearable if there was pizza for lunch*, I thought glumly.

We were just coming up to the serving counter when suddenly there was a lot of clanking and muttering and shuffling back to the kitchen and the queue stalled.

'One minute please,' one of the cooks said.

'Fingers crossed they've run out of COTTAGE PIE,' Libby said, way too loudly.

The woman gave her daggers. 'We have.'

I blushed on Libby's behalf, who was incapable of feeling embarrassment.

'Right then,' a new, smiling supervisor said a moment later. She was carrying a big stainless-steel tray, which she placed under the heat lamp. 'We had a problem with our order from the caterers – cottage pie is out, I'm afraid. We've got this though.' She lifted the lid up, revealing a tray of piping-hot, decent-looking pizza.

Pizza. Just like I had wanted. Just like I had wished for.

Suddenly, I really wasn't hungry any more.

***

'Jessie, your manifesting powers are on fire!' Summer said, as we sat down a few minutes later with our surprise pizza.

I tried to smile, but my *mind* was on fire. Another thing I'd wished for had come true. Surely that couldn't be a coincidence? My magic was definitely regressing and was once again out of my control. How long before I accidentally broke someone out in a rash or made their nose grow? I couldn't go through all of that again.

Callum and Marcus strutted past us then, with their usual swagger and sly smiles. My standard strategy with them was to not break eye contact, to never back down, never let them think they had any kind of upper hand. Today, though, I looked down at the floor, nervous that the slightest surge of hatred would spark something dangerous.

Libby stuck her middle finger up at them as they sauntered past – Callum ignored her but Marcus made some gross gesture in return. 'Callum really has changed,' she said. 'He's almost kind of dull now that he's good. The other night, when he was at mine, I couldn't start an argument with him at all.' I flinched at the mention of Callum being round at Libby's house, I always forgot their dads are good friends. 'I even trotted out the old line about how the England football team should be men and women playing together. Not so much as a frown. Nada. I almost miss the old Callum.'

'You *miss* him?' I said, stunned. 'What exactly do you miss? The open bullying of girls and the constant sexist comments? Or the trying it on with people who don't want his attention?'

'Well obviously I don't mean I want him to go back to doing that stuff,' Libby said, rolling her eyes and taking a big bite of her pizza, a drip of orange grease escaping and running down her chin. 'I meant, like, the other side of him. He wasn't always a hundred per cent awful. He used to also be a good laugh and a bit of a partner in crime. He was the only thing that made those dinners bearable.'

'You didn't mention he was at yours the other night. What dinner?' I didn't like the idea of Libby casually hanging out with Callum again. He was our enemy. *All* of ours. We'd battled him together and we should be standing together against him now too. Even though they had a history that went beyond that.

'They came round for our annual end-of-summer dinner party. It's all kinds of boring, but it's *usually* made more fun by Callum who's *usually* up for pranks, or stealing some booze or something. Not this year though.'

'Wasn't that ... weird, having him in your house?' I asked. I reminded myself that Callum and Libby had been friends for a long time, before everything that happened last year. Not just friends, boyfriend and girlfriend. 'After everything ...'

'Yeah. Kind of. I didn't know what to expect, to be honest. I was on the defensive, ready for a fight, but he seemed ... I dunno, different. And, like I said, dull.'

'Nice isn't the same thing as dull, Libby. That's a really dangerous stereotype that gets bandied about. But that's besides the point, because I don't think that Callum *is* nice. I guarantee you he hasn't actually changed, he's just better at covering it up now. I bet he's finding new ways to attack from undercover. He's probably planning something right now, as we speak, and here we are, just eating our pizza like sitting ducks! We can't let our guard down, not even for a *second*.'

I stopped and they all stared at me in shock, like I'd just said pizza is the Devil's food.

'What?' I asked, taking a breath.

'Are you OK, hon?' Libby asked. 'Been on the energy drinks?'

'I know last year was really tough for you, Jessie.' Summer's voice was gentle and soothing, like she was talking me down from a ledge. 'But I think Callum has changed. We won, dude. It's all good.'

I opened my mouth to protest, but before I could further make my argument, Libby cut in.

'I heard you got an invite to that event Callum's dad is holding,' she said. 'The faux fundraiser which is actually a "look-at-my-son-and-how-he's-changed-his-ways-it's-ok-you-can-vote-for-me-again-now" press event. You going to go?'

'Not in a million years.' I couldn't imagine anything worse, especially if my powers were becoming uncontrollable again.

'You could go for a laugh – and the canapés they serve at those things are always lush.' Libby did a dramatic chef's kiss.

'No amount of breaded prawns on sticks would convince me to go.'

Just then, Freddie walked past, panini and a water in hand. Callum called him over to where he was sitting with Marcus. Freddie smiled, then caught me watching him. He paused for a small, uncomfortable second, an accidental piggy-in-the-middle, before giving me an awkward wave and heading towards Callum. Marcus gave me the middle finger, laughing. My stomach bubbled.

'You OK?' Libby asked, quietly.

'Fine.'

'They've been friends for ever, Callum's a hard habit to break.'

'I'm not going to tell him who to be friends with, it's fine.' I pushed thoughts of Callum away. He didn't deserve my headspace. 'Right then, Fem Soc – let's make it an epic year. What are we going to tackle first?'

'We've got a new Head, which might mean new opportunities,' Tabs said.

'Depending on what she's like – not sure I got the feminist ally, progressive vibes from her,' Libby said. 'She might be worse than Harlston for all we know.'

'No one can be worse than Harlston,' I said, remembering our hideous, ineffective, old-boys-network former Headteacher – the one whose office I had accidentally wrecked in a fit of rage when he ignored my pleas for him to do something about the horrific bullying I was suffering. Another one of my accidental magic incidents. I shuddered.

'We still haven't got the uniform policy officially changed,' Libby said.

'Yeah, but they verbally agreed on that, all they have to do now is sign off on it,' I said. 'I think we need something bigger.'

'Like what?' Summer asked. 'Mixed sports teams? That will never happen—'

'Oh God, here it comes,' Libby groaned, looking somewhere behind me. 'Don't make eye contact.'

I turned round. *It* was Sloane. In uniform this time, but barely – shirt sleeves rolled up, skirt substantially shorter than technically allowed, tie loosely knotted, and a full selection of jewellery: choker, about five earrings in each ear, chunky rings on fingers. Black nail varnish and the green streaks in her hair both very much still present. She was doing the canteen walk-the-plank walk, searching for somewhere to sit while the whole canteen watched on, no one offering her a place or even a smile.

'Libby!' I hissed. 'Don't be such a bitch.'

'Sloane! Over here!' Summer called, waving.

Sloane smiled and I could practically see the relief hit her. I knew the feeling well. It wasn't that long ago I was doing the same walk.

Sloane sat down next to me, in a waft of incense and musk. My body flinched, out of the blue, like she'd given me an electric shock. I hoped it wasn't visible. I glanced at Libby, whose face was cartoon levels of grumpy.

'Thanks,' Sloane muttered.

'Don't worry about all the staring,' I said warmly. 'It eases off, eventually. How are you finding everything?'

'It's been … interesting. Man, I'm pleased it's pizza today though.' She looked directly at me, again for a beat too long. 'I thought it was meant to be cottage pie. Don't you just hate cottage pie?'

'Uh, yeah, don't we all?' I managed, feeling all kinds of weird. There was an uncomfortable pause.

'So where did you move here from?' Summer asked.

'It's a long story, but basically everywhere – we move around a lot.'

'Ah, same as Jessie,' Summer said. 'She was a bit of a nomad – until she found her Island calling, of course. She only joined six months ago, so you're both kind of newbies.'

'Did you?' Sloane asked, still looking intently at me. 'Good to know I have something in common with someone. Is it all you dreamed it would be?'

I didn't know why, but the question seemed loaded somehow. Or maybe it was just the way her eyes were fixed on me, like I was an interesting specimen.

'It took me a while to adjust, but yeah, I like it now.' I put the last bit of pizza in my mouth, feeling uncomfortable, like *I* was the new kid all over again.

Libby hadn't said a word since Sloane had sat down. She was looking at Sloane with a mixture of bored indifference and hatred – like she couldn't work out whether to yawn or pounce.

'Are you in living in town?' Tabs asked Sloane. 'Jessie and Libby are, Summer and I are further out.'

'You live in that big old hotel, don't you?' Sloane asked me. She hadn't looked away, even when Tabs had spoken to her.

'Uh, yeah,' I replied.

'How did you know that?' Libby asked, clearly deciding to pounce. Sloane finally turned away from me to look at Libby. 'Oh, you know, small island. Someone mentioned it, I think.'

Libby wasn't buying it. Or wasn't buying Sloane, in general. 'What do your parents do? I mean, did they move down here for work?'

'Another long story, but yeah, kind of,' Sloane said.

She and Libby stared at each other, neither backing down. 'Well I live just down in Steephill Cove. We were planning on hanging out there later if you want to join,' Summer said, breaking the stand-off.

'That sounds great, thanks for the invite.' She took a big gulp of her black coffee. 'Did I hear you say something about Feminist Society? I'm so on board with that.'

Wow, her hearing was good – Sloane must've been halfway across the room when we'd been talking about it. As I turned to look at her, there was that electric shock again, making me bristle. Our uniforms must have both been full of static.

'Down with boys!' She let out an awkward laugh and I inwardly cringed on her behalf.

'That's not exactly what we're about,' Libby said, the anger making her face harsh and pointed. 'And this is actually a planning meeting, so it's not open to everyone – sorry.'

I cringed again, this time on behalf of Libby. She was being mean and it wasn't fair. Sloane seemed fine. A little awkward, but that was part of being new – who isn't awkward when faced with a canteen of stares?

'Oh,' Sloane said, glancing at the floor, a blush creeping up from her neck. 'Well, maybe when you're up and running. I'm really interested in boys receiving consequences for their actions ... and feminism in general.' She stood up, clumsily lifting her tray, nearly spilling the remains of her coffee. 'But no worries, I'll leave you to it. I've got to go to the office anyway.'

A shout came from the other side of the canteen. Callum was standing up, fuming, his shirt completely soaked. 'Look where you're going, you absolute—'

'Sorry, sorry, it just flew out of my hand, I swear,' a bright-red Year Eight was stuttering.

We all stared for a bit too long. When I turned back to the table, I noticed Sloane was focused on me once again. She looked away quickly and started walking towards the door.

'We'll see you later, at Steephill,' Summer called out.

'What the hell, Summer?' Libby barked, before Sloane was out of earshot. 'I don't want to hang out with that weirdo.'

'You were being mean, Libby,' Summer said. 'I felt sorry for the poor girl. I don't know why you're so against her. I think she seems all right.'

'No, she doesn't,' Libby said. 'She seems like a *freak*. A freak who takes herself *way* too seriously and has no sense of style. She gives me the creeps. And why did she keep staring at Jessie?'

Part of me agreed with Libby – there was something ... *off* about Sloane. I couldn't place it though, and my inner critic was shouting that maybe it was just because she was a bit different. And of all people, I shouldn't be dismissing someone on the basis of being a bit different.

'Summer's right,' I offered. 'We should give her a chance. Just because you don't like the way she dresses, doesn't mean she's not a nice person. In fact, it probably makes *you* not a nice person.' Libby flicked a fleck of pepperoni at me. 'I feel sorry for her, it's horrible moving somewhere where you don't know anyone. Terrifying. I know how that feels.'

'She is nothing like you, stop saying that,' Libby said.

'Um, you didn't like *me* at first either,' I said.

'Um, I did until I thought you'd tried to snog my dickhead boyfriend.'

'Guys, let's not get into that,' Tabs said. 'Libby, let's give Sloane a chance.'

'Fine. But I hate you all,' Libby muttered, admitting defeat gracelessly. 'And I wish a lifetime of cottage pie on your heads.'

CHAPTER SIX

Steephill was looking its usual glorious self in the end-of-summer sun. The busyness of the summer had eased with the throngs of holiday-makers returning home. There were a few families spread out on the sand, down for post-school beach time, and some walkers sitting at the trestle tables in front of the coffee shack – everyone was taking in the last of the warm days.

This was the first September I'd been on the Island and so far it was my favourite time of the year here. There was a shift, a new peacefulness after the madness of the summer crowds. I took a deep breath, trying to push out thoughts of erratic powers and merging families and surrender myself to the feeling of calm.

'Jessie!' Summer called, waving from one of the big rocks where she was sitting with Libby and Tabs. 'Over here.'

Libby was sprawled against the rock behind her, wearing the world's shortest shorts, long limbs soaking up the sun. Tabs was rooting through her rucksack like she was doing a final check before heading off on an excavation dig to uncover a long-buried Viking tomb, eventually pulling out a vat of super-strength strength sun cream.

'Hey,' I said, taking my trainers off and walking over to them.

'Do you want a coffee?' Summer asked. 'I'm back on the counter in five.'

'I'm good, thanks. I could do with a swim though. Who's in?'

'Are we not waiting for your *special friend*?' Libby asked, eyebrows raising above her massive film star sunglasses.

'If you mean Sloane, she's not my special friend, I wasn't even the one who invited her down here – but a) stop being so unwelcoming and b) I'm sure she'll work out we're in the water if she does come,' I said.

'I can look out for her. I have to stay on the beach until we close up, anyway,' Summer said.

'Tabs? You in?' I asked.

'Sure,' she said. 'Let me just put some more sun cream on.'

'It's hardly Ibiza-level sunshine,' Libby said, taking her itsy-bitsy shorts off to reveal an itsy-bitsy bikini. 'Live a little, Tabs, get a tan. It might do you good.'

Tabs aggressively rubbed a massive dollop of cream on to her shoulder. 'Yeah, because skin cancer's known for "doing you good".'

Libby pretended she hadn't heard and ran into the water like some kind of Baywatch water nymph, while I did my usual slow and wimpy waddle in, gasping every time the water got a little bit higher up my body, full on whimpering when it got to boob height, which is, as everyone knows, by far the hardest stage of the process. I could hear Summer chuckling behind me, as she always did when witnessing my ridiculousness. She says it's one of the many signs I'm not a true Islander and that before the year is out I'll be running straight in – I can't see it myself.

I eventually made it out to Libby, as did Tabs once she'd smothered herself in enough sun cream to withstand the sun in the Sahara Desert. I always love the water once I'm in and my body has adjusted to the cold – as long as my feet don't touch anything slimy on the bottom, I don't spot anything moving under the surface, and I don't look back to shore and freak out about how far away I am. Basically as long as I can tread water and stare straight ahead, it's perfect.

Libby tried to get us to swim to the next cove. I refused, but in exchange I offered the next best thing in her eyes – floating on our backs and talking about boys.

'So tell us more about Don Julio or whoever your Spanish hottie was,' I said.

'Juan.' She sighed. 'He had these intense dark eyes that spoke to my soul.'

Tabs and I laughed.

'Spoke to your fanny, more like,' I said.

'What exactly were his eyes saying to your soul?' Tabs asked. 'Jump into bed, love?'

Libby splashed Tabs. 'It wouldn't be fair to give you all the details as Summer's not here. So come on, dish the dirt on you and Freddie, Jessie,' she said. 'The rest of us are so single we're practically Mother Theresa acolytes at this point. As the only attached one of the four of us, it's your duty to give us details. We can live vicariously through you.'

I sighed, closing my eyes to the sun, thinking about Freddie: his sparkling eyes after he's laughed so hard he can't breathe, the way he lets Dave sit on his shoulder even though he's allergic to cats, the silly names he calls me (Bessie, Jazz Hands,

Jelly, Indiana). But also, more recently, the awkward silences, the not getting my jokes and the coming round less.

'There are no details to give – just the regular hanging out and kissing. And before you make any snide comments, I'm fine with that so don't try any of your peer pressure on me.'

I heard Libby do a little intake of breath. 'As if I would!' She was off her back and treading water now. 'Hanging out and kissing is great – the best, actually. I'm not fishing for sexy-time talk. I just want – NEED – some romantic detail. You know, little gestures, sweet nothings, loved-up texts – anything! Right, Tabs?'

'Leave me out of this,' Tabs said. 'You're the prying busybody. I'm here for revision timetable and exam talk.'

Libby splashed her again.

I paused. Did Freddie and I have any of that? Sweet nothings and loved-up texts? I felt like we used to. A bit.

'Well, there isn't any. That I would tell you. We're not ... mushy like that.'

'*Ooohhh,*' Libby said, dramatically. 'Is he friend-zoning you? Oh my God, are you friend-zoning *him*?'

'What?' I rolled over too, so that I could tread water. 'Of course not,' I said, feeling the tinge of a potential lie. I reached for a distraction. 'We're totally fine. I just don't like talking about it – unlike some people. Anyway, if you want romance so badly, why don't we focus on finding you a boyfriend?'

'I honestly cannot be bothered with any of the boys at our school,' Libby said, holding her nose and ducking under the water briefly, before bursting back up and splashing us. 'How about you, Tabs? Is there a literary nerd you've got your eye on – a romantic poet in the making that you're writing sonnets to?'

Tabs blushed, ever so slightly. 'I mean, I hate sonnets, so no. But also, just no. Besides, it's GCSE year – more important things to focus on.'

'Oh come on, surely nothing's more important than boys?' Libby said, winking at me. Tabs, still floating on her back, made a little exasperated huff, not appreciating Libby was only winding her up.

'Ugh, Morticia Addams is here,' Libby said, looking to the shore. I turned and saw Summer standing, talking to a black silhouette that was obviously Sloane.

'Come on,' I said, 'we should go and say hi.'

'Go ahead,' Libby said. 'I'd rather not ruin my last hit of summer vibes by interacting with a mortician, thanks all the same.'

I shook my head. 'Be nice!' I splashed her and quickly swam away with Tabs.

***

'Hi!' I said, wrapping my towel round me and sitting myself down next to Summer and Sloane.

Closer up, Sloane looked even more out of place than she had from the sea. Her pale face, long grey trench coat and dark lips jarred against the picture-postcard British seaside landscape.

'Nice swim, girls?' Summer asked.

'It was, actually,' I said, though I was starting to feel the cold already.

'Where's Libby?'

'She ... wanted to get some more exercise in,' Tabs said, diplomatically.

Sloane squinted out towards the water, looking for Libby on the horizon. I quickly dried myself as best I could and put my layers back on, shivering.

'Jessie Jones, you absolute wimp!' Summer berated. 'It's not cold at all!'

'It is when you've just come from the water,' I protested.

'Do you want a hot chocolate?'

'Please!'

'Anyone else want anything?' Summer asked. 'We're closing up but I can get a last order in.'

'Black coffee would be great,' Sloane said.

'I'll come help.' Tabs folded her towel and swimmers up precisely, placing them in a waterproof bag which then went neatly into her rucksack. I was surprised she hadn't had the foresight to bring her own thermos of hot chocolate.

'So you're into the whole beach life, surfer girl thing then, are you?' Sloane asked, once it was just us. She was perched on the rock, her trench coat spread out behind her like a cape.

'It's not my natural habitat, but I'm learning to love it,' I said.

'Yeah, it's not my natural habitat either,' she said, playing with the ring on her thumb. 'If that's not completely obvious. Which makes it extra rubbish being forced to move down here.' She looked at me from the corner of her eye.

'I completely understand,' I said. 'I felt like that when we first moved here too. It was so not my thing – any of it. I'd been happy living up in Manchester, about as different a place as you could get from here. Busy, multicultural, big. It was definitely a shock.'

'I could kind of tell. That you're different to the others, I mean.'

I didn't know how to take that.

'Totally didn't mean that as an insult,' she said, looking flustered, seeming to sense my confusion. 'Just that, I can tell you're not from here, that you're used to a more ... diverse scene.'

'Well, yeah,' I said, still not entirely sure I got what she meant – or that I was on board with whatever comment she was making about me or my friends.

'How did you manage to adjust?'

I thought about that. How *had* I managed? 'I guess by getting to know these guys.' Sloane's eyes widened, glancing out to the sea. 'Honestly, they're all lovely, even Libby – once you've warmed up to her ... or she's warmed up to you. So that really helped, and ... I don't know, I just eased into it. Baby steps. There's a lot to like.'

'Hmm. I'm not so sure,' Sloane said, her voice barely registering above the noise of the sea.

'So why did your folks move down here? You never said,' I asked.

Sloane paused, looking up from the thumb ring she'd been twiddling. 'Ah look, they're back,' she said, avoiding my question and focusing her attention on Summer and Tabs, who were walking over with drinks.

'I hope one of those is for me.' Libby walked across the sand to us. She must've gotten so cold she had to give in.

'Of course. Here,' Summer said, distributing the drinks.

I sipped mine, cautiously, knowing it would be hot but also

knowing the Cove Café's hot chocolates were the Best In The World – fact. Libby put her Robie and a beanie on, sitting down on our rock as far away from Sloane as she could get.

'Didn't fancy a swim?' Libby asked Sloane.

'It's not my thing,' Sloane replied.

'What *is* your thing?' Libby asked and I could see she was desperate to add some snide remark – I guessed something along the lines of *Watching Tim Burton movies on repeat?* I was proud of her for resisting.

'Let's see,' Sloane said, pointedly. 'I'm into witchcraft.'

My stomach lurched. It took everything for me not to gasp or make some other inadvertent noise.

Libby laughed. Sloane's face stayed expressionless.

'So, what, you're a witch?' Libby asked.

'Not exactly. There's no such thing as witches, right?' Sloane said, taking a tiny pause. My heart pounded. 'I'm a Wiccan.'

'What does that mean?' Summer asked.

'It's a religion based on nature,' Tabs piped up. 'Honouring nature – summer solstice and equinox and that kind of stuff, isn't it?'

'Pretty much,' Sloane said.

I breathed more normally again, my initial panic subsiding.

'So, do you have rituals and do spells?' Summer asked, looking genuinely interested. 'And covens and things like that? Or is that a different type of witchcraft?'

'Oh yeah, lots of rituals – and yes, covens.'

Libby was scowling into her cup even harder. 'So, you can, like, curse people and make people fall in love with you?' she asked, the acid in her voice burning through.

51

Sloane laughed. 'I wish. No, nothing like that, unfortunately. It's all about respecting nature and healing.'

I still felt jittery, even though I knew it was nothing to worry about. Sloane was not talking about my sort of witchcraft. Nothing was going to expose me or threaten me. Still, just the mention of witchcraft around my friends was too much to bear. I finished my hot chocolate and stood up. 'I should probably head, guys.'

Just then two boys came shooting across the sand, heading straight into the water – Marcus and Harry. 'All right, ladies!' Marcus shouted at us. 'Coming for a swim – and a bit of underwater action? Or is it your time of the month?' He did a double take when he saw Sloane with us. 'Not you though, Dracula. How are you even out in sunlight?' They high-fived each other and thrashed past the small children playing in the shallows, water splashing all over them, causing a wake of tears.

'Ignore them,' Summer said to Sloane. 'They're one of the many legions of dickheads we have at Queen Vics whose sole aim in life is to piss people off and be general arseholes.'

Underwater action? I thought to myself. *The only underwater action you deserve is being stung by a jellyfish. Or better yet, bitten by a shark!*

I grabbed my things, annoyed at how the day had ended.

'ARGH! WHAT THE—'

I turned to see Marcus, writhing around in the water, arms flailing, shouting in pain.

A white-hot flash of fear jolted through me. *No, no, no, no. Not again, not again. Oh God, was it a shark? What have I done?*

I dropped my bag and began to run towards the water's edge, where a small crowd was already forming.

It wasn't you, it was me. A voice in my head said.

Not my voice.

Sloane's voice.

And don't worry, it's just a jellyfish.

CHAPTER SEVEN

I'd left Steephill as fast as was humanly possible. It must have looked a hundred shades of weird – running away in the middle of a major drama just as everyone else was concerned for Marcus – but I'd had no choice. It was all too much.

Sloane didn't try and follow me. What even *was* that inside my head thing? It had felt . . . violating. But buried deep beneath my feelings of confusion and fear, I also felt a tiny fluttering seed of something else – excitement.

I'd met other witches on the Island at the coven meetings Nonna had taken us to – but mostly ladies on the more mature end of the spectrum who were all about the wild hair, bold patterns and statement jewellery. Sloane was different. She was my age for one, and she was the only witch who had ever got into my head.

I wanted to ask Mum and Nonna about it, but when I got home Handy Andy was there and it was impossible to catch either of them on their own. What would I have even said? That I'd met a secret witch who summoned a jellyfish to sting a boy according to wishes she'd heard in my head?

And anyway, what was *I* if not a secret witch?

I went to bed that night feeling worried and witch-angsty, thoughts of witches and broomsticks and warts swirling round my head like I'd been transported right back to days of old. In the morning I couldn't face thinking about it any more – again, like days of old. As I plodded down the stairs, I could hear Handy Andy's booming laugh echoing from the kitchen.

'"Nacho cheese", get it? Like "not your cheese", but in an American accent?'

Seriously, did he ever go home? Was this my life now – being subjected to lowest-level dad jokes twenty-four seven? I wasn't sure I was ready for that phase yet. It felt weird having a man in the house so much, especially first thing in the morning when I felt I should be free to roam around in my ancient and too-small *Buffy* T-shirt if I wanted to.

Luckily, I was in my uniform now. I grabbed my bag from where I'd dropped it in the hallway and headed for the door, giving Dave a passing stroke, moving on before she could wind herself round my ankles.

***

'I can't believe you missed that drama – out of choice.' Libby's first words to me as I joined them on the seafront.

Our group WhatsApp had been off the chart last night, but I hadn't been able to bring myself to engage with it, feigning another family dinner.

'It was, like, the best thing to happen this year by a hundred miles. Even better than when I had my hot and heavy session with Juan,' she continued. 'You should've seen his face, Jessie – Marcus's, not Juan's. It was *priceless*. I suggested Harry should piss on him – it's meant to help with jellyfish stings. Wish you guys hadn't rained on my parade.'

'It was a step too far,' Summer said. 'As much as we hate him.'

'And besides that, it's a myth,' Tabs added. 'Urine on a jellyfish sting doesn't actually work. It could even make it worse.'

Revision Facts – Acids and Alkalis (Chemistry)
1. Acids form acidic solutions in water.
2. Acidic solutions have pH values less than 7.
3. Alkalis form alkaline solutions in water.
4. Alkaline solutions have pH values greater than 7.
5. The normal pH level for urine is between 4.5 and 8.0. Therefore it is not acidic enough to do anything but make a jellyfish sting worse.

'Exactly!' Libby said, twirling round, arms in the air. 'An even better outcome – pain AND humiliation.'

They relayed the whole story – how Marcus was wincing and writhing in pain, how he'd had to be helped out of the sea and Summer's mum washed the area with vinegar while he cried, how Summer had to fetch Marcus some water and, later, a hot chocolate, how Libby basically just stood by and filmed the whole thing.

'And can we please take a minute to discuss your little undertaker friend – who left just after you, by the way,' Libby said. 'Can you believe all that witch stuff she was saying?'

'Libby!' Tabs reprimanded.

'Come on, you have to admit it – she's a weirdo. LIKE *I* SAID from the BEGINNING. This witch stuff confirms it. Summer, back me up here.'

I held my breath, my stomach in knots, waiting for Summer's

response. Kind, open-hearted, friendly Summer, who was the least judgemental person I knew.

'It was *kind* of weird,' she said, tentatively. 'But I don't know, maybe we didn't understand it properly. She can't really think she's a witch? That's not what she was saying, right?'

'She totally was!' Libby said firmly. 'We'd better be nice or she'll hex us. I bet she's got a cauldron and everything – collects newt's eyes and bat sperm.'

Summer let out a half-laugh and Tabs shook her head. Part of me knew this was typical Libby – the side of Libby that enjoys letting rip. And I knew she didn't mean all the stuff she came out with – with Libby, half of it was always said to get a laugh – or a reaction. But I felt sick all the same. Sick because I *did* have a cauldron, sick because I *am* a witch, sick because she was saying all those mean, hurtful, nasty things about someone for essentially being what I am. I could hear my heart thumping in my ears.

'She's not *my* little undertaker friend, by the way,' I spluttered. They all looked at me, curious. 'I know her the same amount you guys do. So don't make like out like we're best buddies.' I stopped. I didn't know what I was doing, but I felt the need to distance myself from Sloane, even though it left a bad taste in my mouth.

'Touchy,' Libby said.

Summer put her arm through mine, 'Ignore her. We know you're not friends.'

She was being supportive, but it didn't make me feel any better. We reached the main gates, where Freddie was leaning against the wall, waiting for me, like a beacon of hope. A beacon of hope with a gorgeous smile.

'Hey,' he said, grinning.

'Hi,' I said, as he gave me a kiss, the smell of his shower gel and fresh uniform instantly calming me down. 'See you later, guys.' It was a relief to wave them off.

'After school, yeah? Meet here?' Libby said.

'Sure,' I replied, my heart not in it.

'So I take it you saw it all happen,' said Freddie. 'The famous Marcus vs the jellyfish event of the year?'

'God, not you too,' I snapped. 'It's not that big a deal. People get stung by jellyfish all the time. It's hardly front-page news.'

'Woah,' he said, holding his hands up in surrender. 'Sorry. I guess I thought you'd be kind of . . .'

'What?'

'I don't know – happy? Ish? Or have found it funny at least.'

'Do you think I'm that mean? That I'd want people I don't like to suffer pain?'

He glanced to the floor. 'No, I don't. Come here.' He wrapped his arms around me. 'You're right, it's not a big deal. Sorry I brought it up.'

I found myself tucked up against his chest in a safe little Freddie bubble. I felt bad for snapping at him.

'It's fine. Sorry, I'm just tired.' I tilted my head back to look up at him. 'So Tabs said you shared some of your writing with her? I didn't even know you wrote anything – other than starting line-ups.'

It was meant as a joke, but I could see from his expression it missed the mark.

'I *have* mentioned it before – the writing. It's a new thing, but I'm quite into it.'

'I swear you haven't.'

'I really have, Jess. You didn't seem interested, so I never mentioned it again.'

Ouch. Bad Girlfriend points.

'Well, I'm sorry then – I'd love to hear more about your writing. And I'll pay more attention in the future, Shakespeare.' I reached up to give him a kiss, partly to make up, partly to get one last hit of Freddie before I faced the day. 'We'd better go in.'

***

My head was a sea of push and pull – part of me having a total freak-out and feeling scared by Sloane's dramatic revelation and the other part having a million different questions that needed answering. For now though, I needed more time to think things through. I avoided Sloane all day, on high alert right up until the final bell rang. Then I relaxed.

Which, in hindsight was a mistake. I shouldn't have let my defences down at all, because as I walked out of the gates, there she was. I looked away, whipping my phone out and pretending to be absorbed by something on my screen, hoping she hadn't clocked me. But of course she had.

'Can we talk?' she said, appearing at my side.

I looked around, not wanting people to see me talking to her. 'I can't, sorry, I'm meeting the girls.' At least I didn't have to lie.

'It's important,' she said softly. 'Please.'

She looked different today, or maybe I was seeing her differently now in light of her revelation. I noticed a spattering of freckles in little clusters on the top of her cheeks, a tiny fleck of amber in her dark eyes. She seemed less spiky and imposing now that I knew she was like me.

'I really can't, we're …' I considered lying, saying we were studying, or had some important appointment. But the fear of her getting inside my head stopped me cold.

'I'm sorry if I freaked you out yesterday,' she began. 'I get the impression not all of your friends are super keen on me. But, just putting that to one side for a minute – you must have questions. Give me half an hour, please? Then, if you want nothing more to do with me, I'll never bother you again.'

Her face looked open, pleading, like a puppy wanting to show its master a new trick. I couldn't bring myself to say no. Plus, it was a good deal – half an hour of Sloane and then I could be free of her if I wanted to be. Free *and* guilt-free. Plus, she was right, I did have questions.

'Fine,' I said, keen to get away from school, knowing that if the girls saw me ditching them and heading off with Sloane I would never hear the end of it. 'But only half an hour.'

'This way,' Sloane said, heading away from the seafront and up to the cliffs.

I fired off a text on the WhatsApp group claiming a family emergency I'd have to elaborate on later. I nearly went with a studying emergency but I knew Tabs would be all over it asking for details.

While Sloane and I walked in silence, I made a mental checklist of all the questions I had. I could start with, *Who the hell are you?* Or maybe, *How the hell did you get inside my head?* Or, more generally, *What the hell do you want from me?*

We turned on to the coastal path. The seafront looked small beneath us. It briefly crossed my mind that I should text the girls telling them where I was. What if Sloane was planning on harming me in some way? An image of her carving my leg off before plopping it into a boiling cauldron flashed into my mind. I shook it away, praying it wasn't a vision, and knowing I was being ridiculous. There was absolutely no value to be had from me or any of my limbs.

We walked along the uphill path for what felt like ages. Then, the route started weaving its way down, back towards to the sea. I figured we were well past the town seafront now, though I had no idea where exactly. I had never been this way before, and Sloane was confidently navigating us through short cuts and side paths and hidden entrances. I realised it would be impossible for me to ever return on my own.

'Through here,' she said finally, moving away from the path towards a solid rock face. It had a strange marking gauged into it, barely visible – three straight lines with a crude star through them, but other than that it looked like a perfectly normal rock. As I watched, she laid her hands on it and the rock started shifting, blurring. I blinked. Out of nowhere, a small opening had appeared.

'Come on,' she said gesturing, impatient, like it was totally normal for a rock to suddenly manifest a gaping hole out of nowhere, and then she disappeared through the gap.

CHAPTER EIGHT

I followed her through, saying just one tiny little prayer that I wasn't walking to my death. I gave my leg a pat, wishing it a safe passage.

'How did you—' I started to ask, stopping abruptly to take in the surroundings.

We'd stepped into a small cove, smaller even than Steephill. A tiny, perfectly formed horseshoe cove, its curves marked by large, jutting boulders and a fringe of greenery holding firm against the breeze. Vine-like leaves hung in long, lazy tendrils over the entrance we'd just walked through, giving the scene some serious *Indiana Jones* feels. There was a fire pit carved out of the shingled sand, a few blackened logs lying morosely in its depths, and large hefts of driftwood arranged around it by way of seating.

'I just made a tunnel,' Sloane said, as if she was explaining how she put her socks on.

'But . . . the rock?' I spluttered.

'Oh that's nothing, just an opening. And don't worry, I've put a protective spell on it so no one can find us here. Or even find *here* at all.'

I gulped, not sure if that was a good thing or a bad thing. 'I don't understand,' I said.

She looked me up and down, confused. 'I don't understand what you don't understand,' she said. 'It's just a basic protective spell – and a manifesting spell.'

I nodded, trying to look like I got it, though she may as well have been speaking Japanese to me for all I understood.

'You *are* a witch, right?' she asked. She lowered her voice, like she was talking to a toddler who had lost its mum and didn't want to scare them.

'Yes, I'm a witch.'

'Phew – I thought I'd got completely the wrong person for a minute.' She sat down on one of the bits of wood and I sat next to her. 'Though I knew I couldn't have. I wouldn't have been able to communicate with you telepathically if you weren't in the Sisterhood.'

'The Sisterhood?' All I could think of was travelling pants.

She sighed. 'Jessie, do you know what you are?'

'Yes. *A witch.*' I felt like we'd covered that.

'Not just any old witch though – a really rare and powerful one. You're one of the Sisters of Endor. And so am I.'

The Sisters of Endor. That sounded familiar, but I couldn't place it. Maybe I'd heard Nonna talking about it, maybe it was at one of the Coven meetings. 'Who are the Sisters of Endor?'

'We're elite witches – like the SAS of witches. There aren't many of us – you're only the eighth that I know of. No one knows for sure why we're more powerful than other witches, or why we come into full-time powers early, even though there are lots of theories. But you knew this, right? Tell me you knew at least some of this?'

'I knew I came into my full-time powers early. And I knew I'm ... different.'

'But no one told you you're a Sister?' she said incredulously.

I shook my head, I felt stupid and naïve and betrayed. How could Nonna and Mum failed to have mentioned this strange new subsection of witchery that I happened to belong to?

'I'm quite new to ... this whole thing,' I said, feeling very much on the back foot and not enjoying it.

I looked away from Sloane, picking at the driftwood, digging my thumbnail into it, gouging out lines of crescent moons. I had no idea how to begin, so I decided to start with the basics. 'Where did you come from?' I asked, more bluntly than I meant.

She frowned. 'All over. Kind of everywhere and nowhere. I'm from a travelling coven. We make our home wherever the wind and the need take us.'

Wow, that sounded like even more disruption and uprooting than I'd had to deal with.

'Are they all here on the Island with you? Your coven?'

'My mum is. The others have gone on somewhere else. We wanted to come and try Island living for a bit. Mum's super busy though, she's hardly ever around.'

'Why the Island? Specifically.'

'We fancied a change of scene – sunshine and sea,' she said.

'I thought you said the sea wasn't your scene?' My tone was leaning towards the Libby end of the interrogative spectrum but I couldn't help it, my head was a casserole.

'I said *surfer girl* antics weren't my scene. The sea is fine.'

'OK, so, you're a travelling witch, you fancied a change, and you're here with your mum.'

'Basically, yes.'

'How did you know *I* was a witch? And a Sister of whatever?' I asked.

'Witches know witches. And everyone knows you're a Sister – full-time powers at your age and the stuff you were pulling off?'

'I didn't know *you* were a witch,' I said, offended that she made it sound so easy, so matter-of-fact, and yet I hadn't managed it.

'You probably did, deep down. Did you not sense a different energy that first day? When I walked into assembly?'

I cast my mind back. It was only a couple of days ago but it felt like a lifetime. I *had* sensed something – a definite energy shift. I'd put it down to the excitement of there being a new person, as well as Sloane being generally intriguing.

'You need to learn to be more intuitive,' she said, unhelpfully. I shot her a look. 'Sorry. I keep forgetting you're new to this.'

'You're not?'

'I've been fully fledged since my first drop of period – which was annoyingly early – end of Year Five. But you weren't here, right? You were on the run, with your mum who was denying her powers? So you were late to the party, you have an excuse.'

'How do you know that?' I asked, uncomfortable at her level of inside knowledge.

She shrugged. 'Witch grapevine. It's quite an unusual circumstance, word gets around.'

I wasn't sure I liked the idea of being an *unusual circumstance*. Or of featuring on the witch grapevine for that matter.

'Why did you do that to Marcus?' I asked.

Her face brightened briefly, a smile bursting to the surface, until she saw my expression. 'You're not angry about that, are you? I thought I was doing you a favour – it was what you wished for.'

'No I didn't!' I snapped, instantly realising that of course she was right. I had wished it, kind of. 'I mean, yeah but only slightly. I didn't actually intend it to happen.'

'I'm sorry. But you need to be careful about what comes through your head.'

'Yeah, about that. I don't like you getting inside my head – it freaks me out.'

'Oh.' She ran her hand through her hair, a green strand flopping forward on to her face. 'Sorry. Again. I thought you'd get a kick out of it. It's pretty cool. And fun – and an easy way to communicate, just us. It comes in useful, trust me.'

'Well, it came as a bit of a shock. Plus, I had no idea how to say anything back.'

'Well don't worry about that,' she said, perking up. 'I'll teach you how later. I'm so pleased we're having this conversation – I've been trying to get your attention ever since I started.'

'Wait!' I said, a light bulb switching on. 'Did *you* make Freddie score that goal?'

She nodded, grinning. 'It's normally against my policy to do anything nice for boys, but I thought you'd realise something was up.'

'The pizza! And the drink someone spilled on Callum in the canteen!' I added, my mind racing through all the unexplained things that had happened since Sloane's arrival.

She smiled, nodding.

'Callum was one of the boys who gave you such a hard time last year, right?'

I stared at her. 'Was *that* on the witch grapevine too?'

'You're famous.' Sloane shrugged. 'Callum one hundred per cent deserved it. And Marcus too. Boys like that – I know their kind. I know what they're like, what they're capable of. They need to be taught a lesson, and not just a jellyfish sting either – something they won't ever forget, something that will make sure they never offend again.'

Her eyes had clouded over as she stared out towards the sea, the waves now rising and crashing in violent peaks against the shore.

'I dealt with that last year,' I said. 'It's better now. I think they've learned their lesson.' Did I actually believe that? Maybe not; but, for now, it *was* better than last year. I had to try to believe they'd changed.

'Have they though?' Sloane asked, echoing my thoughts. 'Because in my experience, boys like that never learn and they certainly never change. Once a misogynist, always a misogynist. The only thing to do is keep putting them in their place. Until you can get rid of them altogether.'

I snapped my head up, hoping she hadn't said what I thought she had. 'What do you mean, *get rid of them*?'

'Get rid of their *behaviour*, I mean. You need to chill, Jessie,' Sloane laughed.

A ball of uncertainty formed in my stomach. I studied Sloane's face, not knowing her well enough to tell if I had just misunderstood – or if I had understood perfectly and now she was just trying to cover it up.

'You can't do that stuff,' I said. 'Revenge, making people suffer – it's . . . bad. And mean. And not what magic is for. One of the many things I learned last year!'

'Of course not,' Sloane said. 'I'm passionate about making sure that girls and women feel safe, that's all. I saw Marcus being a jerk and it was instinct to act against him – for *protection*, not revenge. But if you say things have changed overall, then that's great. I won't need to take action again.' She began to run her finger along the tattoo on her wrist.

I let myself relax a little.

'I can control myself, you know,' Sloane said. 'I held off doing anything to Libby, which was actually very hard to resist when she was being such a bitch to me.'

'Please don't, that would be—'

'I didn't! Even though I was really angry,' Sloane said, sounding pleased with herself. 'Pretty duff choice of friends, by the way.'

'Libby is great,' I said. 'She's loyal and funny and always there for her friends.'

'Well, that's not exactly the Libby that's coming across to me, more savage pitbull desperate to tear into me.'

'Her bark is worse than her bite.' I thought back to earlier in the year, the looks Libby would shoot me, the fear I carried round with me every day coming into school, going to my PE lessons. 'And she's working on the bark thing.'

'Look, I wouldn't know much about friends, I've never really had any – we always moved around too much. But . . . I just feel like if I did, I wouldn't choose someone so . . . mean.'

I considered telling her about the time I was off with a

stinking cold and Libby had brought round homemade chicken soup – it was pretty disgusting soup (she's a terrible cook) but she'd read that chicken soup was good for colds and had spent hours making it. Or the time she bailed on a date to help me finish my Media Studies coursework I was stressing about. Or when she wrote me a funny poem about sisters after Bella and I had fallen out over something.

But I didn't tell her any of that, because that was how Libby was with *me*. Sloane was right; Libby had been horrible to her – almost indefensibly so. I totally understood how awful that felt. But I also knew Libby was decent – deep down. It reminded me of Freddie's words about Callum: *He's decent, he's just had a tough time of it.*

'I never really had friends before here either,' I said, not knowing what else to say. I felt torn. I wanted to defend Libby but I understood how Sloane felt.

'Do they know?' she asked, turning to look right at me. The question felt like an arrow. Pointed. What she was really asking was, *do your recently made friends, who you're trying to forge a normal life with, know that you're actually a through-to-the-bones witch, who was responsible for all kinds of weird shit last year?*

I stuttered, fumbled, not wanting to answer.

'Ah,' Sloane said, a glimmer of a smile showing.

'I haven't known them that long. I don't want to . . .'

'Scare them off?'

'It's not that, exactly,' I said, thinking that actually it *was* that, exactly. 'They'll be fine with it, we're good friends. I just want to find the right time.'

'But are they really your friends if they don't know the real you?' The question was a bullet this time.

'They do know me. There's more to me than magic and being a witch. That's not what defines me.'

'But it's such a huge part of us – it's our foundations,' Sloane said.

'It might be for you. It's not for me.' Anger pinched at my corners. How dare Sloane just rock up out of the blue and start making assumptions about me and my friends. She didn't know anything about us. About me.

'OK.' She shrugged. 'You know yourself and your friends better than I do.'

A chill spread straight through me – had Sloane been in my head again? Surely not – I'd know. *Wouldn't I?* I shivered. I hadn't known the other times.

'So if they don't know about your powers, does that mean you haven't been able to do magic around them? That must be awful – and DULL.' Sloane waved her hand and flames suddenly rose from the fire pit in front of us, flickering and jumping and dancing to the beat of her hands as she twirled and twisted them. She looked alive, all of a sudden, no longer awkward or shy, like she owned the space she inhabited and everything around her.

'How did you . . .' I stuttered, not able to take my eyes of the flames.

'Oh come on. Fire is like the first thing you learn.'

I nodded. 'I've only started fires and put them out – but never controlled them.'

'Your mum and grandma have been teaching you, right?'

'Yeah, but we've been going slowly. They said it's complicated and that some things are for much later, when my power is balanced and I understand it more. Like learning to drive, or whatever.' I heard their standard refrain echo in my head – *'it's complicated'. 'Not yet, it's complicated.' 'Maybe soon, it's complicated.' 'All in good time, it's complicated.'*

Sloane scoffed. 'Your power is as balanced as it needs to be, Jessie,' she said, her dark-rimmed eyes glowing. 'They've obviously been keeping things from you – they haven't even told you about the Sisters. This is all yours for the taking – now. No more waiting. You can drive a goddam Lamborghini! You are a powerful, badass witch and you deserve to know all that you can do – and be.'

My insides fizzed like lemonade, her words ringing in my ears. I thought of the tea leaves and my anger flared. All those health and safety assessments I'd had to endure and the whole time they'd been lying to me – or keeping things from me, at least. I *had* been ready, I knew it.

'Try it with me,' Sloane said encouragingly. She made fists with her hands, and the fire went out, the heat disappearing like someone had yanked a blanket off me. 'Start a fire like normal, but just stay linked to it – feel the connection, breathe it in, and, when you can sense it in your fingers, start moving.'

It sounded too simple. And if it was that simple, why hadn't I done it before?

I concentrated, starting my own fire like I had many times before, my eyes focusing on the lick of the flames, the connection I felt to the fire. I centred myself, still staring at the flames, the reds and oranges melding into a moving, blurred mass. And then, when I'd normally let the connection go, I held on to it instead, breathed into it. Sure enough, the buzz made its way to my fingers, to every part of me. I waved my hand, gently, a slight wrist twist – and the flames did the same, dancing to my beat. A fire conductor.

'Oh my God!' I shrieked. 'I'm doing it!'

'Yeah you are!' Sloane shouted. Then she let out an ear-piercingly loud shriek, which echoed around the cove.

'Shh! We don't want anyone to see us,' I said, panicking, my flames lowering.

'I told you.' Sloane's eyes gleamed. 'Protective spell – no one can see us, hear us, or find us. We're in a bubble. Our own little freedom bubble. We can do whatever the hell we want.'

'Really?' I asked, nervous and excited at the thought.

Sloane's flames shot into the air, reaching into the sky, towering over us. 'Yes!' she said. 'And you've got so much still to learn.'

My stomach leaped, feeling as high as the flames. I was absolutely terrified and ridiculously excited. Something felt so right about this. I felt alive.

And seen.

And powerful.

CHAPTER NINE

The next morning, I went out to the potting shed to find Nonna. I was glowing in the light of Sloane's magic revelations and all the fun we'd had. After the flames, we'd moved on to waves and rocks and even animals. At one point, Sloane had summoned a legion of crabs who had come scuttling out of the sea in tight lines, like an army battalion swarming over the brow of a hill. And most amazing, most thrilling of all, was the fact that I could do that too. Not yet, obviously, because no one had taught me how; but I knew it was there, inside me, ready and waiting. And I was determined to get Nonna to start taking me seriously and teach me some proper magic. The kind Sloane had showed me was possible.

'Good morning,' Mum said as I walked in. I hadn't realised she would be out here too. 'You're up early. Have I missed something? It's not a revision club day, is it?'

Mum and Nonna were standing side by side, leaning over the counter and forming a sort of plant repotting conveyor belt – Mum handing small seedlings to Nonna, who eased them into bigger pots and covered them with soil. The ancient radio was blaring out Motown tunes, and their hips moved in sync to the music. Combined with the beams of glorious sunshine that shone through the glass ceiling, the whole scene was pretty heartwarming. They must have made up.

'Come and join us, sweetcheeks,' Nonna said, doing a twirl with a seedling in her hand. 'We're doing the herb bundles next.'

'Tempting as that sounds, I've got to get ready for school.'

'Oh, you big spoil-sport.' Nonna flicked some soil at me. 'You're hardly ever out here. You need to learn this stuff – I won't be around for ever. I could be hit by a bus tomorrow and you'll never know how to make a herb bundle.'

Mum elbowed her for that. 'Are you all right, darling? Did you need me for something?'

I thought I'd give them one more chance. 'I was just wondering if we could squeeze in an extra magic lesson today. I'm quite keen to try some manifesting. Or protection spells, maybe?'

Nonna stopped dancing and turned towards me, sapling in hand. 'Jessie, sweetheart, we've been through this.'

UGH. Same old, same old. I knew what the response would be and I couldn't bear to hear it again. Sloane had taught me more in twenty minutes than they'd taught me in six months. They were stopping me fulfilling my potential. It wasn't fair.

Nonna sensed my frustration. 'Come and help us with the bundles and I'll teach you all about the cleansing power of sage.'

That was SO not what I had in mind.

'I've got to get to school,' I grunted.

'Have a good day, love,' Mum said.

I was a few stomps away when I stopped and turned back.

'What kind of witch am I?' I asked.

'What do you mean?' Mum said, going very still.

'I'm more powerful than some witches, and I got my full-time powers earlier. That's not normal is it? Am I not a normal witch?'

'You're a very powerful witch, Jessie,' Nonna said flatly, exchanging a look with Mum. 'Which is wonderful. But no matter how powerful we are, we all have to learn the basics and build our understanding and our strength step by step.'

'Right. So, I'm not a Sister of Endor?'

It had the desired effect. They both stood suddenly statue-still.

'Where did you hear that?' Nonna asked, all serious now.

'I was doing some research online,' I lied, not wanting to throw Sloane under the bus. 'It sounded a bit like me – coming into my full powers early, that sort of thing.' I had no idea if there really was anything online. I could tell by Mum's face and the way she was keeping her eyes on the floor I was on to something though – Sloane had been right. 'I *am*, aren't I? Why didn't you tell me? Do you not think that's like, vital information you're keeping from me – *about* me!'

Nonna put her sapling down and stepped towards me, putting her arm around my shoulder, giving my arm a gentle squeeze. 'Jessie love, of course we were planning on telling you, explaining it all, in time. It just seemed like a lot for you to take in. We wanted you to concentrate on finding your magical feet first.'

'Knowing you're a Sister would've just given you more to get your head round, darling,' Mum said, finally making eye contact. 'A complication you didn't need.'

'You would've ended up like Justin Beaver,' Nonna said.

My mind whirred. 'What?'

'Well, he had all that success and fame and then look, he ended up arrested and completely out of control.'

'Nonna, that's not exactly ... and it's not Justin *Beaver*!' I sighed, not even knowing where to start. The disappointment pinched at me. They had been actively hiding this from me and now I knew why. They didn't trust me.

'Ignore Nonna,' Mum said. 'That wasn't a helpful comparison – we're not suggesting that you're going to—'

'You don't trust me,' I snapped. 'That's what you're both saying. Isn't it?'

They were silent. A little bubble of anger sprung up in me.

'Why don't we go inside now and talk about it?' Mum asked.

'I need to get to school,' I said, storming off. Sloane had been right all along – they had been lying to me and holding me back.

It was time to take matters into my own hands – time to get behind the wheel of that Lamborghini.

***

In assembly, I was barely able to listen. Ms Pritchard was saying something about revision timetables and mocks and was looking very serious, but all I could think about was the fact that Mum and Nonna had been lying to my face. Maybe not openly lying as such, but lying by omission.

Did they seriously think I'd get all power-happy and too big for my boots? What would that even entail? Demanding special dinner privileges and insisting on not doing any chores? I could handle the truth. And I could certainly handle some more magic lessons – proper ones. I thought back to the fire and the waves and the crabs and all the rest of it and got a little surge of excitement.

I still wasn't sure how I felt about Sloane herself, only sure that I didn't quite have the measure of her yet. There was the shadow of a thought nagging at me, the sense that she wasn't revealing everything about herself – though she'd been honest about being a witch, which was more than I had been at first. And she'd answered all my questions. I had no obvious reason to doubt her. I was aware however, of the giant headache that was awaiting me in the form of Libby if I did want to see more of Sloane.

Check out the eyebrows on her. Sloane's voice suddenly popped into my head and thrust me back into the dull assembly. *They've got a life of their own. I swear they're going to take off in a minute.*

I tried to stifle a laugh, which ended up coming out as a snort.

Ms Pritchard glared in my direction.

Careful, the eyebrows will come for you.

Sloane had taught me how to communicate with her – and how to block voices out when I didn't want them in my head, which made me feel a lot better about the whole thing. And she was right, it did have its perks – like being able to have a laugh during a dull-arse assembly!

You'll get me in trouble, I thought-spoke.

Yay! You did it. Man, this is boring. Do you want to skip out after?

No! I've got Maths.

Yawn.

Not to me. And besides, we're revising ratio and proportion – which always comes up.

Yawn again. After school? At the cove?

I told Libby I'd go shopping with her.

Who wants to go trudging through boring shops when you can make waves. LITERALLY MAKE WAVES.

I had no idea how she'd managed to raise her thought-voice, but I was impressed.

There was a shift in the hall and people started fidgeting in their seats, adjusting themselves from their slumped positions. I zoned back in.

'I hope these pointers have been useful. And a reminder of exactly how important this time – this year – is to you all. Know that all the work will be worth it in the end,' Ms Pritchard said, finishing up with a flourish, waggling a finger like a cut-price Winston Churchill.

The form tutors sitting on the sidelines stood up and started overseeing the mass exit. I dutifully plodded out with my form, running through the day in my head – I was looking forward to getting stuck into Maths revision, less so English.

'Hey,' Sloane said. No longer in my head but in person, appearing in front of me in the corridor, taking me by surprise. 'So I can't convince you to bail?'

'Never,' I said, hoping Libby wasn't seeing this.

'But after school is a maybe?' She looked hopeful.

'I don't know, I don't like bailing on people – especially not twice in a row.' I glanced around, making sure no one who mattered was in earshot.

I saw Sloane's face fall. 'I get it,' she said, looking down. 'You have friends already, no worries.'

My heart tugged for her, taking me right back to when *I* had zero friends and didn't know a soul. That stuff is HARD. 'We can definitely hang out soon,' I said quickly. 'I just don't want to let my friends down. But definitely soon.'

She snapped back into a smile, safely recovered from the verge of tears.

'You know we'll have fun.' She grinned, turning the streak in her hair from green to purple to blue in the time it took me to blink.

The second bell rang and just at that moment Libby emptied out of the hall with her form. She did a double take when she saw me talking to Sloane and raised her eyebrows at me.

'Gotta go,' I said, hurrying away from Sloane.

I marched into Maths in a fluster, Libby's face imprinted on my mind like some kind of frowning hologram. Why did I even feel so bad? I was allowed to be friends with whoever I wanted – Libby wasn't the boss of me. Just bossy.

Although, I reminded myself, it wasn't like Libby – or anyone – had *said* I wasn't allowed to be friends with Sloane. Maybe I was overthinking it. Overreacting. Maybe it was all fine. In which case, why did I feel this icky, pulled-in-two-directions perma-guilt? Guilt for being friendly with Sloane, and guilt at practically disowning Sloane in that moment. I just needed to put my big girl pants on and woman up to Libby, explain I was capable of deciding for myself who I do and don't want to talk to, thank you very much. I shouldn't be feeling this guilty. It wasn't like I had anything to hide. Except, I remembered with alarming clarity, I very much did have *something* to hide.

'You all right?' Tabs asked as I slammed my books down on the table and sank into the seat next to her. I gave Freddie, who was grinning at me, a cursory wave from across the classroom.

'Yeah,' I said. 'Actually, no. I was just talking to Sloane in the corridor – she grabbed me after assembly – and when Libby saw us she gave me the biggest dirty look. Like I'd doomed her to a life devoid of hot boys.'

Tabs laughed.

'OK maybe not quite that dirty a look, but it was punchy. It pisses me off – how she acts like she's the boss of us all. And she's so mean sometimes. She's been about as welcoming to Sloane as a punch in the face.'

I took a breath.

'Wow, you're really not all right,' Tabs said. 'I know what you mean about Libby, and yes, her mean streak is definitely making itself seen again. But, I dunno ... as weird as this may sound, I don't think she's trying to boss us around when it comes to Sloane. I think she's maybe trying to protect us? Or thinks she is.'

'Protect us? From what?' I said. 'Developing a penchant for black lipstick? Because there's nothing else dangerous about Sloane.' Deep down, I knew that wasn't true – but I also knew that Libby didn't, so my concern couldn't possibly be her concern.

'I think she just gets a bad vibe from Sloane.'

'She got a bad vibe from her the first day she set eyes on her, before she even spoke to her, with nothing at all to base it on other than how Sloane looks. That's not being protective, it's being prejudiced.'

'If you want to be friends with Sloane, be friends with her. No one can stop you hanging round with whoever you want,' Tabitha said gently. 'But whatever you do, please don't actually doom her to a life devoid of hot boys – we'd never hear the end of it!'

'I just can't face an argument with Libby about it,' I said, the thought of it making me wince.

Mr Anstead came bustling in then, a KeepCup of coffee in one hand, a pile of precariously placed books in the other, both looking like they were on the verge of spilling over.

'So you reckon Sloane's decent?' Tabs whispered.

'Yeah. Maybe?' I replied. 'I think she's different, but we should give her a chance. She's actually quite fun.' Though after I said it I realised that making fires dance and summoning crabs from the sea might not be everyone's idea of fun.

'Have you been hanging out with her then?'

'A bit,' I said, remembering that I had bailed on the girls claiming a family dinner the night before. 'I bumped into her on the front last night after . . . sorting out some stuff at home. We had a coffee.'

'Quiet please!' Mr Anstead boomed. His lidless coffee cup was perched on the very edge of his desk, next to the tower of books that were inching closer to the cup with every move he made. He turned his computer on, the cup edged closer. He leaned across to get a pencil, the cup edged closer. His elbow nudged the books, the cup—

I righted the swaying, about-to-spray-coffee-everywhere cup, saving Mr Anstead from the embarrassment and the hassle of cleaning it up, saving Eleanor Landy from having coffee-soaked tights and saving the class from wasted learning time. My good deed for the day.

Towards the end of the lesson, while I was working out what proportion of the £60 from the doughnut sale Pierre, Andrew and Lisa were all due, according to how many hours they'd put in (I don't know what Pierre's excuse was, but the lazy git clearly did not care about this doughnut sale), Angela Wright passed me a note.

I took it with trepidation. It had been a long time since I'd had a note passed to me in class.

Can I have a quick word with you after class pls, Callum.

I did a double take, blinking a few times to make sure I'd read it correctly, and when I was sure – Was it the Apocalypse? What was happening? – I scrunched the note up and dropped it on the floor. I could sense Callum was watching me, possibly trying to catch my eye. I focused on Pierre and making sure I gave the dosser as little of that £60 as he deserved.

***

I was ahead of the curve, poised and ready to go by the time the bell went at the end of Maths, having already closed up my books, got my things together and given Tabs a cursory goodbye. But apparently, Callum had done the same. He was waiting for me right next to the door.

'Can I talk to you quickly, please?' he asked, forcing the words out like he was eating ants.

'No.' I started walking away.

'It's important.'

I carried on walking, refusing to even engage. There couldn't possibly be anything Callum and I had to talk about.

'Jess, wait up!' Freddie called, running up to me.

He put his arm around me, it felt like a nice protective gesture.

'Did you ask her yet?' Freddie asked Callum.

I bristled at the fact they'd obviously had a conversation about me.

Their relationship was complicated – mainly by me. But also by Freddie having had a bit of an epiphany about Callum last year – also caused by me. They'd always been close – football buddies, classmates, even the rare kind of boy friends who share some feelings – until me. Until Callum being such a massive dick was too much for Freddie, who is not a dick (just a bit of a sheep sometimes).

Since then they'd kind of made up, keeping up a form of friendship, but not a friendship like they used to have – although recently I'd noticed that they seemed to be spending more and more time together. Freddie had always insisted that Callum was essentially decent, that he's just 'had a tough time', but I'd never bought it. Some people are rotten to the core. So I knew they still talked, but I didn't like that they apparently talked about *me*.

'Ask me what?' I snapped, feeling betrayed.

Callum glanced around him. People were staring as they walked past us, whispers echoing through the halls. He waited until the coast was slightly clearer, leaning closer.

'This event tonight, the one my dad is hosting for the paper?'

I nodded. Yes, I knew the hell-fest to which he was referring.

'Look.' The discomfort was practically sweating off of him. 'I know it's probably your idea of hell.' I nodded again – he had that right. 'But I was wondering if there was any way you would come.'

I stared at him. Then Freddie. Then back to Callum.

'Uh, that would be a hard no. Why should I?'

Callum rolled his shoulders and ran his fingers through his hair, clearly wishing a hole would open up in the floor and swallow him. He looked genuine and sincere ... almost vulnerable? It was throwing me – this was not the Callum I was used to.

'You'd be helping me out,' he said at last, in a quiet voice.

I laughed. I couldn't help myself. Was Callum being serious? He scowled at me.

'And why would I want to do that?'

'You're right,' he said, his face back to normal Callum, the raw meanness in his eyes. 'You wouldn't. Forget it.' He turned to Freddie. 'I knew this was a stupid idea,' he said, then stormed off.

'What the hell was that?' I asked, shaking off Freddie's arm, which now felt manipulative rather than protective.

'That was Callum reaching out.' He looked disappointed. In *me*?

'Well he chose the wrong person to reach out to. Why on earth would I go to that hideous event?'

Freddie paused, on the verge of saying something but deciding against. He frowned, lowered his voice. 'Would it really be that bad?'

'Um, let me see. Yes, yes it most definitely would. They humiliated me, remember? Why does Callum even want me there?'

Freddie sighed. 'It's not my story to tell and it's complicated, but ... basically his dad is a bellend – a nasty one – and this particular event is quite a big deal to him and you being there ... is also a big deal to him and it would help things.'

'Like father, like son,' I muttered.

'Since the whole video story broke last year he's been giving Callum a really hard time. Like, a *really* hard time. He thinks it's damaged his chances of getting re-elected and he's ... taking it out on Callum.'

'And? Are you suggesting that's my fault?'

84

'No – *of course* not. Not at all. The video was good for him, for all of us, overall – it gave everyone a wake-up call. But for Callum, things have been tough . . .'

I was too angry to listen. *Poor Callum, such a hard life Callum.* As far as I was concerned, Callum deserved everything he got. Him getting a hard time from his dad wasn't anything that required my sympathy; it was justice. A justice that he'd managed to slither away from at school.

'Have you experienced some kind of sporting injury or bang to the head? Do you not remember how disgusting he was to me last year? Maybe not, as you were standing right beside him through most of it.'

Freddie's face dropped, wounded. 'That's harsh.'

'That's true.'

'I'm not asking you to become best friends, I'm asking you to do this one thing. He apologised. He's been trying. Haven't you noticed?'

'A dickhead leopard doesn't change its spots.'

Freddie's face was hard. 'You're so caught up in hating him, you're not seeing him clearly. You've got a set idea of who he is and you're wrong.'

And with that, I turned and walked away, refusing to listen to any more.

CHAPTER TEN

I was still fuming – and confused – at lunch. The whole thing had been brewing in my head all through infectious diseases in Biology, like an infectious disease itself. An infectious disease like Callum Henderson.

Revision Facts – Communicable Diseases (Biology)

1. A pathogen is a microorganism that causes disease.
2. All types of pathogens have a simple life cycle: they infect a host, reproduce or replicate, then spread from their host and infect other organisms.
3. They have structural adaptations which enable them to remain successful at completing their life cycle and spreading to other organisms.
4. Diseases caused by pathogens are called communicable diseases. This means they can be transferred between organisms.
5. There are different ways that the communicable disease known as Callum is spread effectively. These include, but are not limited to: being an MP's son, being a sporting superstar, generally being untouchable, opening his mouth, existing.

Although, to be honest, it wasn't Callum asking me for help that had upset me so much. It was *Freddie*. Freddie rekindling the bromance with him. Freddie taking *Callum's* side. That look on Freddie's face – like I was the one who was out of order, like I had done something wrong.

It wasn't *me* who had come on to Callum, reacted badly to him rejecting me and spread false rumours all round the school. It wasn't *me* who had kept scores on the opposite sex and talked about them as if they were worthless objects to be passed from person to person. It wasn't *me* who tricked Callum into going to a party with the sole intention of recording something that could humiliate him in front of the whole school. It wasn't *me*—

'What's up?' Summer asked, falling into step with me on the way to the canteen. 'You're stomping to lunch like you've got a fight to pick with the cook. You upset it's not your beloved pizza again?'

'Not the cook,' I grunted. 'Callum. And Freddie.'

'Uh-oh. What's happened?'

There was no queue so we walked straight through to the counter, where colourless ladles of macaroni cheese were dumped on to our trays. I explained what had gone down earlier.

'Weird,' Summer said, as we sought out Libby and Tabs who were on our first-choice table – away from the kitchen and the area the Year Sevens liked to congregate in. 'I wonder why Callum wants you to go to this party?'

'That's not even the point, though.' I plonked myself down at the table next to Tabs.

'Well hello to you too,' Libby said.

'We're having a drama,' Summer said. 'Or Jessie is.'

'Ooooh. Fill us in.'

'It's nothing major,' I snapped, annoyed at the excitement in her tone. This was my life, not some gossip. 'Callum asked me to go to this newspaper event tonight – which of course I said no to. But he'd obviously been talking to Freddie about it and Freddie got involved and . . . basically seemed to be suggesting that I should go and that I was mean for not helping Callum out. Which just seems crazy to me. Like, why would *I* do anything to help Callum out? Anyway, Freddie and I have now fallen out about it – and the whole thing is just . . . annoying.'

I dug my fork angrily into the congealed mass of macaroni, trying to chisel out a mouthful.

Libby didn't reply. When I looked up I saw she was deep in thought, ruminating on my anger-vomit. 'That does seem strange,' she said slowly. 'Callum asking you for a favour.'

'I know, right?' I was pleased that she understood. 'Like, HELLO, you made my life a living hell, why would I do anything for you?'

'Well, yeah. It makes me think it must be important.'

'Huh?'

'You know what Callum's like, all strong and silent. You hate him, for obvious reasons. He hates you, also for obvious reasons. You collapsed his safe little misogynist-terrorist reign. It must've been his worst nightmare having to ask you for help.'

'And?' The macaroni stodge was lodged in the back of my throat.

'Well, I just think, if he still asked you for help, given all that, then he must have a really good reason.'

I looked at Summer and Tabs, incredulous. Was I really hearing this?

'I don't care what's important to Callum Henderson! I wouldn't help him if he was' – I reached for the worst situation I could think of – 'drowning. Or falling off a cliff. Or on fire.'

'Jessie,' Summer reprimanded. 'Bit harsh.'

'I'm not saying he's a saint,' Libby said. 'I'm just saying he must have a reason to have asked you. Maybe you should think about it.'

'Freddie has your back,' Tabs added. 'He knows your history with Callum. Maybe you should talk to him and find out more.'

'You have all lost the plot.' I felt the anger biting at me. How dare they? Callum had made my life a misery. Why did I owe him anything at all?

Just then, I felt a swish of air behind me. I turned around to see Sloane towering over me, tall and ominous, the bright redness of the Slushie in her hand looking like misplaced optimism. My heart sank. Sloane was not what I needed right now.

'Sorry, I didn't mean to interrupt. I was just . . . can I sit here?'

As much as I wanted to, there was no way I could say no. 'Sure.'

I watched Libby's face darken as Sloane sat down next to me.

'Everything OK?' she asked me. 'You look upset.'

'I'm fine,' I muttered. The situation was making me feel like I had ants crawling all over my skin. 'It's just . . . a minor drama.'

'That doesn't sound good.' She took a big slurp of Slushie.

'It's nothing,' Libby said. 'Jessie's being dramatic.'

'I hardly think it's dramatic not wanting to go to an event with the boy who made my life hell,' I snapped.

'Wow, that doesn't sound like a good idea,' Sloane said. 'Do you mean Callum Henderson?'

'Yeah,' I sighed.

Sloane's eyes widened. 'For what it's worth, I think you should stay well away – that boy is nothing but bad news. I've worked that out already and I've only been here a few days.'

Libby looked like she was about to actually fire darts out of her eyes.

'Like you said,' Libby spat, 'you *have* only been here for a few days. And actually, although he is a prize knob, Callum can be OK. And he's had a tough time of it. So maybe don't get involved in things you don't understand.'

Summer and Tabs were nodding along. *Oh here we go again*, I thought. *Just like Freddie – let's everyone get out their tiny violin for Callum and his hard life.*

I know, right. Sloane said in my head, making me jump. *Where does she get off? Why don't we go to the party together tonight? We could have some fun. Teach Callum a lesson he won't forget?*

NO. No.

'Think about it, Jessie,' Libby said. 'Why don't we go and talk to Callum, find out more about why he wants you there. I really think there must be more to it. And if you decide to go, I can go with you for moral support if you want. I know how to deal with his dad too.'

Not as well as I could deal with him, Sloane said. *I can't believe they're defending that low life over you.*

'Or I could go with you?' Sloane offered, out loud this time, taking a final slurp of her Slushie.

They all stared at her then, like she'd just offered to kill their firstborns.

'I think I've got her covered,' Libby scoffed. 'Thanks all the same.'

Sloane smiled. 'You know where I am if you need me, Jessie.' And with that, she stood up and walked away.

CHAPTER ELEVEN

'Today we're revisiting representation in the media,' Ms Simmons said. There were groans. 'I know, we've looked at it quite a bit but it will come up in your exam and you need to be prepared.'

I'd crept into Media Studies at the very last minute, wanting to minimise any potential Freddie-confrontation time. I had firmly focused on Ms Simmons since then, refusing to let my eyes wander and risk meeting his. I was still fuming – but now I was angry with even more people: Callum (always); Freddie (for talking about me with Callum); the girls (for siding with Callum and Freddie and acting like I should give him any kind of a break); and even Sloane (because although she was trying to have my back, she was making things more complicated). I was a spiky ball of Velcro, anger sticking to me everywhere I rolled. I wasn't sure who was Top of the Pops on my anger list, but I was sick of all of them.

'So,' Ms Simmons continued, 'last year, we looked at the representation of women across different forms of media.'

'Page Three,' Marcus shouted out, kissing the tips of his fingers like he was a chef having tasted the finest produce.

Ms Simmons let out an exhausted sigh. 'We did touch on that Marcus, yes.'

Revision Facts – Gender Stereotypes in the Media (Media Studies)

1. Representations of women in the media are often stereotyped and defined by how men see women (the 'male gaze') and how women are expected to look and behave.

2. Representations of women have traditionally been focused on sexuality, beauty, emotions, relationships and the home.

3. In *The Mouse That Roared*, Henry Giroux used examples of Disney characters to show how female characters are sexualised but delicate princesses, who need to be saved by a male character.

4. Case studies: Snow White (cleans the house, is rescued by a prince because she is pretty), Ariel (gives up her voice to win the prince with her body, a prince who then has to save her from the evil sea queen), Mulan (manages to win a war almost single-handedly . . . but then returns home, where her 'happy ending' involves, you guessed it, being romanced.)

5. WHAT HOPE DO WE HAVE WHEN WE'RE BROUGHT UP ON THIS SHIT?!

'Our practice question today is going to be thinking about these ideas and expanding them to look at the representation of men in the media. We're also going to be looking back at older issues of magazines to see if and how representation has changed. As you would get in the exam, I'm going to give you four magazine covers in total. Two of the publications were made for a target audience of women, one historical, one present day. Two are from the same time periods, but made for men.

'I want you to examine these covers in detail and compare and contrast. Look at all aspects of the covers please – the images, the headlines, even the fonts. You may be surprised at the extent of the gender stereotyping. Think of who the publications are trying to attract and what they're trying to tell that audience, just from the cover.'

The idea of solo, practice-paper focused work to get stuck into filled me with calm. It was just what I needed – not to speak to a single soul. Ms Simmons, my guardian angel.

'I'm going to give you fifteen minutes' group brainstorming time to discuss and then we'll go to silent working.'

Ugh. Ms Simmons, I hate you.

'Group One – Marcus, Tommy, Kate and Izzy,' Ms Simmons began, reading from a printout in front of her. 'Group Two – Tabitha, Claire, Zoe and Alex. Group Three – Olivia, Michael, Ethan and Catherine and—' I knew what was coming. Of course, because today was obviously a TOTAL SUCK-FEST OF A DAY. 'Group Four is … Jessie, Freddie, Charlotte and Josh. Fifteen minutes – make the most of it – off you go.'

The class sprang into action, chairs scraping, people moving, Marcus messing around, as always. I dragged my chair over to where my group were congregating with all the enthusiasm of someone walking the plank.

'So, what do we think?' Charlotte asked, turning the printouts over, keen to crack on with the activity.

I silently thanked Charlotte for being even more committed to learning than me. The first cover was an *Ideal Woman* magazine cover from 1982. The image was of a celebrity I didn't know, wearing a swimming costume with legs cut so high they were almost touching her armpits and a front so low it was almost touching her crotch. She had BIG glossy hair, bright blue eyeshadow and perfect (airbrushed) make-up. The headlines around the image read: *Get Beach Body Ready in Five Easy Steps; Satisfy Your Unbridled Lust Without Threatening Your Man; Colour Match Your Life; Sizzling Summer Recipes That Won't Break Your Budget or Your Diet.*

Wow.

I looked at the recent women's mag cover: *Celebrity Hair Hacks; This Season's Must-Have Styles; Best of the New Tweakments; High-Speed Hookups and Online Orgies.*

Wow, again. Slightly more subtle, but basically the same messaging: *Must Stay Hot to Attract Man.*

I scoffed under my breath and turned my attention to the men's covers. There was one for a magazine called *His Monthly* – I'd never heard of it, but judging by the image on the front of a woman with her boobs practically out (covered by her arms, but only just) it looked like a top-shelf dirty mag. This couldn't have been just an everyday magazine hanging out on the supermarket stand, surely? I studied the article titles: *Chat-up Tips to Bag a Hottie; Picnic Like a Man – the Best Beer Coolers Put to the Test and Outdoor Sex: Girls Reveal All.* I was speechless at the blatant sexism, my mouth gaping open in absolute wonder.

The final cover was for a modern-day magazine, *Men's Motivation.* Its cover image was of a shirtless guy, full-on six-pack and muscles of almost Popeye proportion. The headlines around it read: *Abs Special – How to Get Them and Keep Them;*

Get Rich Quick – the Best Investment Advice; Why Football is The Best Sport On Earth.

'God, look at these!' Charlotte said, shaking her head. 'I mean, where to even start.'

I jumped straight in, my head full of ideas, my mouth word-vomiting them out. Fuelled by my anger and the worry that any pause would give Freddie an opportunity to try and talk to me, I ranted about the pressures on women to look a certain way, the expectation that we 'perform' for men, the fact that things hadn't really changed in forty years (no matter how much we're told they have) and that if anything, they've just become more subtle, more *insidious*.

And all the while, in my head I was having my own boy-centric drama – and being annoyed at myself for it. If Freddie *did* have a chance to talk to me, would it be to apologise or to try and persuade me again to go to the damn event?

When I did finally stop for breath, just as Ms Simmons sent us off to do the practice paper, I risked a glance at Freddie. He didn't look like he had been trying to get my attention at all, or like he even registered I was in the room. He looked distanced, closed off, his face hard.

I didn't like it.

CHAPTER TWELVE

After school I went straight home, where I trudged around feeling sorry for myself, boiling the kettle for a pity Pot Noodle while Dave curled herself between my feet meowing at me, and Chicken strutted round the kitchen clucking.

'I know, right?' I said to them. 'It all sucks.'

Bella was at an A Level revision session, Nonna was with a client in her annexe and Mum was – I actually didn't know where Mum was, but I was relieved to have the house to myself for once. I checked my phone. Nothing from Freddie. Which was unusual. He usually sent regular texts – just silly memes or gifs or little check-ins, which I was only realising I enjoyed now that they were absent. Not that I *wanted* to hear from him, I told myself – I was still angry. But a grovelling apology text telling me he had thought about it and now totally understood where I was coming from wouldn't have gone unnoticed.

As I poured the water over the rock-solid noodles I heard a key in the door. My alone-time bubble burst. Though maybe it wouldn't be a bad thing . . . maybe talking to someone I actually trusted might be just what I needed.

'Hello?' I called out, hoping for Bella.

'Well, hello there,' a deep voice called back. Handy Andy. Since when did he have his own key? Isn't that something

Mum should've run past us? I definitely couldn't be dealing with naff jokes and small talk right now.

'Ooh, is that Pot Noodle I smell?' he said, coming into the kitchen.

'It is.' I willed the noodles to hurry up with their softening. 'Mum's out by the way, I don't know where.'

'She's been looking at possible shop locations with Kate,' Andy said.

Shop location? I knew she'd branched out from making headbands and scrunchies into bigger stuff but I didn't know it had got to that point. His superior knowledge of my mum's whereabouts stung slightly. 'We said we'd meet back here – we're going over to that reclamation yard in Ryde to look for some pieces for the lounge.'

I stabbed my fork into the noodles aggressively. We didn't call it the *lounge*, we called it the living room. And what was *he* doing choosing 'pieces' for it?

'Have fun.' I grabbed the Pot Noodle and made a break for it.

'You all right, Jessie?' he asked, before I'd made it to the stairs. 'You seem a bit . . . tense. I'm a good listener you know, if you want a sounding board. I help Neve with her problems all the time. Including love woes – those are my specialist subject.'

I turned to look at him, standing in the kitchen doorway in his paint-spattered work trousers, his pot belly pushing against the Oasis tour T-shirt from 1996, a gold chain nestling in a bird's nest of chest hair that was escaping up towards his neck. His face was an unpleasant mixture of sympathy and hope. Was he *hoping* I had some love woes so that he could help me with them? My Velcro anger-ball found some space for a new addition.

'I'm fine.' I turned to go upstairs. Seeing his smile slip, I added, 'Thanks though.'

Dave was waiting on my bed, her 'I can smell food' face looking longingly at me. She must've anticipated my movements. Poor old Chicken couldn't make it up stairs, which was probably just as well – my Pot Noodle was chicken and mushroom.

'Dude, it's not for you.' I swore she looked disappointed.

I rearranged some pillows to lean against and sunk into my bed, checking my phone again. Nothing from Freddie, a few on the girls' WhatsApp chat and one from Summer. I couldn't face the group chat, but I opened Summer's.

> You OK? Sorry if you felt ganged up on earlier. We love you! Do whatever you think best mate, listen to your gut and ignore everything else.

Oh, Summer. Lovely, kind, reliable Summer.

I pictured Summer's face and I knew, for sure, that she really *did* have my back. Even if I couldn't always see it. I tried tuning in to my gut, attempting to work out what it had to say, other than, 'Feed me more noodles.'

Had I been too harsh with them? Maybe. I'd still been reeling from the whole Callum interaction and hadn't had a chance to think rationally. He did have a way of turning me into a raging, steaming pit of irrational. Did I really think they would suggest something that wasn't in my best interests – or harmful in any way? Absolutely not. Maybe it had been Sloane's presence and her words creeping into my head, making it feel like it was an 'us vs them' situation.

Libby was right, Sloane didn't know the back story. Whereas these girls did. I knew I could trust them. And Freddie. If Freddie thought I should go to this thing, he must have a good reason, and he must know that it wouldn't put me at risk in any way. I thought back to his face in Media Studies. I didn't like that coldness, that detachment. I wanted my always-smiling Freddie. I decided to text him.

> Hey. I'm sorry about earlier – it caught me off guard. If you really think I should go tonight, I will.

The Writing Bubbles of Anticipation appeared instantly.

> That's really kind but I don't want you to do anything you're not comfortable with. Honest. And I'm sorry too.

> It's fine. I trust you. But it's for you, not him. You'll owe me.

> That I can do. Chips and a Cove hot choc?

> Perfect.

> I can come with tonight if you want?

> Thx but I'll ask Libby. She's used to Callum's dad.

***

'Hey, guys.' Libby was leaning against the wall to the car park at the top of town. 'Ooh! Check you out, Miss Corporate Lawyer!'

The truth was, I felt wildly uncomfortable in the pencil skirt and pussy-bow shirt Bella had lent me. She'd done my make-up too, really going whole hog with the kind sister thing, even walking me over – though I think part of that was to escape the tension at home.

We'd had an awkward dinner when they'd got back from furniture shopping, during which Handy Andy kept coming up with reasons why Bob Henderson MP was a wonderful person, valuable member of the community and all-round good egg, while Nonna shot each one down with progressively harsher insults.

'See, I told you it looks good,' Bella said, nudging me.

'Thanks.' I felt like I couldn't express my hatred of the get-up with Bella right there. 'I just feel weird.'

'Well, get used to it, you're about to feel a whole lot weirder,' Libby said. My face fell. 'I'm *joking* – it'll be fine! Fun, even – who knows. Free food at least.'

'You sure you want to do this?' Bella asked. 'You totally don't have to.'

I thought of Summer's text, of Freddie – and of having Callum being in my debt. 'I'm fine. I'll do a quick in and out – show my face, eat a breaded prawn, run like the wind.'

'That's my girl!' Libby said. Bella eyed her up, uncertain. She'd never particularly warmed to Libby after the events of last year. Probably not helped by the fact Libby thought that Bella, in her beauty blogger capacity, was super cool. Libby always came across as way too keen whenever Bella was around.

'I'll be at Maddy's, which is right around the corner – call me if you need anything. OK?'

'OK.' I nodded, feeling like a child on my first day at school. 'And thanks.'

'C'mon,' Libby linked her arm through mine and we started walking. 'Let's do this!'

It felt nice to feel the full supportive force of the Libby I knew and loved again – no snide comments, no mean streak. That's the thing with Libby. If she likes you, she loves you and she'd do anything for you, but if she takes against you ... well, you're screwed. I was lucky last year in that I eventually managed to chisel down far enough to find the Good Libby. Though I had to endure her nastiness first.

I thought about gently broaching the subject of Sloane, taking advantage of the fact it was just us, no audience, and asking her to lay off a bit. But then I remembered the girls' conversation the other day – the things they were saying about Sloane and her Wiccan declarations – and that was when they didn't even know the full story. I didn't want to get into that. It was better to keep Sloane at a safe distance and just bask in the warmth of Good Libby for now.

Town still had a little of the summer buzz left, even on a Thursday night – people eating dinner at the few remaining outside tables along the street, loud groups spilling out of pubs, enjoying the last of the light evenings. Still, there was a definite chill in the air – though maybe the chill I felt was more dread than autumn setting in. The thought of being near Callum on his own ground was enough to give me frostbite.

'And did I tell you about the time he had some big-wig company director over?' I zoned back in to what Libby was saying, not realising I'd zoned out in the first place. 'He was trying to cut some deal with him to base his company on the Island and, honestly, the arse-kissing was grade-A gross. Callum thought it would be funny to put a saucy website up on his dad's laptop so when he went to present to the director guy it would come up. He saw it in time, sadly, so the joke never paid off and, as you can guess, it didn't go down well. I got kicked out and Callum got in BIG trouble. He was always doing stuff like that to his dad, winding him up. He hates him, blames him for driving his mum away.'

We were walking up the hill to the houses at the back of the town. The *top* of the town, really – with the big, expensive houses, with the full-on sea views and wraparound balconies.

'Is his mum not around then?'

'She left a while ago – out of the blue. Don't ever mention her in front of Callum – he goes mad.'

'Does he not see her at all?' I asked. The thought of not having contact with Mum gave me goosebumps.

'Not as far as I know. When we were together she'd call once a week but Callum would never answer. She was always texting too and I never saw him reply. He was angry with both of them – with his dad for forcing his mum away, with his mum for deserting him.'

'Why does Callum think his dad forced his mum away?'

'I don't know exactly. He's not the biggest of talkers, but from what I can gather, I think his dad had affairs and was generally a bit of an arse to her.'

'Does he have any brothers or sisters?'

'A younger sister – but his mum took her with her when she left. I don't think Callum's seen her since. Can you imagine? Being the one she didn't choose?'

I shivered.

'Right then,' Libby said, as we turned on to a large gravel drive. 'This is it. You ready?'

CHAPTER THIRTEEN

The drive was lit with soft, warm lights nestled into the bushes, its curves leading to a grand, double-fronted house whose vast windows gave the impression it was staring at me. Our house was big, but a messy, run-down, hasn't-been-loved-in-a-while big. This house was big in an imposing, dignified kind of way, a stately master to our house's slovenly servant.

A uniformed caterer opened the solid door for us, holding out a tray of drinks. 'Good evening. Can I interest you in a champagne, sparkling water or elderflower and mint spritz?' Her limp smile told me she didn't see why she had to bother with these pleasantries for two unimportants who were probably the same age as her.

Libby reached for the champagne, but I gave her a steely look and she grudgingly took an elderflower spritz.

'Killjoy,' she whispered.

I grabbed a water and let Libby lead me through the entrance hall, with its chequerboard floor and sweeping staircase, towards the noise. The noise was that very particular sound of groups of pompous men charged with their own importance, speaking too loudly, guffawing and generally enjoying the sound of their own voices. It made me feel queasy. I sipped my water, readying myself, hoping Libby would find us a quiet corner to cower in until we could reasonably leave.

'Mr Henderson,' she said, matching the loudness as she walked us straight up to Callum's dad who was holding court in the centre of the room. He looked smart – in a try-hard, has a stylist type way, every detail precisely considered. His dark hair was slicked back in exact, neat sections, an acceptable smattering of grey whispering around his temples, making the forest green of his eyes more pronounced and as sharp as his designer suit. It was easy to see where Callum got his looks from – and his coldness.

Mr Henderson's eyes flickered dark on Libby before he corrected himself, putting a smile back on his face. 'Libby. Well, what a nice surprise, I didn't expect to see you here this evening. Are you and Callum ...'

'God no,' Libby said. 'The headline star here invited me along. That's OK, isn't it?'

Mr Henderson smiled at me with the assurance of a tiger who has caught its prey. I tried to tell my mouth to smile back. It did more of a quiver. 'Ah, Jessie. So pleased you made it.'

He gave me a two-handed handshake, complete with Tom Cruise intensity. A gold signet ring with some intricate crest on it caught my eye, its ostentatiousness making me cringe. 'Clive, Derek, this is Jessie Jones – the young lady who made that wonderfully brave film – the one that exposed the terrible culture at Queen Victoria Academy under that old Headteacher.'

The way he talked about it, you'd have thought *that wonderfully brave film* hadn't prominently featured his own son.

His cronies looked as confused as I felt – but they dutifully nodded their recognition and offered me their damp hands to shake. I wished my powers extended to being able to magic myself out of there.

'I can't tell you how relieved I am that the Head has left and we have all been able to move on from such a terrible time,' he continued; his eyes were focused and shining with lies. 'And that your piece enabled others – including my Callum – to see how they had been influenced. It gave them the chance to change their ways.'

I nearly spat my drink out. This was some serious propaganda.

'Callum, come and say hi.' Mr Henderson waved his hand regally as he shouted loudly enough for everyone in the room to hear. I guessed he wanted people to witness the grand reunion. Callum walked over, his face wearing a strange, pliable, accommodating expression that, in combination with the chinos and shirt he was sporting, made him not look like Callum. Our eyes met and buried beneath the hollow glaze, I saw the faintest trace of something else there – I couldn't read if it was apology or appeal.

'Hi, Jessie,' he said, trying for friendly and falling short. 'Thanks for coming.'

A whiff of booze landed with his words.

'Ahem.' Libby said, from beside me.

'Both of you, thanks for coming.' I could sense his uncertainty at Libby being there, like she posed a threat.

'Callum tells me he's been tutoring you with your maths again,' Mr Henderson said.

He said WHAT?! My nerves instantly morphed to pure anger. Libby gave my hand a subtle squeeze.

'More like studying together,' Callum got in, quickly, his eyes full of desperation now.

As if I would ever study with him, I thought, flashing back to our 'tutoring' session last year when he had first tried it on with me. I so wanted to say something, to set the record straight, could almost feel the words forming like vomit at the back of my throat.

I swallowed. I didn't want to cause a scene. I was here, I'd shown up, I was Doing the Right Thing, Mr Henderson was getting his moment. Five more minutes and I could leave.

'Well, it's great to see you two are all made up now. And great that Callum is helping you out. Not a bad apple after all, hey?' He gave Callum a rough back-pat. I saw him flinch. 'Where's Brian? We should get a photo.'

A lank-haired photographer was summoned and we huddled in for a photo – Mr Henderson in the centre, his muscular arms wrapped behind me on the one side and Callum on the other, the waft of his expensive cologne catching in my nose. I smiled for the photo – it may have looked more like a grimace – and then it was done. I was done. My duty was done.

Apparently, so was Mr Henderson's. 'Thanks. Enjoy the food,' he said, turning his megawatt smile and charm on to someone the other side of the room.

Callum and I were left alone – Libby having wandered off somewhere when we were taking the photo. He shifted uncomfortably, like he didn't know where to look, apparently deciding on the floor. 'Thanks for coming,' he mumbled again.

'Freddie asked me to.'

'Don't worry, I knew you hadn't done it for me.'

'Am I free to go now?'

'Please do,' he said, eyes glancing up from the floor to give me a parting stare before walking off.

I looked around for Libby, desperate to leave. The mingling colognes suddenly smelling stronger, the booming voices sounding louder, the overdose of testosterone making the air thinner. I guessed she'd gone to the bathroom as there weren't any hot boys she could have been sidelined by. Pushing my way through the suited shoulders, I did a slow circuit of the room, searching for her with no luck.

Eventually, I flagged down a caterer to ask the way to the toilet. She pointed vaguely towards the back of the house, where, I saw, there were two different corridors leading off. By the time I turned back around to ask for clarification, she had gone.

I picked the direction that looked the most likely – slightly better lit, less imposing – and edged my way along it, taking in the photos on the wall as I went. They mainly showed a younger, sweet-looking Callum, with a grin that looked more mischievous than menacing, often with his arm wrapped around a little girl who I guessed must be his sister. There were a few lone hooks where frames had obviously once hung, now standing empty, a past erased.

And then, suddenly, in the following photographs, the sister was gone. No more Callum and his sister, just Callum. Callum sitting puffed and proud as the captain of the football team, Callum mid-run in the middle of a match, Callum at some kind of formal event, Callum looking small next to his dad outside the Houses of Parliament, their matching cold eyes seeking me out from behind the glass. I really needed to get out of there.

Picking up the pace, I headed for the first door I could see. Muffled voices came through the slight opening, an opening just big enough for me to catch sight of the figures beyond.

'What the fuck was that?' Mr Henderson hissed, towering over Callum, who was sitting on the deep leather Chesterfield. There was dark panelling and walls of books, a large, grandiose desk at the far end. 'All you had to do was smile and be nice to her and you couldn't even manage that convincingly. I told you how important this is to us.'

'To you,' Callum said, all ice.

His dad slapped him, hard, around the back of the head, his signet ring catching on Callum's skull with a *clunk* that set my teeth on edge. Callum hardly flinched. If it wasn't for a lock of his hair being out of place, I'd have thought I'd just imagined it. I slunk back, flattening myself up against the wall of the corridor, wanting to sink to the floor.

'Important to me *is* important to us, you impertinent fool. If that stupid little girl and her jumped-up ideas lose me this election, it will be your fault. I told you to stop.'

'You told me not to get caught.'

'It's the same thing.' I heard movement, the clink of ice cubes in a glass. 'Get back out there and make nice. It's not for ever, just until—'

'What if I don't want to play along any more?'

There was a pause. I could sense the tension in the room from outside of it – weighted, suffocating.

'It is not playing, as you well know. And you'll do as I say or you know the consequences. Now, go!'

Panic clawed at me. The absolute last thing I wanted was for them to walk out and see me here. Suddenly, my abdomen cramped. Oh God, OK; so actually the *absolute* last thing I wanted was for my powers to accidentally do anything.

Mr Henderson was still talking, but his voice was creeping closer to the door. I tiptoed further along the corridor, finding the first open door I could and practically running inside, my breath short and shallow, my insides wobbly.

I looked around – I seemed to have landed in a sitting room of some kind. This one had the feel of a comfy, not-for-show sitting room – worn rugs, colourful paintings, a big TV and a plush cream sofa overcrowded with bright cushions. I perched myself on the edge of the sofa, listening out for footsteps heading in the other direction. I found my phone in my bag, needing Libby and needing, more than ever, to get out of there.

WHERE ARE YOU? I need to leave.

The bubbles appeared. Just as the door slammed and Callum walked through, rubbing the back of his head, seeing me at the last minute, his face contorting as he did.

'I'm sorry – I . . . got lost.' It sounded pathetic, even to me. I felt pathetic.

He laughed, a strange, eerie laugh. 'Perfect!'

He shook his head, walked round and reached under the sofa to retrieve a bottle of something – whisky, it looked like. He took a giant swig, wincing slightly as it went down. He slumped himself on the other end of the sofa, looking me up and down, his steely eyes assessing me. I shifted, uncomfortable, itching to escape.

'You wouldn't know.' He said the words more to himself than to me. 'Looking at you, you wouldn't know.'

'I wouldn't know what?'

He blinked then, as if waking up from a trance. 'Honestly, I couldn't give a toss whether you're here or not. Jesus, sleep over if you want!' He offered me the bottle, looking defeated. I took it, though I wasn't sure whether it was out of sympathy, camaraderie or fear.

I swigged, the alcohol burning my lips before going on to burn my throat. 'I need to find Libby, then I'm going.' He held his hand out for the bottle. 'I'm sorry,' I added, barely a whisper.

'For what, exactly?'

I didn't know, exactly. Mainly I was sorry that his dad was so disgustingly horrible, but I couldn't say that. I was sorry that me existing had made his dad worse towards him too. I couldn't say that either.

'Sorry for . . . everything that happened last year. Kind of. I mean, sorry that it got to that place.'

He looked at me, frowning, as though trying to work out what I was saying, what the words coming out of my mouth meant. He shook his head again, his own words forming slowly. 'Look, last year was . . . bad. I was . . .' He sighed. Deep and heavy. 'I'm sorry too. For lots of things. I didn't mean . . .' He itched at his chin, clawing at a non-existent beard. 'Thanks for coming tonight. I know it was for Freddie, but thanks.'

Serious Callum was making me uncomfortable. I found normal, mean Callum easier to deal with. 'I'm always available for free breaded prawns,' I said, by way of lightening the mood.

'Oh, you mean the "prawn tempura with a cayenne batter and aioli." He put on an exaggeratedly posh accent, dragging out the word *aioli*. 'Only the best for the red-faced, sweaty, bad-haired kiss-arses who swarm to these things.'

'Talking of bad hair, did you see—'

'Wig-guy! Yes I did!' His eyes lit up. 'Bizarre. I think he's going for a Donald Trump look.'

'Very misguided.'

'And that's not even the worst of it. Another one, one of Dad's fellow MPs, who wears bad cravats and has wandering hands – Handsy Harry. His name isn't actually Harry but Handsy Quentin didn't have the same ring to it. When I was twelve he gave me an in-depth lecture on the best porn sites to visit.'

I looked at him incredulously.

'And there's one guy who's known for getting his cock out at the end of every party and laying it on women's shoulders for shits and giggles.'

'Ew! What's his name – Cock-Out Colin?'

Callum laughed, his eyes gleaming.

'Nice one, Jones.' He took another swig. 'Welcome to my world. Or Bob Henderson MP's world, I should say.'

'Here you are!' A young, smart-looking woman holding a clipboard bustled into the room. 'Your dad's about to make his speech, you need to be there.' She glanced at me dismissively, before hurrying back out of the room as Callum stood up.

I stood up too, smoothing down my ridiculous pencil skirt which felt even more awkward than before. Callum did a double take, something on the sofa where I'd just been sitting catching his eye. I looked down, my whole body tensing when I saw it – a small, but obvious, blood stain. You had to be kidding me – not *again*.

'Oh my God ... I'm so sorry, I ...'

I wanted to run.

Or die.

Or just catch fire. I was furiously, fiercely red.

He laughed. A laugh I couldn't gauge – exhausted? Menacing? Friendly? He took another swig.

'I'll sort it – I'll just get . . .' I spluttered, rooting through my bag for some tissue, or salvation, of any kind.

'Callum, we're waiting,' Smarty-pants called from further down the corridor.

Callum turned back to me. 'It's fine. Just go.' Then he walked out of the room, leaving me to sink into the full extent of this horror.

Revision facts – Reproduction and Menstrual Cycle (Biology)

1. During the process of the menstrual cycle, the uterus prepares for pregnancy. If the egg is not fertilised and implanted in the womb, the uterus lining is shed – this is called *menstruation*.

2. Oestrogen is involved in repairing and thickening the uterus lining.

3. Progesterone maintains the lining of the uterus during the middle section of the menstrual cycle.

4. Menstrual blood is different to normal blood due to its composition and physical properties.

5. However, like all blood, menstrual blood is an absolute arse to remove from any fabric – for most people. Though luckily, not so for witches.

CHAPTER FOURTEEN

Libby, of course, thought it was hysterically funny once my texts had finally managed to entice her away from the food table and to come to my rescue. I'd magicked the stain away and run out of that house Usain Bolt levels of fast, frantically chain-texting her only once I'd made it to the end of the drive. My skin felt sticky and hot and itchy and ice cold all at the same time and my mind was working overtime – cringing at the flashbacks *and* worrying about what would await me at school the next day.

'I just can't,' she laughed as we walked back through town. 'It's too good!'

'*Good* is not the word for it.'

'Maybe it's too soon now, but I promise you'll see the funny side – someday.'

'Do you think Callum will tell people I bled all over his sofa?'

She thought for a minute. 'I think maybe he's changed enough to realise that's not cool.' I breathed a sigh of relief. 'How did he seem when it happened?'

I thought back. 'He seemed ... OK? He laughed. He was pretty drunk though.' I bit my lip. I wanted to tell Libby what I had seen, between Callum and his dad – but I wasn't sure whether I should or not.

'So, Callum's dad . . .'

'Ugh. Bob the knob.'

'You said him and Callum don't get on.'

'Yeah, Callum's never quite lived up to the all-star impeccable standards that his dad expects. It's caused some . . . friction. I think that's another part of the reason his mum left too.'

Friction. Was it 'friction', that I had seen? Did I need to report it to someone – and if so, who?

'And Callum doesn't seem to give a shit,' she continued. 'Like I said, sometimes he winds his dad up on purpose, to get a reaction.'

Well. He had definitely got a reaction.

'Do you think he'd ever hurt Callum – like, seriously hurt him?' I asked.

'Bob? God no. His bark is worse than his bite.' She glanced at me. 'Why? Did something happen?'

I hesitated. It made me feel better that Libby, who knew the family much better than I did, seemed to think things were OK. Maybe it had been a one-off, or not as bad as it looked. Maybe Libby didn't need to know – I could talk to Freddie about it instead. Bob Henderson was a powerful man and I had to tread carefully.

'I just don't get a good vibe off Bob,' I said at last. 'I almost felt sorry for Callum at times tonight. And actually, we had about half a minute of semi-civilised chat just before Periodmageddon happened.'

Libby stopped in her tracks, turned around and grabbed both my arms, a look of faux-horror on her face. 'Are you saying you and Callum . . . bonded?'

'I wouldn't go *that* far. But we had a conversation that didn't involve either of us wanting to kill the other one.'

Libby grinned and walked on. 'Progress. As I keep saying, Callum's not all bad, always. I remember once in Year Four, Summer was really upset because Luke Rollins had broken her model of Hampton Court Palace she'd spent three weeks making so Callum went and broke Luke's model of a Tudor house. It was sweet.'

'Uh, I'm not sure I'd call that *sweet*, necessarily. Destructive maybe.'

'You know what I mean, sweet in his own way. There are seeds of decent in that boy, they're just buried deep.'

'Hmmm, jury's out on that.' We'd arrived at the crossroads where we split, our houses in different directions. 'Thanks for coming tonight by the way.'

'Any time, doll-face. I got your back.' She swept me up in a big hug. 'Now, go and wash your skirt and find a super plus, hey?'

***

'Hey.'

It was Sloane, swinging round at me from the wall in front of our house the following morning like some kind of stalker. I jumped. Then inwardly sighed – I could so not be doing with this right now.

'Sorry, didn't mean to startle you. Thought we could walk to school together?'

'Um, I always meet up with the ... others, but sure?' It was about as nice a way of saying, 'Please God, no' as I could manage. My headspace was totally not with Sloane right now. After

Summer's supportive text yesterday and Libby's actual support last night, I was all about the status quo – keeping things stable and normal and calm. I didn't want anything – not Callum, not Sloane – to threaten that. I had my girls, they had my back, all was fine. No complications, thanks very much. And Sloane was definitely a complication.

'So you ended up going to the event last night after all?' she asked.

'How did you . . . yes, I went last night.' I felt trapped.

'You should've called me – I would've gone with you.'

'I went with Libby,' I said, imagining the looks I would've got if I'd turned up with Sloane in tow.

'*And?* How was it? Please tell me you did some sick magic and gave that hideous boy some of what he deserved?'

'Ssssh!' I said, aware that we were getting closer to the seafront where the girls would be waiting with every step. 'No, I didn't. It was actually OK with Callum. We had our issues, and now they're sorted – or sorted enough that we can all get on in relative peace. Besides, I think he's changed.' As I said the words, I willed them to be true, aware that today would reveal if they were or not.

Sloane shrugged. 'For the record, I think you're wrong – people like that don't change. But good luck.'

We walked in silence for a few steps.

'I gave myself a solo tour of the town last night,' Sloane said, eventually. 'It was good to get a feel of the place – at least I know where I'm going now, even if I don't have anyone to go with!' She left a pause, which I didn't fill. Was she waiting for me to suggest hanging out? I felt guilty. I should have been trying to be a better friend to a new girl – a new *witch* no less. But I had too much on my mind right now for town tours. 'Anyway,' Sloane went on, after an awkward beat, 'Do you fancy some more magic lessons after school? I've got this super cool—'

'I'm busy today,' I said. Sloane's faced dropped, the excited gleam in her eye gone. The prickles of guilt intensified. I had really enjoyed the magic we'd done. It was great spending time with someone who totally got it – got *me*. We'd had fun. But the pull of the normal and safe and calm was too much, especially not knowing what was going to happen at school today. If Callum did do something … I needed my girls by my side. I couldn't risk the complication. 'Look, now's not a great time for me. Mocks coming up and all that. Maybe when things have settled down, we can hang out a bit then.'

I stopped, knowing that once we rounded the corner we'd see the girls and, more importantly, the girls would see us together and that would be a whole new headache in addition to the Callum-shaped one. Sloane noticed me stalling. Her big, kohl-rimmed eyes went forlorn for a second – just a second though.

'Sure, let's do that then,' she said, walking off back the way we came. 'Here if you need me.'

***

The girls tried to distract me on the way in with plans for our horror movie sleepover/Feminist Society planning meeting. They insisted that everything would be fine and Callum wouldn't tell anyone – and, even if he did, we would get through it.

Despite their best efforts, I was a wreck. I was listening to my gut, but my gut was a quagmire of confusion. Yesterday, I would one hundred per cent have expected some kind of retribution for my period blood on his sofa, but today, I wasn't quite so sure. Not that I agreed with everyone about his decent side, but I had glimpsed some sort of other side to him – a blink-and-you'd-miss-it size glimpse, but still something.

I practically held my breath walking to my locker: nothing.

Media Studies: nothing.

Break time – including walking past Marcus and Harry: nothing.

Maths was a double holding-my-breath, quaking-in-my-boots/school shoes moment, as it was my only lesson with Callum. This would be it – the moment of truth. White peaks of fear pulsed through my stomach as I walked into the classroom, my sweaty hands clutching my textbook, willing it to be some kind of arsehole shield. Mr Anstead wasn't there yet, as evidenced by the noisy chat, people perched on desks and general milling around. I scanned the room for Callum – and found him, leaning up against the far wall, huddled over in concentrated chat with someone.

Freddie.

I did a double take, studying the scene properly – was that, in fact, my boyfriend, head bent in secret discussion with my enemy? Yes, yes it was. Callum was probably filling Freddie in on how his girlfriend perioded all over his sofa. I knew he wouldn't have let me get away scot-free.

'Hey,' Tabs said, walking up next to me. I grunted in response, making my way to my seat, but unable to take my eyes off them. 'Ah, I see,' she said, following my gaze. 'It's nothing to worry about – they're friends, you know that. And anyway, if he's just telling Freddie, who cares? Freddie has your back.'

I knew she was right, but I couldn't tear my gaze away. Callum was looking angry, and gesticulating, Freddie was nodding and looking concerned and then I was sure – SURE – I caught the words 'blood' and 'sofa'. They were keeping their voices down, and there was other noise in the room, but I was absolutely, swear-on-Dave's-life certain Callum had said 'blood'. Then, as Mr Anstead bustled into the room clutching a pile of papers, Callum and Freddie laughed and gave each other a manly fist bump.

I felt the heat rising from my chest, a blush blooming. My nightmare was coming true – and it was worse than I imagined.

CHAPTER FIFTEEN

It was hard to concentrate on the past paper Mr Anstead had us doing. All I could think about was Callum and Freddie.

My insides were churning. Mainly, I was angry with Freddie. If he and Callum had been laughing at me – after everything that had happened . . . I could feel the rage rising up. I fumed my way through my paper, not even double-checking my answers. At one point I glanced up to see Callum looking at me with something that almost resembled a smile on his face. Possibly a conniving, evil, sly one – I looked away before I had the chance to ascertain its position on the villainy scale.

'Papers to the front please,' Mr Anstead called out over the shrill of the bell and the scraping of chairs. I'd only just finished, further proof, not that it was needed, that my head was not in a good place.

'Have you got a minute?' I accosted Freddie as soon as we were out of the door.

'Uh . . .' He looked at his watch, avoiding my eyes. 'I've got a team meeting and have to grab lunch first . . .'

'I'll be quick,' I said, not giving him the chance to squirm away.

'OK, sure. What's up?'

We were walking and talking, verging our way towards the boys' changing rooms. 'I saw you and Callum talking earlier.'

'We were chatting, yes.'

'It looked like more than chatting, it looked like a deep and meaningful.'

'Jessie, can we not do this now?' He sighed.

'Do what?'

'I know you have a thing about Callum – sorry, I didn't mean it that way,' he quickly amended, seeing the expression on my face. 'I know you and Callum have issues – justifiable ones – but he is also my friend. We were just . . . catching up. Talking about the match later.' He was lucky we were walking side by side so he couldn't see my response to the elephantine lie I was sure he had just casually trotted out. 'I've really got to go.' Still no eye contact. 'I'll catch you later.'

***

I'd calmed down slightly by PE, my last lesson of the day. The high-risk times of Maths and lunch had passed without event, and the girls had talked me down about the whole Freddie/ Callum thing. So what if Callum had been telling Freddie about what had happened? Freddie was pretty cool about that kind of stuff.

At lunch earlier, we'd spent at least twenty minutes trying to analyse the smile Callum had given me during Maths. I gave them a detailed description ('like he'd seen a friend he once liked but had fallen out with and that friend had just tripped over and was lying flat on their face, mixed with the Joker's smile, but the inner one made by his actual lips, not the big red painted-on ones').

Summer opted for the smile being friendly, Tabs hypothesised that it wasn't even directed at me. After I recreated the smile, Libby concluded it was a stunned, scared 'My eyes! My eyes!' sort of expression, a Callum-appropriate response after finding period blood on his sofa.

None of them thought it was a sly or cunning or villainous smile. While I was aware that none of them had actually seen the smile, and my description of it possibly left a lot to be desired, their reassurances made me feel a bit better anyway.

So by the time I went into PE, I felt fine – relieved even. All in all, the day had gone better than I had expected.

'Hello hello!' I beamed at Tabs when I saw her in the changing room. One of the perks of me finally being moved down a set for PE was that Tabs and I got to be rubbish together. Mainly we tried to avoid the attention of Ms Price and any balls.

'Um, hi? You know it's PE, right?'

'I do!' I said, taking my uniform off and hanging it on a peg. 'And what a joy it will be to avoid balls and talk shit with you all lesson.'

Tabs looked me over. 'You're worrying me, but OK.'

'Count me in for the avoiding balls and talking shit,' a voice behind me said. Sloane. What was Sloane doing in our PE set? 'I got reassigned,' she said, as if reading my mind, waggling a slip from the office at us. 'Guess it only took them one session to work out they'd way overestimated me.'

She was already changed, her dark hair pulled into two short messy pig tails, green streaks loud and proud, a faded band T-shirt underneath the school PE top. Her face was still tinged with licks of darkness – dark lips, dark-rimmed eyes, dark shadows. It was unsettling having her there, though I wasn't sure why. Libby wasn't in this class so there wouldn't be any tension there; plus, it wasn't like Sloane would spill any witch secrets in the middle of a PE lesson.

Maybe it was guilt from earlier, from shaking her off when she'd asked to meet up. I hadn't *completely* shaken her off – more just parked her for a bit, until my footing was firmer. Having a fellow witch around – especially one who wanted to hang out with me and my friends – was a big step and I needed time to see how I felt about that. I figured that was fair enough.

'TWO MINUTES, GIRLS! On the Astro in two, please!' Ms Price shouted.

'We'd better go, guys,' Tabs said, leading the way.

'You OK?' Sloane asked, as we made our way to the Astro.

'Yeah, fine,' I replied, forcing a smile and trying to be friendly, reminding myself it was all fine.

'Warm-up time,' Ms Price boomed, once we were all out.

I liked Ms Price. She knew what she was dealing with in this group and had leaned into it – no pressure, no frustration, no expectations – and not a trace of the discriminatory dictator energy of her predecessor, Coach. We were doing hockey at the moment, second to last of my least-favourite sports (only cross-country was rated lower in my mind). Hockey's saving grace was that it was possible to lurk and avoid too much physical activity – which is exactly what Tabs and I did for the majority of the lesson.

Sloane, I noticed, was surprisingly good at it though – maybe the goth aesthetic had fooled me, or maybe she was just *relatively* good, compared to the absolute state of the rest of us bottom-setters. Either way, she looked pretty capable, zipping round after the ball and doing some neat little tackles. She may have even scored a goal, though I couldn't be sure as I wasn't paying enough attention.

The whole lesson went by in a relatively pleasant blur and by the end of it the revision talk with Tabs and non-hassle with Sloane had me in a decent mood. I was looking forward to the sleepover that night and feeling fairly positive about everything as we took our time walking to the changing rooms at the end of the lesson.

Which was why it caught me off guard.

I heard the commotion before I saw it, the buzz of drama like a swarm of bees, rising in volume and excitement the closer we got to it.

'Jessie.' A grim-faced Manda Burton headed us off in the corridor. 'You'd better come and see.'

Tabs and I looked at each other and sped up. Whatever it was, my gut was screaming at me that it wasn't good.

A small group, gaining in numbers as people from other PE sets finished their lessons, had amassed at the far end of the changing room. Near where I'd got changed. *Exactly* where I'd got changed actually, I realised as I reached them. Some of the girls looked excited, some angry, but most just looked horrified. They backed away to make space for me to come through.

And there, hanging up where I had left it, was my school uniform, covered in blood, pools of deep red gathering on the tiled floor beneath it.

CHAPTER SIXTEEN

It took me a minute to understand what I was seeing, to take in the full extent of it. Fleeting thoughts ran through my head – Maybe it was paint? Or had someone had an accident, an injury? – and were just as quickly dismissed. It was definitely blood.

My uniform, covered in blood. Who could have done this?

I knew, of course. *Callum.* The misogynist leopard never changes its spots.

'What the—' Sloane appeared behind us. 'Oh my God! Is that ... that's blood!'

'I don't know what it is, but it was like this when we all came in.' Manda was fluttering around, wanting to be useful. 'I'll go and get Ms Price.'

'No, don't.' I snapped out of my head-spin. 'I'll deal with it, it's fine.'

'Jess? You sure?' Tabs asked, quietly, uncertain. 'That looks like real blood. You need her to see this – you have to report it.'

'I'm sure,' I said, cutting her off. I knew Callum had done this, and I knew why, and I felt sick to my stomach about it; but I also knew I couldn't face the pointless, ineffective chain of bureaucracy I'd thought was the answer last year. Maybe it would be better with the new Head, maybe what happened last year meant I would be taken seriously this time . . . but maybe not. I needed time to think, to work out what I wanted to do about it before making any moves.

'What do you think happened?' Tabs asked tentatively.

'It's not what happened. It's *who*,' I said darkly.

'I can't believe he would do this,' Sloane murmured.

I felt everyone's eyes on me, waiting, expectant. Then Tabs went into full helpful mode, shooing people out of the way, retrieving a tote bag from her rucksack. 'Put your uniform in here,' she said, handing it to me.

Sloane went and got a mass of damp toilet paper and the three of us knelt down, the nobbles of the tiles digging into our bare knees, a wad of paper in each hand, trying to soak up the blood as the chaos around us eventually dissipated and the changing room emptied out.

We could be doing this the easy way you know, Sloane's voice said inside my head.

In front of Tabitha?

We could get rid of her somehow. You shouldn't be down on your knees scrubbing blood off the floor because of that arsehole. He should be licking it off.

I ignored her. It took us three loads of toilet paper before the earthy smell of the blood dissipated, the final stubborn streaks of watery pink disappeared and the now-empty changing room no longer looked like a crime scene.

'Thanks, guys.' I slumped on the floor, my back against the wall.

'No problem,' Tabs said, sitting down next to me.

Sloane stayed standing, hands on hips. 'You all right?'

'Not really, no.'

'WHAT THE HELL?' Libby came storming into the changing room, Summer running behind her. 'We just heard. Sarah Holdness said she heard from Fay Dury that there's red paint all over your uniform. What happened?'

'It was blood,' I said.

'*Blood?*' Libby and Summer echoed.

'That's right, Callum cocking Henderson strikes again.' I pushed myself up from the floor, offering Tabs my hand to pull her up. 'I can't believe he actually did this. I mean, I can believe. I just ...'

'He's a dick,' Sloane said, rubbing my back. Libby caught sight of her for the first time, her face immediately morphing into sharp annoyance.

'Are you sure it was him?' Libby asked, focusing on me and ignoring Sloane.

I stared at her. Was she being serious? She looked serious.

'Who else is it going to be? Coach, back from the hinterland? Cole Sprouse?'

'Weird options, but whatever.' Libby sighed, choosing her words carefully. 'I don't think Callum would do this. Not now – not ever actually, it's not his style. It's way too dark for him. And besides, where would he even get real blood from? And where would he have stored it all day – the logistics don't add up.' This time she looked directly at Sloane. 'Maybe don't jump to conclusions?'

My head throbbed. 'Not his style?' I said. 'Let's see – I leak blood onto Callum's sofa and the next day my uniform is covered in blood – from God knows where. Yeah, massive parkour level of jumping to conclusions going on there, Libby.'

He has a network of boys all at his beck and call – I'm sure one of them has connections with a butcher or something – I don't know! I don't think logistics is the problem here – Callum can always find a way.'

'I think she's just saying let's look into it first,' Summer said, stepping towards me, reaching for an arm-pat. I swerved. I couldn't believe them – *all* of them. Even Tabs was standing quietly, looking at the floor.

'For what it's worth, I think it's pretty obvious it was him,' Sloane said. 'And yes, I don't know him like you all do, but who else would have a reason to do it?'

'You can sod off,' Libby snapped, hands on hips, facing off. 'We've got Jessie covered.'

'It doesn't seem that way to me,' Sloane said. 'I'm just trying to support a friend.'

'Like Libby said, we've got her covered,' Summer was defensive.

Tabitha was looking at me, a pleading expression on her face. She hated arguments.

I felt trapped, backed against a wall. My friends said they supported me, but it didn't feel that way. It actually felt more like they were doubting me, ganging up on me, gaslighting me even. Only Sloane was on my side.

'I know it was Callum, I just know it.' My shout echoed off the tiles. 'Sloane's right, WHO ELSE WOULD HAVE DONE IT?'

'Dude, calm down,' Libby said. 'There are other arsehole possibilities in the school. Marcus? Harry? Anyone Callum might have told.'

'I did see Callum out of his lesson earlier ...' Sloane said quietly. 'I was on the Astro. I thought it was weird as he was over by the quad, which isn't anywhere near the toilets or anything.'

'See, I told you!' I said, the righteousness neon bright.

Libby's face had turned crimson – not with embarrassment at being proved wrong. With anger.

'It's very interesting you only thought to mention this now,' Libby hissed at Sloane.

'Leave it, Libby,' Summer said, quietly, warning.

'Have you got any proof of this Callum sighting?' Libby took a step closer to Sloane, ignoring Summer.

Sloane edged back, her eyes widening. 'I was in the middle of a PE lesson, I didn't have my phone with me – if that's the kind of proof you mean.'

Libby laughed nastily. 'Of course you don't have any proof. I don't know what exactly you're playing at, coming in here with your sad, throwback dark-arts look but if it's wanting to be friends with us then you can forget it – go back to whatever wannabe witch, weirdo rock you crawled out from and leave us alone. Jessie's fine. And you? You're a freak.'

A freak.

I wished Libby hadn't said that.

More than that, I wished she hadn't had those thoughts, let alone aired them. My body sagged with a weighted blanket of disappointment, shot through with a surge of anger.

'Let's go,' I said to Sloane. And then, picking up my bag and the tote with my ruined uniform in it, I ran out of the door before the room could close in on me.

CHAPTER SEVENTEEN

'My God, those girls!' Sloane said, following behind me as I stormed down the corridor, trying to catch my breath. 'I really don't understand why you were friends with them.'

I flinched at her use of the past tense – it felt wrong, uncomfortable.

'I need to find Callum,' I said, concentrating on my mission.

'Why? He'll only deny it.'

'Yeah, I'm sure, but I want to confront him. I want to see it in his eyes.'

'*Or* why don't we go down to the cove and work out our anger through some awesome magic?'

It was tempting – the thought of not having to see Callum's smug face and burying myself in feeling powerful instead – but there was something driving me on. The need to prove Libby wrong, the need to see it for myself written on his face, to not back down. Sloane grabbed my hand as we broke out of the front doors, the sunlight too bright and warm for my mood.

'Seriously,' she said, 'leave it. Him lying to your face won't make you feel any better. In fact it'll probably make you feel worse.'

People were standing in groups, milling around, muffled voices, animated faces – that became more animated when they saw Callum walking over to me, flanked by Freddie. *Great.* Yet again, I was in the spotlight.

'It wasn't me,' Callum said, not bothering with small talk.

'I'm so sorry, Jessie,' Freddie gave me his usual greeting kiss, putting his arm around me.

I shook him off, furious that he was at Callum's side, that I'd listened to him about going to that event in the first place. He bristled, confused.

'Of *course* it was you,' I said to Callum, my arms crossed. 'Who else would it have been?'

'I don't know,' Callum said. 'But I swear, it wasn't me.'

Sloane made a noise – something between a grunt and a scoff.

People were watching, some with phones out, interest piqued, probably hoping for more showdowns like last year. 'Can we ... not in public?' Callum said, gesturing to around the corner.

I complied, walking round to the side of the building where it was empty. Freddie and Sloane followed.

'Why would I do something like that, Jessie?'

'Oh, I don't know, because I had the audacity to accidentally bleed on your sofa? Because I saw a snapshot of your life and it made you uncomfortable?' His face darkened at that one. 'Because I thought I saw an inkling of decent in you and you wanted to remind me you're a dick? Or maybe just because, oh yeah, that's it – you *are* a dick.'

'Jess,' Freddie said. His voice had a patronising, parental tone. *Ugh.* 'Hear him out. I was angry with him too, when I heard about it, but I really don't think he's lying.'

'Of course you don't,' Sloane said.

They both looked at her, as if realising she was there for the first time. 'Sorry, what has this got to do with you?' Callum asked, glaring.

'I'm Jessie's friend – her only decent one, apparently.'

'And she saw you out of class, near the girls' changing rooms right around the time when it must've happened,' I said. 'Care to explain that?' Slam dunk.

Callum looked startled, caught out, a flush creeping up his face. 'Yeah, I was there. I got a note from someone saying to meet them ... look.' He swung his rucksack round and rummaged in the front pocket producing a crumpled piece of paper – small and grey with a border of stars, and two lines scrawled in childish writing.

Revenge on JJ for last year.
Meet me by locker 113 at 2.15. Don't be late.

I studied it, decoding the words. JJ – that had to be me. That first word, *revenge,* was a punch in the gut. Freddie didn't even look at the note, which meant he must've already seen it – and apparently didn't have a problem sticking up for Callum anyway.

'Really?' I said, the same old Callum-sickness throbbing in my veins. 'What is this supposed to prove? That you can forge a note? That you want revenge?'

'No! I thought Marcus must have sent the note. I was worried he'd do something bad. That's why I went – I was trying to *stop* anything from happening. I don't want any more trouble.'

'Let's go, Jessie,' said Sloane, protectively. 'You don't need to listen to these lies.'

134

'I don't want any more trouble,' Callum repeated. He looked tired. Exhausted, even. Which was exactly how I felt. Except my exhaustion was painted in anger.

'Well then maybe you shouldn't have covered my uniform in blood,' I said, and turned away.

'Whatever – it wasn't me.' Callum's tone had changed. All stone and ice now. 'I knew you wouldn't believe me. I don't care if you do or not, but I'm telling you – I. Didn't. Do. It.'

Do something to him, Sloane's voice in my head.

I shouldn't. He's not even worth it.

It'll make you feel better.

Maybe she was right, again. I hadn't listened to her before when I should have done.

'WHAT THE—' I heard Callum behind me.

I felt a thrill – a flash of pleasure, fulfilment.

Sloane turned round to look. *Nosebleed – nice, I like the symbolism!*

CHAPTER EIGHTEEN

Sloane suggested we stop off at her house then head to the cove, but I managed, somehow, to get out of it. My head was treacle, I had a dull, heavy pain pushing on my chest and I needed to be alone.

I promised to call Sloane when I was feeling up to it and left her, with a strong sense of having kicked a lost puppy. I was too exhausted for guilt though. By the time I'd closed our front door, I felt as if I'd just finished a marathon. While wearing one of those ridiculous mascot costumes.

I heard the whir of Mum's sewing machine from the sunroom and had a sudden urge to go to her. I dumped my bag in the hallway and made my way through to the back, slumping on the old saggy sofa and only just managing to hold in the tears. She was feeding bright patterned material through the machine, a list of orders printed out next to her.

'Oh, hello, love,' Mum said, pausing her sewing. 'I didn't hear you come in. How was your day?'

How was my day? Let's see – my nemesis poured blood all over my uniform as revenge for leaking period blood on his sofa, my so-called friends and boyfriend all deserted me in the blink of an eye and the only person who is still on my side is a powerful witch who might expose my innermost secret. Though maybe that doesn't matter anyway, seeing as all of my friends are apparently not actually my friends.

'Rubbish,' I grunted. It seemed like a fair summary.

'Oh no. I'm sorry to hear that, sweetheart.' Mum took her glasses off, properly focusing on me. 'Would it help to talk about it? I'm a good listener.'

The treacle was too thick; just imagining trying to shape it into words made my head hurt even more. 'I don't think so,' I said. 'I'm a bit drained to be honest. But thanks for the offer.'

She got up from behind her machine, carefully walking around the mountains of multicoloured material that were lying in heaps on the floor, and sat next to me on the sofa, pulling me in for a hug. I had to dip my head to be low enough for it to nestle on her chest.

'You can never be too drained for a cuddle,' she said, stroking my hair, transporting me back to being ten.

I blinked back the tears and breathed in the Mum smell – clean laundry, her musky perfume and warmth. We sat there for a while, my head bobbing with the rise and fall of her chest, letting the calm wash over me as the sun cast warm tendrils on me. There were a limited number of days this glass-walled room was usable – in the winter it was too cold and in the summer it was like a sauna. But today – today the glass took the cold edge off the day, squeezing all the heat from the sun until it was just perfect. I could see Nonna pottering away in her shed at the back of the garden, hear the faint beat of her music coming through her tinny speakers.

'Have you and Nonna made up properly?' I asked.

Mum sighed. 'Hmm. You know that being too drained to talk about it thing . . .?'

'You seemed all right the other day.'

'Well, it's complicated. Nonna . . .' She paused, trying to find the right words. 'Nonna has very set ideas about how things should be done. She always had Gramps, who knew about her being a witch from the beginning. She doesn't quite understand . . . that it can be a bit more complicated. She was lucky.'

'I think she was brave,' I said. 'To tell him.'

'Maybe a bit of both. Lucky and brave.'

'Do you ever think that Nonna might be a bit right – that maybe people don't really know us properly if they don't know we're witches? Like Andy? And Freddie? And my friends?'

Mum's hand paused the hair stroking. 'I *don't* think that actually. I will tell Andy at some point because if we do go further down this route, I don't want to have any secrets between us – been there, done that, got the hideous T-shirt.'

'Hey! Are you calling Bella and I hideous T-shirts?'

'Of course not, darling. You know what I mean.' I grunted in response. 'But in the meantime, before I know if our relationship is going anywhere, there's no point. Andy can still get to know me properly, I am the sum of my parts. Yes, being a witch is one of those things, but it doesn't define me. I'm also good at sewing, I'm an ambitious but terrible cook, I love reality TV and long walks and Special Brew – but only one, never more. I like Motown and historical fiction and catching leaves in the autumn and none of that has anything to do with me being a witch.'

When she put it like that, it all made sense and seemed totally logical.

'Why are you asking?' Mum said. 'Are you thinking of telling Freddie?'

'Ugh, no.'

Mum sat up straight, my head rudely ejected from its perfectly comfy resting position on her chest. 'Oh dear. Is that why you're upset? What's happened?'

'I've fallen out with him. And with the girls.' Was *falling out* even the right term for being stabbed in the back and totally betrayed? 'They all took sides against me on something and it was really annoying and now I just feel like they don't understand me. They're in this little tight-knit Island bubble and have been friends for ever and share shiny, happy memories and I'm this strange new girl and I'm never going to be able to infiltrate the bubble, no matter how hard I try. Even though it was kind of me who brought them back together after they stopped being friends for so long, that doesn't seem to matter now. And I'll just never get there with them because they have all this shared history and really, deep down, they're bosom buddies and I'll always be an outsider, as per usual.'

I took a breath.

'Oh, honey. That sounds rough.' Mum was framed in a halo of sunshine coming through the side window, dust motes dancing in the rays. 'I'm sure they weren't doing it on purpose and would feel terrible if they knew it was upsetting you. They're nice girls and they've always been so supportive. You've got the sleepover this evening, haven't you? Why don't you try talking to them about it then?'

'No way am I going to the sleepover.'

'Well, Jessie, how on earth are they going to make new shiny,

happy memories that feature you in them if you're not there?'
Mum tucked a loose strand of hair behind my ear. 'I really
do think you should give them a chance. Was it a heated
moment? Is it possible there may have been some kind of
miscommunication happening?'

I grunted in the affirmative. *Heated* was an understatement.
More like layer-of-the-sun hot.

'Well then, it sounds like you should talk to them about it,
now you're all calmer. Take it from someone with a history of
running away and not giving people a second chance.'

Her words worked their way into my muddled brain and
made a kind of sense. 'I'll think about it,' I said.

'And, in the meantime, would you like me to make you a hot
chocolate?'

'Yes, please.'

***

I stood outside Libby's front door for a solid five minutes,
running Mum's lines over in my head like a mantra: *they're nice
girls and have always been so supportive of you.* But a voice in my
head kept reminding me that none of the nice, supportive girls
had messaged me to check if I was OK or to apologise or to see
if I was still coming tonight.

Sloane had messaged me, though. Asking how I was, asking
if there was anything she could do to help.

I shook the thought away – this wasn't a competition between
Sloane and the girls, this was about getting to the bottom of
what I sincerely hoped was just a miscommunication and not
the back-stabbing it felt like. This was about trying to get back
to normal.

I took a deep breath, trying to breathe some courage into me. I knocked. I waited for what felt like for ever. Eventually, Libby's mum opened the door.

'Oh hi, Jessie,' she said, smiling, glass of wine in hand. I remembered Libby saying her dad was away on a work trip – which explained the unusual smile from her mum. 'I didn't realise you were coming.'

'Um, yeah.' I felt on the back foot already – did she not realise I was coming because Libby hadn't mentioned me? Were they hoping I wouldn't come? Was I disinvited?

'Come on in,' she said, opening the door wide. 'They're rehashing their Year Five talent show dance routine – the return of the Bieberellas. A big moment!'

I could just about see them in the background, at the back of the fancy kitchen extension. They were completely wrapped up in each other – laughing and joking and dancing in time with the ease of people who know everything about each other, who know each other's foundations. The ease of people who are not in the slightest bit concerned about a falling-out earlier in the day. Mum was wrong – they were not supportive and there had not been a miscommunication and I was an absolute fool for coming here.

'Are you coming in?' Libby's mum asked, looking at me questioningly.

'Actually, I ... forgot ... I've just go to ...' I said, not even knowing what I was saying. And with that I turned and ran away.

CHAPTER NINETEEN

I met Sloane at the top of town. She'd sent me a text about thirty seconds after I'd left Libby's, which felt like a sign. I was angry at myself for going to Libby's – but not as angry as I was with my friends – or former friends, as I supposed I should start calling them. In that one moment, standing at Libby's door, the reality had hit me – I was an outsider to them and I would always be an outsider to them, because at the end of the day, how can you compete with shared history?

You can't.

I think I'd always known that, deep down, but seeing them dancing happily together, after how they behaved earlier to me, made it crystal clear. I'd felt alone and powerless – until Sloane's name had flashed up on my phone screen.

'You made it!' she said, as I approached. She wore a big grin and eye make-up three shades darker and heavier than usual. She looked genuinely pleased to see me, which felt good. At least someone was.

'I did.' I was grabbing for enthusiasm but my stomach felt sour. 'What's your plan? We could chill at yours maybe?'

'I mean . . . we could do that. But my mum's home and she's pretty knackered.' Sloane fiddled with her choker. 'Maybe we could head to the cove? Practise some magic?'

'Do you know what? That actually sounds pretty good,' I said. What better way to shake off the feeling of powerlessness, after all?

'Perfect! Let's go.'

We walked in silence, me trailing along behind Sloane like a puppy dog while she stomped along roads and pavements and paths. I didn't recognise a single landmark from last time, other than the lone footpath signpost perched at the top of the hill, but just as we eased off the path, the solid-but-suddenly-not-so-solid rock face with its small secret mark appeared once again. In an instant we were through the other side, the Cove of Magic waiting for us in all its sparkly glory. I breathed it in, the salt water tang filling my nose, steadying me.

'Do you want to do the honours?' Sloane gestured to the fire pit, looking exactly as it had when we left it. It wasn't dark yet, but the cold was beginning to set in.

'Sure.' I took a breath, and as I exhaled, the flames flickered into life. The power of the simple act made me buzz.

The sand was dry enough to sit on and we settled ourselves down around the fire, leaning back against the driftwood. Sloane unzipped her bulging rucksack and pulled out a bottle of wine and two plastic cups. She poured wine into one and passed it to me.

'I'm fine, thanks,' I said.

'No disrespect, but I don't think you *are* fine after today. Not drinking is totally cool though. I just need something to help me unwind.'

She took a big sip and let out a sigh of appreciation. I *did* need some unwinding, that was true.

'Oh, go on then,' I said. 'Just a small one. I'm not really a big drinker.'

She handed me a cup. 'Cheers,' she said.

'What are we toasting to?'

'To friends.'

I scoffed.

'To *proper* friends,' she corrected. 'Ones who know you and are always there for you.'

'I'll cheers to that,' I said.

I took a sip, the tartness causing my cheeks to pucker.

'So . . . what are you going to do about Callum?' she asked.

I'd been focusing so much on the girls, I had almost forgotten about Callum. 'I don't know. I could report him again, I suppose,' I said half-heartedly.

'Yeah, good idea,' said Sloane. 'Did that work last time?'

'Not exactly,' I said. Which was an understatement. 'But that was with a different headteacher – who was an absolute dick. Ms Pritchard might take it more seriously.'

She shrugged, looking unconvinced. 'Well then I guess it's worth a try.' She picked up a stick and leaned forward to poke the fire, letting the tip of the stick catch fire then blinking to make it disappear.

'I just don't know if I have the energy to go through that again. It was . . .' I searched for the right word to describe it – horrendous? Soul-destroying? Like my insides had been ripped out and hung on display? 'A lot. It was a lot.'

'I totally get it,' Sloane said. 'But if you don't do anything now, he'll just keep bullying people. Girls, especially.'

I took a sip of my wine, considering the prospect of Callum

let loose and emboldened by success, free to cast his toxicity on whoever crosses his path, safe in the knowledge that there would be no consequences.

'I know what *I* would do,' Sloane went on.

'What would you do?' I asked.

'Now, listen, before you say anything, I know I wasn't here last year and I know I don't have the shared history you do ...' My stomach flipped at that phrase – had I made Sloane feel as much on the outside as *I* had felt with the girls? 'But I've known boys like Callum – and I know they'll keep doing that stuff until something, or someone, makes them stop. They need to be taught a lesson.'

'I thought he had. Learned his lesson, I mean.' How stupid had I been to believe there was even a chance Callum had changed? And how ridiculous that everyone else still believed he had – even though the proof was right in front of their eyes, flashing like a neon danger sign.

'Well, clearly not. He poured blood all over your uniform to humiliate you. And then he had the audacity to deny it to your face, even though I'd seen him out of his lesson. That *proves* he's learned nothing. He still thinks he can swagger around, doing whatever he wants, whenever he wants, with no repercussions. This is what men *do* – they're mean, bullying, arseholes who do terrible things that have terrible consequences for people, and then they saunter off and carry on with their lives, unscathed.' She took a big gulp of her wine, stared into the fire. 'It's not OK. The endless cycle of men being hideous and women suffering because of it. Something has to be done. And who better to take things into their own hands, to make these men accountable, than us – kickass witches!'

It was a passionate speech, if a little extreme. It stirred something inside me. Sloane was right – Callum *hadn't* learned anything. Why would he? He'd got a temporary suspension, lost a few friends, received a bit of hassle, but nothing that actually affected his life. He was still captain of the football team, he was still popular at school, and he would still go on to some fancy university on a sports scholarship, hob-nobbing with all the other rich white men and getting in with the old boys' network who would eventually give him a good job he was completely underqualified for. He was untouchable.

Except, he hadn't factored in me.

'Sod it.' I took a gulp of my wine, ignoring the sourness, enjoying the buzz. 'You're right. Callum Henderson needs to be taught a lesson.'

'YES! Cheers to that!' We tapped our plastic cups together. 'Revenge is a dish best served by a witch!' Sloane's eyes gleamed, the reflection of the fire lighting them up in all their darkness. She looked resplendent, glowing.

Revenge. Revenge. That word. It made my gut squeeze.

'But we shouldn't,' I said, my shoulders dropping. 'We can't use magic for that – it's bad. It will unbalance things, cause a chain reaction.'

Sloane leaned forwards. 'But *is* it bad if we're doing it for the greater good? You have to look at the bigger picture. A little bit of magic now will stop a lot of hurt in the future. It's *preventative* magic. Which is actually good magic.'

'I hadn't thought of it like that.' The wine was working its way to my head, rounding the hard edges, softening the worry.

'But the last time I did stuff like this all kinds of bad things happened. There were storms. My nan got sick.'

Sloane waved her hand airily. 'Oh that's easily got around. We cast a protective spell.'

'What?' I was shocked.

'Yeah, piece of cake. Before we do the big magic, we do a little sub-spell. It acts as a balancing act. Like ... replacing money on the scales with stones, so they don't tip.'

I couldn't believe it – if it was so easy, why hadn't Mum and Nonna told me? Another thing they'd kept from me. A flash of anger shot through my chest.

'So what do we think, for Callum?' Sloane asked. 'What would teach him to behave?'

'Um ... ' I thought. 'Maybe another nosebleed? One that lasts a month?'

'Bit dull. Arsebleed?'

'Too harsh. He could lose his football skill?' I was warming to this now.

'Hmm. That feels a bit underwhelming.' Sloane drew a figure of eight in the sand with a stick, guiding it round and round the figure. We sat staring at the fire, deep in thought, the crashing waves providing a suitably atmospheric soundtrack. 'I still can't believe he did that to you.'

'I know. He makes me sick.'

'That's it!' she said, standing up with a flourish. 'He makes you sick – so let's make *him* sick.'

An image of Callum sprang to my mind – a slightly diminished Callum, looking pale and weak and queasy. Maybe even vomiting a couple of times. It filled me with joy.

'Let's do it!'

'Excellent!' she said. She paced around the fire, plastic cup of wine in one hand, waving her stick around with the other and frowning in concentration like she was a half-cut eccentric inventor on the verge of something big. Then, throwing the stick on to the fire, she turned to me. 'I think I have most of the things we'll need.'

She balanced her cup on the sand and dug around in her bag, pulling out various items à la Mary Poppins: something small wrapped in tinfoil, some jars with herbs in, a wooden spoon. She yanked out a notebook, battered and leatherbound. Something fluttered out of it on to the sand, and I picked it up.

It was a photo of Sloane – a less goth, lighter-haired Sloane, but definitely Sloane. With her arm lovingly slung around . . . another Sloane. Two Sloanes – grinning and standing in front of a sign that said, '*Welcome to Berwick.*'

Sloane saw me looking and grabbed it out of my hand abruptly.

'Sorry,' I said. Then, curious, 'Who is that?'

She glanced down at the photo in her hand, her face softening – but only briefly. 'It's my sister. My twin sister, obviously.'

'Wow, I didn't realise you had a twin! Where is she?'

'Not here.' Cold and hard. She carried on unpacking the rucksack, focused, concentrating, bringing out some old nails (the rusty kind, not the finger kind, thank God), a shovel, a black candle. Then she glanced up at me. 'Sorry. She's with the coven – long story, but I miss her.'

'Of course.' I didn't know what else to offer.

'Anyway, we have work to do!' Her smile was back.

She took more things out of her bag: some thick-glassed, murky-looking jars, pots containing all kinds of who knows what and last, but in no ways least, a small cauldron. A travel cauldron, if you will. I laughed, the wine and the excitement warming my insides.

'A mini cauldron – are you kidding?'

'Of course not,' Sloane said. The flames reflected in her eyes, licks of red and orange dancing, making her look like a cat in the muted light. 'Have you tried lugging a real cauldron around – they're heavy!'

She laid everything out carefully and reorganised the fire, placing the cauldron carefully on top.

'What's in this?' I asked, picking up a small Tupperware container, the kind that normal, non-witch people would use to store salad dressing.

'Shrew's blood,' she said, like it was, in fact, as everyday as salad dressing.

I dropped it. 'What the f—'

'Shrew's blood is no big deal! Sometimes, for powerful spells, small sacrifices have to be made. Our little friend – Shona, let's call her – was one of those sacrifices. She was a feminist (all shrews are – ever since Shakespeare gave them a bad name) and she'd be pleased, honoured even, that she gave her life to a good cause.'

Sloane chuckled, but I wasn't finding it funny. 'I don't know if I like this,' I said, a cold sweat coming on. 'It feels a bit creepy. And wrong.'

'Jessie, it's *magic*. It's life. It's part of the cycle.'

'Isn't this, like, *Dark* Magic though?'

'Is that what you're worried about?' Sloane asked. 'Really don't be. There's no such thing as Dark Magic. That's a myth spread about by male oppressors who made up reasons to persecute us. Think of this as a ... Light Grey Magic – the colour of the cliffs.'

That was not entirely reassuring. Light grey still felt a shade too dark.

Seeing my expression, Sloane put her arm around me. 'Seriously, witches do this stuff all the time – you just wouldn't know that because you've been lied to and haven't been allowed to experience your full power. I guarantee your grandma will have a ton of shrew carcasses buried somewhere round your house. And remember what Callum did to you. Imagine what he might do in the future.'

As Sloane was talking, Callum's face appeared again and all the feelings of rage flooded back, a dam broken, the water gushing out at full force. That sealed the deal for me. That and the half a bottle of wine. Sod the shrew. It was for the greater good.

'Cool,' said Sloane. 'I think it's the right decision.' She sounded almost casual. She arranged everything (surprisingly) neatly around the fireside and set to work, unwrapping packets of herbs. 'Can you do the refills?'

I poured the last of the wine into both our glasses, keeping half an eye on what Sloane was doing. I felt a morbid pull towards it while also feeling repulsed. Like watching a car crash.

I drained my wine – it seemed to be helping with the whole not thinking too much about what was happening thing and had a nice numbing quality to it, despite the furry tongue. Sloane opened up the tinfoil packet, revealing a dark heap of . . . something.

'What is that?' I asked.

'This,' she said, holding the contents aloft between her fingers, 'is a lock of Callum Henderson's hair.'

'What?! How did you get that?'

'I have my ways. He didn't notice.'

'Why do we need it?'

'My God, they really haven't taught you anything, have they?' She sighed. 'It binds the spell to him.' She bundled the hair with the herbs, deftly tying the batch together with a piece of yarn and handing it to me. 'That's everything. Are you ready?'

'I think so?' I said, thinking exactly the opposite. The Other Me was floating outside of me and was wondering what the hell I was doing, but the Wine Me was just going along with it.

'One last thing,' Sloane said, pulling a bottle out of her rucksack. Rum. 'I knew we'd need something extra warming.' She poured a generous helping into both our cups. 'Cheers!'

I took a sip, the alcohol burning on my lip, leaving a pleasing heat. Sloane dipped her forefinger into the pot of shrew's blood and ran it across her face making war stripes – a line on each cheek, one on her forehead – offering me the pot to copy. I did the same, the blood warm and sticky on my cheeks, leaving my skin underneath tight.

'OK, serious now. Let's concentrate.'

She opened one of the jars and placed the nails inside before adding some drops of the shrew's blood from the Tupperware. 'See this candle?' She showed it to me. 'I've carved Callum's name into it.' In my wine-and-rum haze, it only vaguely worried me exactly how prepared she happened to be for this particular spell scenario. 'We light this – and the bundle of his hair and sage and then put it all in the jar and bury it.'

'Ohhh, that's what the shovel is for?'

'What did you think it was for?'

'I was scared to ask – burying a body?' I laughed.

'This is a travel shovel, we'd need a proper-sized one for that,' Sloane said, completely straight-faced. 'But before we do the lighting – and this bit is really important – we have to set our intention. That means we have to visualise Callum and really concentrate on his punishment. Imagine that smug face of his, the way he just dismissed you, lied to your face, and then imagine the smile being wiped off that face. How good it will feel for you.'

'Yikes, OK,' I said. I wondered if I'd ever said 'yikes' before. It totally felt like a 'yikes' moment.

'You ready?'

Sloane reached for my hand, giving it a quick, sharp squeeze. I took a deep breath. The flames shot up, instant heat cutting through the chill I felt at my core.

'OK, let's set the intention then. I'll squeeze when we're ready to cast the spell.'

I did as she'd told me – pictured Callum's face, with the smug grin. His self-assured strut. Other images of him tried to creep in – him in the sitting room in his house, looking sad and bitter and hurt. I shook them off – I wasn't here to feel sorry for Callum.

I refocused, back to finding my blood-soaked uniform, my thoughts like creeping tendrils of smoke searching for the red-hot anger I knew was there. And, further back still, to last year, his face when I rejected him – the disgust layered thickly on it. He *was* disgusting. He deserved to be punished – and properly, at last.

I imagined him how I wanted to see him – weak and pathetic and grovelling and humble and most of all, SORRY.

Sloane squeezed my hand. I opened my eyes, shaken from my reverie, my head and heart dry and pounding. She smiled at me, easing her hand out of mine to pick up the candle and light it, then handed it to me to do the honours. I placed the lit candle carefully inside the jar, which she then rested by the fire.

'Now for the spell. We need to say it five times. Here, I've written it down.' She produced a piece of paper torn from a schoolbook, neat rows of sharp, angular writing floating and criss-crossing in front of my eyes. When had she even written this?

'I scrawled it down when I was getting the stuff together at mine,' she answered my unspoken question, holding the paper between us, close enough to the fire for the flames to light it up. 'Let's do it.'

I started reading, the words feeling cumbersome in my dry mouth.

'For the evil you have caused us, Callum Henderson, we, the
Sisters of Endor call on The fates.
We curse you and send you to hell,
Sisters of Darkness, make him unwell,
For being an absolute dick,
Sisters of Darkness, make him sick.
Teach him a lesson, make him know fear
Let this spell last one lunar year.'

With each round, I felt better and better. A tingling sensation was spreading and growing, blossoming, sending electricity driving through me, turning my anger and fury into something solid and tangible, weaponising it. By the last round, the last word, I felt like I was on fire – alive, strong. The strongest. I checked to make sure I wasn't levitating because I one hundred per cent felt like I could be. It was the same buzz I'd felt when I'd first used magic successfully to light a candle – but times a thousand.

Sloane looked at me, eyes wide and shining. 'Feels good, huh?'

'It really does.'

'This is proper magic, my friend. Welcome.'

'Now what do we do?'

'Now, we bury it. And then – we go for a swim!'

CHAPTER TWENTY

Sitting around the fire post-swim, so cold I couldn't feel my face, I almost felt like a new me. Or a me I wasn't familiar with yet.

I'd gone in the water practically naked – Sloane's idea, which I had uncharacteristically agreed to. It had been liberating. And for some reason – adrenaline, a post-spell high – I'd gone straight in for the first time ever too. No fannying about, waiting for the sea to lick the tops of my ankles or taking it in whimpering stages. The water had been a cold, numbing blast against my skin which had instantly turned to a throbbing, satisfying warmth. I'd dipped my head under the water, enjoying feeling cocooned by it, relishing the sensation as it reached every part of me and absolutely not giving one fleeting thought to what creatures and underwater creepy-crawlies were under the surface. Where was the old Jessie and what I done with her?

'This'll warm you up,' Sloane said, handing me the rum bottle. 'And I'll put this on too.' She took a can of soup out of her bag and poured it into the cauldron.

'*That's* why you brought the cauldron!' I realised we hadn't actually used it for the spell.

'I knew we'd need something to warm us up. Cauldrons are multifaceted like that.'

I laughed, shaking my head at her. 'But we can warm things up ourselves – no cauldron needed.'

'I like the symbolism of it. Plus, I didn't know what spell we'd end up doing – better to come prepared. We also didn't need the blood on our faces, but I thought it added a certain . . . je ne sais quoi.' She stirred the soup. 'Bet you're feeling on a high right about now, aren't you?' she asked. 'Magic is like that – it's a powerhouse.'

She was right. I did feel pretty amazing. 'I do feel pretty good.'

'You'll have a crash in a bit, probably tomorrow, but you just need to eat your way through it – and drink plenty of water.' She glanced at the rum bottle. 'Which you'll need anyway.'

We drank our soup from fresh plastic cups, the liquid burning the roof of my mouth and, as Nonna would say, warming my cockles. I looked up, taking in the blanket of stars shining clear in the sky, the moon sturdy and solid, the parent keeping a sage eye on its offspring. We'd never had skies this clear in Manchester, skies like you imagine them, storybook skies. The cove looked magical now that it was properly dark – all perfect natural wonder and atmosphere. The booze and the magic and the swim and the soup were all dancing together inside me, giving me a hazy-round-the-edges happiness.

Sloane smiled at me, her eyeliner still surprisingly in place. I wished Libby and Summer and Tabs could see this side of her – not necessarily the killing-small-animals, cursing-people side, but the warm, fun, free-spirited part of her that you wouldn't know was buried underneath her hard-as-nails exterior. I knew this whole thing must be tough for her – moving to a new place, trying to make new friends. And on top of that having to leave family behind too.

'Do you and your sister get on?' I asked, softly. 'Is it weird not having her around?'

Sloane lowered her cup, a darkness setting over her face. A wave crashed on the previously calm sea. 'It's complicated.' Her voice was quiet, cracked. 'My sister is quite troubled. Our relationship has ... changed. She had a terrible accident and she's now in a wheelchair – something not even fixable by magic. I was there and I felt really helpless about the whole thing. It's tough.'

A chill struck me. 'I'm so sorry. That's terrible. When did it happen?' I thought back to the photo, which couldn't have been taken that long ago.

'It was eighteen months ago. Actually, eighteen months, two weeks and four days ago, to be precise. And it was terrible.' Sloane didn't look at me, just kept her eyes focused on the fire, pain making her features hard and dark.

I felt awful for prying, for bringing up something so obviously raw still. 'Don't feel you have to tell me, I'm sorry I asked. I didn't know.'

'I want to tell you. I trust you, we're friends. That's what friends do, isn't it? Tell each other secrets, including the horrible ones. Support each other.'

I nodded. 'Totally.'

She took a deep breath, readying herself. 'Isla – that's her name. Isla was amazing. She was fun and fierce and full of life. She never took shit from anyone, always knew her own mind, always had a plan or some new adventure for us to go on. She was the sociable, lively, fun one and people saw me as the intense, boring one – but I didn't care. I enjoyed bathing in her light as much as anyone else. She made me feel stronger, better, just by being near her.'

I had to look away from the pain on her face.

'But a couple of years ago, something changed in her,' she carried on. 'I don't know why, exactly. Maybe she got sick of being the golden child. She got into Dark Magic – and I mean, *really* Dark. She became obsessed with it. Everyone warned her – Mum, the coven, me – we all told her to stop, that it was too dangerous, that she would go too far. And then, one day, she did go too far.

'She'd been on a date with a boy from school, Dylan Morris. He was like Callum, always walking around thinking he was king of the castle, Billy Big Balls, but for some reason Isla liked him. The next day, he told everyone they'd done ... certain things. Which they hadn't. It was all the usual lies and slut-shaming – tale as old as time. Isla said she wanted to teach him a lesson, asked me if I wanted to help. I said yes. I thought if I was there I could keep an eye on her, make sure she didn't go too far. We tracked him down after school ...'

Sloane rubbed at her face, like she was trying to erase the memory, to rub it out of her head. I wanted to go and hug her, to reach out to her in some way, but it felt like she needed to finish uninterrupted. I shuffled closer.

'When we found Dylan ... it was like Isla was possessed. I thought we were just going to scare him, but that wasn't enough for her. I tried to stop her, but she just kept going. She wouldn't listen. She would have killed him. I grabbed her, to make her stop . . . and she fell and hit her head. That crack – that sound – I can still hear it, every day. She'll never walk again – because of me.' A huge wave pounded on the sand, the fire flickered and rose.

'Sloane, I'm so sorry.' My words felt feeble – as empty and fragile as the washed-up shells by our feet. I moved next to her, tentatively putting my hand on her back. 'You can't blame yourself. It was an accident. You were trying to protect her.'

'It shouldn't have happened.' Her voice was flat. 'She should never have been put in that position in the first place. And now . . . I miss her. God, I miss her.'

We sat in the moment, the gentle lapping of the water and crackle of the fire the only sounds riding on the night. I rubbed her back, wishing I knew the right thing to say.

'Anyway. Enough of that!' She shot her head up, the bright, engaged Sloane back and ready for action in the blink of an eye. 'Pass me that rum bottle and let's talk about *you*.' She took two deep gulps, not even wincing as it went down. 'How are you feeling? Looking forward to seeing Callum getting his comeuppance?'

I smiled, picturing him looking nauseous and not his usual overly confident self. 'Hell, yeah.'

'Now, are we going to do anything about those jerk-off friends and boyfriend of yours who completely threw you under the bus? Maybe teach them a lesson too?'

'No!' My stomach did a little pull at the thought of the girls and Freddie. I was angry with them – but I wanted them to be safe. 'No, we leave them alone.'

Sloane hesitated, then nodded. 'All right. They're ancient

history though, right? You've got me now – you don't need waste-of-space bitches who don't support you when *I've* got your back.' She nudged my shoulder and topped up our rum cups, holding hers out for a toast. 'Here's to badass witches who have each other's backs.'

The fire and rum were making me warm-hearted and heavy-eyed. It was good to be around someone who got me – the *real* me, not the one who has to hide a huge part of myself every single day.

'I'm glad I met you,' I said, the words falling out of me, merging with each other. 'That sounds cheesy, but I mean, it's nice to hang out with someone . . .'

'Someone who gets it?'

'Yeah. Exactly.'

'I'm your saviour, Jessie. Here to save you from the mundane, non-magical dreariness you were trapped in. Think of me as your Fairy Witchmother.'

'Fairy Witchmother?'

'Here to make all your wishes come true.'

I laughed. 'I'm so here for that!'

Her eyes widened, looking all cat-like and intense again. 'Well, if I'm to be a true Fairy Witchmother, then I need to know what your deepest desires are, and your deepest fears.'

'Let's see, my deepest fear? That's easy. Another round of Callum Henderson torturing me. Definitely. My greatest desire?' I thought about it. There was so much that I wanted. I wanted my friends to accept me, though I knew they never would. I wanted to stay here and feel alive, ride this wave of power and all things magic. I wanted some water, for sure.

'Well, for a start, I want to break up with Freddie.' It came out of nowhere, but as I said it, I knew I'd thought it for a while. 'I just can't be with anyone who chooses to be friends with that scumbag. I can't trust someone who would choose him over me. You want your boyfriend to be a ride or die and, as he's clearly shown, he's not. Freddie can be really nice, but there's ... something missing.' I giggled. 'I feel like that's a waste of a wish though.'

'There'll be plenty more, don't you worry – Fairy Witchmother doesn't have a wish limit. Granted and granted, by the way.' She grinned at me – a grin that was big and hearty and mischievous and ate right into my soul. 'Now, let's dance around the fire like the motherfucking witches that we are.'

CHAPTER TWENTY-ONE

Revision Facts – Alcohol and the Human Body (Biology)
1. The alcohols are a homogenous series of organic compounds.
2. Ethanol is the alcohol found in alcoholic drinks such as beer, wine and rum.
3. Ethanol is also mixed with petrol for use as a fuel.
4. Short-term effects of alcohol include drowsiness, impaired vision, reduced reaction time, bad judgement calls and severe dehydration.
5. Long-term effects of alcohol include damage to the liver and brain and severe regret at unauthorised use of magic while under the influence.

My dry-as-a-badger's-arse mouth woke me up in the morning – my tongue lying like a beached whale, helplessly flailing in the Sahara, desperate for moisture. I tried to generate some but failed – it seemed my saliva glands had gone on strike.

I grappled around on my side table for some water, not ready to peel my eyes open yet. My head thumped into action with a searing, pounding, bulldozer heft, like fifty weightlifters trampolining on my cranium. Actually, like fifty weightlifters, all carrying ACME weights, trampolining on my cranium. It felt as though my head might actually collapse in on itself and my eyes pop out of their sockets. My hand finally touched a glass of water and I raised myself enough to take three deep, desperate gulps, relishing the sweet, sweet relief of liquid, which was too quickly replaced by a swell of nausea.

Sinking back into my bed, I risked creaking my eyes open. Faced with a swirling ceiling and lurching seasickness, my body screamed that was a mistake. All I could do was lie still and pray for salvation. I was one hundred per cent not feeling like a kickass witch this morning – more like a kicked *in* the ass witch.

I thought back to last night, or the snatched clippings of it I could grasp at. I remembered the early stuff – the spell, the swim, the soup. I remembered feeling sorry for Sloane moving around a lot and not having any friends. I remembered how good it felt to be with someone who knew I was a witch and could relate. I remembered Sloane telling me about her sister and how devastated she had looked. I remembered her wanting to hex the girls and Freddie and me telling her not to. Ah, yes. And I remember saying I wanted to break up with Freddie. Did I actually want to break up with Freddie? I wasn't sure. I was definitely angry at him, *that* was for sure.

My head did a double-pound, not enjoying my intense, tumultuous thoughts. Maybe now was not the time to be making life decisions. Maybe now was the time for paracetamol. Maybe I could magic some up. *Oh, I wish I felt better. I wish this headache would go away. I wish I could open my eyes again.*

There was a knock at the door and before I managed to grunt a reply I heard it open.

'Good morning, petal,' Nonna said. I edged my eyes open enough to see her standing next to my bed, holding a tray laden with various items. 'Oh, you silly thing. Come on, sit up, this will sort you right out.'

I let her wrangle me into an upright position. She passed me a truly disgusting-looking drink, a speckled, beige gloop.

'This will replenish you,' she said. 'Just don't smell it – and don't ask me what's in it.'

That didn't fill me with confidence but I took a tentative sip, expecting the worst. It was actually bearable, if a little thick, and not in a good, McDonald's milkshake type way. Nonna's crazy teas and drinks always did what they were supposed to though, so I made myself take some big gulps, holding my nose and concentrating on swallowing and keeping it down, repeating until I'd drained the whole glass.

'Good girl. Now, I've got you a bacon sandwich, some pickled onion Monster Munch and a pint of ice water.'

'Paracetamol?' I creaked.

'You won't need paracetamol after my drink.' She waved her hand, dismissing the suggestion. 'You'll be right as rain.'

I had to admit, I *was* starting to feel better already. With my new clarity of mind, it occurred to me that I didn't remember coming home last night, or getting into bed and ... I *certainly* didn't remember changing into my ancient and way-too-small One Direction pyjamas.

'How did I ...' I was stuck with the horror that Mum might have seen me drunk and I would be in serious, World's Biggest trouble. 'Did Mum ...?'

'Your Mum's staying at Andy's – they're off early to an

independent market forum on the mainland. I let you in – Bella and I could hear you scrabbling around outside the front door, you couldn't find your keys and were making a right racket. We helped you to bed. I held your hair while you threw up and Bella got you changed.'

Ah, that explained the pyjamas then – *ha, ha, Bella*.

Every atom of me cringed with the shame of it – and not just because of the pyjamas. I focused on the pattern on my duvet, not wanting to make eye contact with Nonna.

'Do you want to tell me how that happened?' she prodded gently, when it became clear I wasn't going to say anything.

Let's see ... did I want to tell her that I'd made a new friend who happened to be a powerful witch, who had taught me things Nonna told me I'm not ready for, who hates my friends, has taken me to a secret cove no one can access and likes to drink and do Dark Magic and skinny-dip while off her face on rum? I *probably* didn't.

'I was just hanging out with the girls and—'

'The girls, hey?'

I nodded, which turned out to be a bad move for my head.

'Well, that's interesting because Summer came here last night looking for you.' *Damn it.* 'Do you want to try telling me the truth now?' Nonna's eyes were steely and straight-talking. I was sprung.

I squirmed. 'OK, so, I've made a different friend – a new girl, Sloane. She's just moved down here and doesn't know anyone and is having problems making friends so, you know, we have a lot in common.' Another little white lie – or omission. 'And I felt sorry for her, so agreed to hang out and basically we just got

165

a bit carried away. I didn't actually have that much to drink . . .'
(ANOTHER LIE) 'But I guess I'm not used to it so it just
went to my head.' I reached for the bacon sandwich as a
distraction, even though I wasn't sure my stomach was ready for
it. I could feel Nonna's eyes on me.

'And the magic?'

I gulped. 'What magic?'

Nonna sighed, like she was dealing with an exasperating
toddler. 'I'm not a fool, Jessie. Please don't treat me like one.
This isn't a regular hangover. So I'll ask again – and the magic?'

Oh, crap.

'It was nothing really, I just did some small things – making
our food hot, lighting a fire, protecting us from a nasty boy.' I
read once that the closer a lie is to the truth, the more believable
it is. Those were not a hundred miles away type lies. 'No one
saw me do any of it and it was all for valid reasons.' That, at
least, was definitely true. It *was* for valid reasons.

Nonna paused, doing that aura-reading, freaky-perception,
analysis thing she does so well. I squirmed again.

'Look, you're doing what teenagers do,' she said, eventually.
'We've all been there, we've all done it. I remember throwing up
chunks after downing the best part of a bottle of ginger wine –
all over the kitchen floor when Great Granny Maud had guests
for dinner. Not my proudest moment. But that doesn't make it
right – or *safe*. It's nice that you are making this girl Sloane feel
welcome, but you need to think about whether she's got your
best interests at heart, Jessie. If she's encouraging you to do
things like this, then maybe she hasn't. Maybe you'd be better
sticking with the people who you know care about you.'

The people who I know care about me? Did she mean Libby and Summer and Tabitha? The people who 'care' about me so much they completely stabbed me in the back and sided with my one true enemy? Those people? As if. Sloane *absolutely* had my best interests at heart. To punish Callum. To be true to myself and my power. To develop my magic in the way it deserved.

'I'll leave you to your sandwich, love.' Nonna eased herself up off my bed and started walking to the door.

'Nonna,' I said. 'When do you think I'll be ready to manifest? Or cast my own spells?'

She narrowed her eyes. 'Why do you ask?'

'I've just been thinking about it.'

'It won't be for a while yet, petal. It's quite a tricky area of magic and you're not ready for it yet. These things take time – you have to earn them too. With great power comes great—'

'Responsibility, yes, I know. So you don't think I'm ready?' *You don't trust me,* I wanted to add.

'Everything in time, love, everything in time.'

But that was where she was wrong. I was ready. *Now* was the time, as I'd already proved – if only to myself.

CHAPTER TWENTY-TWO

'Hey, Boozehound.' Bella knocked at my door and let herself in. It was a few hours later and I felt miraculously better – to the point where I'd even showered and was now walking and talking and generally functioning like a normal, living human being. Nonna should seriously think about selling those drinks – she'd make a fortune. 'Summer's here. Do you want me to send her up?'

My stomach knotted at the thought of seeing Summer – remnants of anger and new flashes of dread.

'I'll come down,' I said, thinking that some fresh air wouldn't go amiss.

I grabbed a jumper, giving it a sniff to make sure it was clean (enough) and padded down the stairs, my stomach knot growing gnarlier and twistier with each step. Summer was in the kitchen chatting to Nonna; to my relief, they were discussing the sleep-inducing benefits of lavender and not my drunken exploits.

'Hey,' I said, hovering in the doorway. 'Can we go grab a coffee? I could do with some air.'

'Sure. Nice to see you, Nonna – and thanks for the advice, I'll definitely look into it.'

'I'll make you up a pillow spray, love, that'll sort you right out,' Nonna called, as we headed out the front door.

We set off down the hill towards the seafront. It was a beautiful day outside. So beautiful I felt bad for having missed more than half of it.

'We missed you last night.' Summer said. 'Libby's mum said you came and then left without even coming in. I was hoping we could all sort things out. You didn't reply to any of our messages – or answer our calls. We were worried about you.'

'You didn't look like it,' I said.

'What do you mean? You didn't even come in.'

'I saw you when I was at the door. You were doing a dance routine or something – from the golden before times. You didn't need me there.' I felt childish saying the words out loud, knowing that they sounded slightly ridiculous and petulant. My argument had seemed more ironclad when it was just in my head.

'Whaaat? You're not seriously upset about us doing a stupid dance routine from a hundred years ago are you? Dude, we can teach you the routine! We were just feeling nostalgic.'

'Exactly. Nostalgic for a time when I wasn't around.'

Summer sighed. 'OK, I get it, you felt left out. But you know, our history doesn't mean that there isn't room for you. In fact, you arriving a) brought us back together in the first place and b) made the group complete. Not all the memories are good, you know. We just choose not to reminisce about the time we fell out over the Great Christmas Production Disaster of Year Six or Skirtgate in 2016. So please stop being silly and missing out on fun.'

Her words made me feel nice and warm, landing on me like a reassuring back rub. Maybe I *was* being silly – and paranoid.

'So are we all good now?' she asked.

'I was angry with you even before I saw you all dancing,' I said, knowing if I didn't air it, it would eat me up.

Summer frowned. 'Because of that thing in the changing rooms?'

I gritted my teeth. 'Yes, because of "that thing in the changing rooms". "That thing" where Callum *soaked my uniform in blood* as a way of period-shaming me and you all defended him.'

'Look, I'm sorry if you felt like that.' Ah, great, the rage-inducing, not-taking-any-accountability non-apology. 'We weren't defending him. We just . . . didn't want to rush to any conclusions.'

I stopped and glared at her. 'Do you at least realise *now* that it was him?'

Summer paused. 'Honestly, Jess, it just doesn't feel right. It's like Libby said. It doesn't feel very . . . Callum.'

'Yeah, cos he's not known for doing shady, horrible things to girls – to me?'

She sighed. 'Callum can be a dick. But it's usually when he's got swept up in the moment, carried away – I'm not excusing it, but this . . . this was premediated. And very, very dark. Someone went to the effort of getting hold of animal's blood! That's too dark to be Callum. I know that's hard to understand, but we've known him a long time and—'

'There you go again!' I exploded, cutting her off. 'You guys know him, know that deep down he's decent, and I don't and will never understand. Whatever. That's not what you were saying last year.'

'The only thing he denied last year was that he came on to you – and did Tabs or I believe him then? No, we didn't. Even

170

Libby didn't, deep down, she just tried to fool herself into believing it. He can absolutely be a dick, but he *mostly* owns his shit. And when he doesn't, it's easy to see when he's lying.' She took a breath, slowed down. 'Look, who did it doesn't even matter. What matters is that we're here for you.'

'It doesn't matter? It matters to me!'

'Sorry, that came out wrong. Of course it matters. I just want you to know we're here for you, and I'm sorry if it didn't come across like that.'

I scowled. 'It really didn't.'

'Maybe we didn't handle it well,' Summer said. 'But Sloane being there really didn't help – she made it worse. I know you won't want to hear this, but I think she was *trying* to make it worse, actually. Pushing everyone's buttons.'

'Of course, blame it on Sloane. It was nice that *someone* actually had my back.'

'I dunno, Jessie. I get a bad vibe from Sloane. Don't you think it's strange that you guys were in the same lesson and yet she was the only one who saw Callum?'

I looked her in the eyes to see if she was being serious. Turned out she was. 'You have got to be kidding.'

'I'm not saying she had anything to do with it, I'm just asking the questions.'

'And why on earth would she do that to me – her friend?'

Summer chewed at a nail. 'Well, maybe because she wanted *this* to happen.'

'What do you mean?'

'Look at what it's done. We've fallen out. You're angry with us. You were out with Sloane last night, I assume?'

I nodded. 'Yes, I was. And as a matter of fact, we had a great time.'

'I don't trust her, Jess.' I could see the worry on her face, but I didn't buy it. This was fake concern. 'I know you don't want to hear it, but I just don't trust her.'

'Because she dresses differently? Because she's not from here? Because she's into different things?' I specifically didn't mention what those different things were. 'Well guess what, any of those sentences could describe me too. And I *do* trust her – a lot more than I trust you guys at the moment.' I couldn't stand there and listen to any more. 'I'm done with this.'

And with that, I stormed off in the opposite direction, taking the deepest of breaths to stop the witch in me from raining down a plague of locusts on her head.

CHAPTER TWENTY-THREE

I sat in the Beach Café (I had deliberately avoided The Quay), nursing my second flat white. The hot coffee seeped into the final fuzzy corners of my brain and completed my revival, though the caffeine wasn't exactly helping my rage issues. I scrolled all the missed messages and voicemails from last night on my phone, knowing I should respond in some way, but feeling unable to bring myself to.

Freddie had started the evening with heartfelt missives about how he was sorry *if I felt* he hadn't taken my side (again with the no-accountability apology!) and asking if I was OK. He was worried about me, apparently, but the worry didn't seem to last too long – the texts had got gradually less apologetic in tone and more snappy. His last text had said that if I was going to be childish enough to ignore him rather than trying to sort it out then fine, so be it.

There was no point in replying to him – to any of them – Summer, Libby, Tabs – as I knew it would be exactly the same conversation I had with Summer. I didn't understand, because I didn't know Callum like they did. Because I was – and always would be – an outsider.

Just then a message came through from Sloane:

> Hey Witch Sis. You wanna hang out? Do some cool witchy shit?

I instantly felt a little shot of happiness when I saw it, relishing in its perfect timing. I went to reply with a big fat yes, but then my annoying responsibility-chip kicked in and I remembered I actually had a lot of revision to do over the weekend. We had a bunch of pre-mock mocks coming up next week and I was already half a day behind due to my elephantine hangover horror of this morning. I couldn't risk losing any more time, as much as I was tempted – which was a whole lot.

> I can't today. I've got to revise.

> Revise? Have you forgotten you're a witch? Witches don't need to revise. C'mon, I'll teach you something fun. Like how to move mountains – literally.

My head was a wrestling match, all twisted limbs and jumbled bodies, the right and wrong of it pushing and pulling with no slam dunk in sight. Or whatever a slam dunk translated to in wrestling.

> Sorry, I also promised Mum I'd help her with something. See you on Monday x

It was a lie – which seemed to be my schtick today – but I knew if I'd stuck with the revision excuse I wouldn't hear the end of it.

***

I knocked on Bella's door and waited for a reply – unlike she normally did.

'Come in,' she called.

'Hey.' I slumped in and flung myself on her bed, blinking at the multitude of fairy lights strung around every possible wall and surface. She was sitting at her desk, fat textbooks laid out in front of her next to all her beauty products and make-up. Of course *she* was revising.

'What's up? You still hungover? Looking for some hair of the dog?'

'Funny. I'm not actually. Nonna's drink was amazing.'

'You should've seen yourself. You were a hot mess. In fact, no hot, just mess. Stumbling about, muttering about a fairy witchmother and Callum Henderson. Or "Callum Bellenderson", as you called him.'

I blushed. 'Yeah, well, I hadn't had that much to drink, I'm just not used to it and I hadn't eaten.'

'Oh, you're trying that line, are you? Who were you even with? It obviously wasn't the usual Spice Girls you hang out with.'

'A new girl at school. You wouldn't know her.'

'Well, I reckon she might be a bad influence, so just be careful.'

A scream broke out in my head – if one more person said that about Sloane, I'd explode. 'I forgot I was talking to Miss Never-Put-a-Foot-Wrong,' I snapped.

Bella gently caught my wrist. 'Don't be a drama queen, I'm just trying to give you some big-sisterly advice. And of course I've put a foot wrong. To the tune of drinking half a bottle of Malibu and many tequila shots. With people who weren't really my friends. So I'm just saying.'

I was surprised. How did I not know about this misdemeanour? I wish I had witnessed it so I could keep it in my things-to-mock-Bella-about bank – like I was absolutely sure she would do with my performance last night.

'And oh my God, how lucky are you that Mum wasn't home – can you imagine?' She laughed and I did too. She was SO right.

I took in her textbooks and immaculately written-up colour-coded index revision cards, in awe at the perfectionism of her – the wholesome (frustrating) *goodness* of her.

'So, was there anything specific you wanted?' she asked after a minute. 'I've got a tonne of revision to do and about five videos to record.'

'I need to revise too, actually.' I pushed myself off the bed, looking at the photos that were plastered all over her wall as I walked to the door. Bella with her mates, all big smiles and gestures of affection. It made my throat tight. 'Have you ever thought about using your magic with your . . . revision?' I knew it was a stupid question as soon as the words had left my mouth.

'You mean, cheating?'

'Well, not exactly, I guess if it's helping with revision rather than in an actual exam.' The words sounded limper out loud than they had done in my head.

'Jess, it's still cheating. I really haven't – and neither should you.' She gave me a parental stare. 'Remember what Dad used to say?' *Here we go, another one of Dad's empty motivational sayings.* '"If you have to cheat to win, you're still a loser."'

'That was about Snap.'

'It still applies though.'

'All right, Mum-clone, thanks.'

I was already out of the door and halfway up to my room when I heard her yell after me. 'SERIOUSLY, JESSIE, IT'S NOT WORTH IT.'

She was right. And that was very, very annoying.

CHAPTER TWENTY-FOUR

I struggled with my English for hours. I could absolutely, whole-heartedly, stick-pins-in-my-eyes *not* be bothered with writing an essay about how much of a wet blanket Macbeth was. English was so not my thing. Numbers and science and cold hard facts I could do; fannying about with words and meaning and subtext and trying to work out what on earth the long-dead author was trying to get across all those years ago? No thank you. The words all blurred into a big ball of bleurgh.

I scrolled through my phone, put it down, tried to write the essay, picked up my phone, scrolled. I looked at my messages from Sloane from earlier. Maybe I *should* try using my magic. Just as an experiment though, not to use in actual exams. Just to see if I could even do it. I probably couldn't, but it wouldn't hurt to try.

I closed my eyes, not sure exactly what to do. I considered texting Sloane for help but I knew she'd want to meet up. Deep breaths. I let a sense of calm descend, swiping away the panic and the images of jumbled words. Deep breaths, channel, release. Deep breaths, channel, release. Deep breaths, channel, release.

I sat there for a full at least four minutes. I was deep breathing and channelling like a total lemon but nothing was happening. Eventually I gave up, opened my eyes, gave my shoulders a roll and made a mental note to ask Sloane about it on Monday.

I was about to get up from my bed (my chosen workspace) and find something to faff about with when I was struck with an overwhelming urge to ... work. My hands placed themselves on the keyboard and, before I had a chance to fully register what was happening, started typing so fast it was like I was some kind of secretarial school graduate from the 1950s. I was half-expecting smoke to come off the keyboard.

Thoughts and ideas and words were coming to me with the same ease that numbers normally come to me. Yes, of course I could write an essay on whether I think Lady Macbeth has power over her husband throughout the play and I could also slip in a neatly insightful bit here about what sort of commentary Shakespeare was making on the concepts of power and ambition. It was joyous, like I was on a rollercoaster, only going up – none of the stomach-dropping-downward dives.

Revision Facts – The Character of Lady Macbeth in *Macbeth* (English)

1. Lady Macbeth is presented as more ambitious and ruthless than her husband.
2. In order to find the strength to murder King Duncan when her wimp of a husband can't, Lady Macbeth renounces her femininity, calling on the spirits to 'unsex' her – take the milk from her boobs and make her infertile. 'Cos apparently femininity and murder aren't compatible.
3. She's cunning and manipulative and uses all the tricks on her husband to get him to do what she wants. See also: all women.

4. And, of course, because she's a woman and not meant for this murderous crap (which is better left to men) once the deed is done she unravels, big time, and develops a raging conscience.
5. Predictably, because of her evil deed, she meets a gnarly end, taking her own life.

By the time Mum called us down for dinner (she and Andy had picked up fish and chips and Jake and Neve on their way back) I had what I was pretty sure was a top-grade essay written up – and with time to spare. I practically skipped down the stairs and into the kitchen. Mum and Andy were dishing up, Bella was filling a jug with water, Jake and Neve were hovering awkwardly and Nonna was sat at the head of the table pouring herself what looked like a pint of wine.

'Hello, darling,' Mum said, shuffling a mass of perfectly greasy chips onto a plate. 'How was your day?'

'Really good actually!' Nonna narrowed her eyes at me and I had a brief panic she could tell exactly what I'd been up to. 'I had a good revision session.' I fought off the guilt-blush that was trying to force its way on to my face.

'What have you been revising?' Neve asked. 'I've been struggling with linear interpolation. My head is swimming!'

'*Macbeth*, but all done with it for now,' I said, keen to move the conversation on before anyone asked me any in-depth questions.

'That's what I like to hear. You hard-workers must be in need of some brain food,' Mum said, passing us both a plate with mountainous amounts of steaming fishy, chippy goodness.

I hadn't realised how hungry I was until my mouth started full on watering at the smell of it, reminding me that the last thing I'd eaten was the bacon sandwich and Monster Munch. 'And how was the horror film sleepover?'

'Oooh, me and Jake love a good horror film,' Andy chipped in. He scrunched his face up into a weird, distorted expression and stuck his fingers up in a claw-like pose. Mum laughed and I gave him a blank look. 'Was it *A Nightmare on Elm Street*? Get it? I'm being Freddy Krueger.'

'It was supposed to be *The Exorcist* but we cancelled it in the end,' I said, tucking into my chips and avoiding Mum's eyes. 'Too much revision.'

'You missed out then,' Jake said, taking his plate and finding a seat at the table. 'That's a classic.'

'Maybe we can watch it all together one time,' Andy said, giving a big, hopeful smile.

'How was the fair?' Bella asked.

'Amazing, actually,' Mum said, a proper big grin on her face.

'Your *mum* was amazing.' Andy put his arm round her back and pulled her into him. 'Everyone who stopped by the stall loved her stuff and she did a bloody good – excuse my French – job of selling. We're so proud.'

I blanched. Since when was *he* officially part of our 'we'? I glanced at Jake and Neve, who were smiling. Did this not bother them? Was I just being mean? I looked at Bella, who seemed to be focusing very hard on her food.

'Well done, love,' Nonna said, raising her glass to Mum. 'You deserve it, you've worked hard. I'm glad you've found your calling.'

'Well, on that note,' Andy said, squeezing Mum tighter, looking like the cat who got the cream, 'can we tell them now?'

Well, now of course he had to tell us – you can't go dropping a line like that and not following it up. I mentally rolled my eyes. Bella shot me a look and I realised I might have *actually* rolled them.

Mum stood beside Andy, smiling like a shy schoolgirl, looking up at him and his bald patch like he was Brad Pitt. 'So, we have some news. Well, kind of news, it's not a big deal – baby steps really, but we've decided that . . .'

Oh God no. No. Please no. For the sake of all that's good in the world, no.

'We're moving in together!' Andy finished.

There was silence. We all sat with our mouths gaping open like fish, mine with a bit of actual fish still half-chewed in it. I definitely saw Jake and Neve's smiles drop. We didn't risk eye contact, but it gave me some relief to know I wasn't imagining the madness of it all. Bella was the first to correct her face.

'Wow, that's . . . great news! Congratulations!' she managed before the rest of us, except Nonna, chimed in with false cheer.

'It's not a sudden, all at once thing,' Mum added, reading the room. 'We're going to take it slowly and—'

'We haven't finessed all the details,' Andy said, his cheeks flushed with excitement. 'And don't worry, my guys, I'll be keeping my place on so we'll still have our weekends together and we can work out where we want to spend them. But this is us moving forward.'

Mum was looking anywhere but at us and Nonna, who was glaring at her. Andy, oblivious, raised his glass at me and Bella. 'So, girls, we're going to be housemates!' he said, rubbing a speck of ketchup off his *'Hard as Nails'* T-shirt.

It was the end of days – our family bubble bursting. I felt a chip lodge in my suddenly dry and tight throat.

CHAPTER TWENTY-FIVE

One small mercy was that it turned out it would just be Andy moving in with us and not his kids, as they spent most of their time at their mum's (though apparently every other weekend we'd have the pleasure). But it was only a teeny-tiny, sliver-like mercy – other than that the whole thing was a raging nightmare.

I didn't want Handy Andy to move in with us. I wasn't naïve enough to be holding out for a Mum and Dad miracle reunion or anything like that, but I had been hoping Andy and his novelty T-shirts were a short-lived rebound for Mum. Yes, he seemed to make Mum happy, but she hardly knew him – and he *definitely* hardly knew her.

Nonna was absolutely fuming. She had eventually managed a good show of congratulations at dinner, but as soon as Andy and his kids had left, she'd let Mum have a piece of her mind. It was the same argument they'd been having on a loop – Nonna angry that Mum hadn't consulted us at all and was taking such a giant step without having told Andy about the tiny little fact that we're witches, and Mum in total denial, saying she'd get round to it but it wasn't time yet. Bella and I had sulked on the outskirts of their shouting, eavesdropping and angrily muttering to each other.

The revelation hung over me all weekend like a thundercloud – dark and depressing and weighty. And Monday morning brought a whole new set of worries with it to add to my woes. I didn't know where I stood with the girls – would they be waiting for me that morning or not?

'Happy Monday!' Sloane was perched on the wall outside my house, drinking a can of Red Bull and smiling like we were off to a party.

My heart sank a bit, which was promptly followed by a surge of guilt. She'd been a good friend through everything – surely I should feel happier to see her?

'Hi,' I said, trying not to sound too disappointed. 'I wasn't expecting you.'

'Thought I'd surprise you.' She passed me a can of Red Bull. 'I figured you'd probably be walking in on your own and could do with the company.'

I tried for a smile, but inside I felt sticky. Why was she so sure I wouldn't have made it up with the others?

'How was the rest of your weekend?' she asked. We were walking now – I deliberately led her the long way round, so we wouldn't risk bumping into the others. 'Did you get your mum's thing sorted?'

It took me a minute to realise what she was talking about – the lie I'd spun her about helping my mum with something. 'Yeah, yeah, all sorted. How was your weekend?'

'Not great actually,' she sighed. 'Mum was working most of it so I was just on my own. It made me really miss my sister. It's hard, you know?'

I felt that surge of guilt again. I should have texted her.

'Anyway,' she said, brightening. 'It's a new week and a beautiful morning, one which will be made even more beautiful when we get into school and soak in the glory of a diminished Callum Henderson. Are you looking forward to seeing him looking less than his usual sprightly self?'

I imagined a humble Callum Henderson, looking all pale and sickly. 'Yeah, I guess I am actually. Cheers to that.' I opened my Red Bull and downed a few gulps, enjoying it in all its chemical glory, only wincing a tiny bit at the synthetic, cloying aftertaste it left behind.

'So what's up, buttercup? Why the sad face?'

'Just some annoying home stuff.' I didn't have the energy to get into it.

'You can confide in me, we're Witch Sisters. A problem shared is a problem halved and all that.'

Halving the problem did sound appealing. 'My mum's boyfriend is moving in, which she announced with great fanfare on Saturday night, and I'm not sure ... I dunno, I'm guess I'm bummed about it. He's OK, but I like it just the four of us.'

'Ah. Handy Andy is making the big move?'

I nodded, though I didn't remember ever mentioning Andy by name before – maybe it had been when I was drunk. 'Yup.'

'Men ruin everything good, don't they? Leave it with me.' Her eyes gleamed dangerously.

'God, no. Like, really, no.' For all of Andy's flaws, he was essentially a bumbling innocent. 'I don't want to do anything like that – not with, you know, *magic*.' I said it under my breath, practically a whisper, as we were getting closer to school. 'Besides, he's making Mum happy.'

'Jessie, that's your family he's inserting himself into. *Your* family, *your* life, *your* house. Has your mum stopped to think about you and Bella? Did she ask you if it was OK first?'

'Not exactly . . .'

'That's not cool. It's probably all his doing too. That's what men do, crawl into women's lives when they're at their most vulnerable, taking advantage, making it so the woman thinks she couldn't possibly live without them because then – oh no – who would change the light bulb or fix the boiler?'

I frowned. 'My mum's really good at that stuff—'

'He's probably a career conman and pulls this kind of stuff all the time. Next thing you know he'll be getting your mum to sign over all her bank accounts and be putting his name on the deeds. That's men, that's what they do.' We turned the corner to school, my body tensing in anticipation. Just at that moment I felt a sharp *ping* on my back, followed by a loud, throaty laugh as Marcus ran past me with a gaggle of mates.

'What the—!'

'Sorry, Sabrina, I thought you were someone else – someone with a sense of humour!' Marcus shouted. He'd taken to calling me Sabrina ever since the stupid witch video last year.

'Grow up!' I managed to shout back. The fact that they still found pinging bra straps funny just made me feel exhausted.

'Oh man, you have GOT to let me do something to him!' Sloane's eyes were on fire with excitement.

'He's not worth it.'

'Jessie! What's wrong with you! We've got to wage a war against these shitdogs.'

'That's what I wanted to do with Fem Soc – but in a more

constructive, less magic way. We need to go by the book if we want to properly change the culture.'

Sloane shook her head at me. 'Who cares about uniform or sports teams – none of that is going to make any real difference. Boys will still be arsehole misogynist boys, intent on making girls' lives hell at every opportunity.'

That had basically been what I'd thought. 'So what would you suggest?' I asked, excited to hear some fresh ideas.

'Well,' said Sloane, excitedly, 'for a start—'

We saw them at the same time. Freddie and Callum, outside the gates, talking to each other in hushed tones, heads bent together in a way that suggested yet another deep and meaningful.

'Speak of the devils,' Sloane said, too loudly.

I looked at the ground, embarrassed. She was worse than Libby with her no filter.

The boys looked up and I took the opportunity to examine Callum. He looked . . . surprisingly, disappointingly, OK. Not a pinnacle of health, he was definitely paler than usual. But he didn't look like he was ill or experiencing any kind of pain or suffering. He was well enough to shoot me a death stare before muttering something and storming off.

'Jess, can I speak to you for a minute?' Freddie asked, his face hard and drawn.

'She doesn't want to speak to you, jackass.' Sloane put her arm around me, trying to usher me forward, away from Freddie.

Freddie ignored her, fixing his eyes on me. 'Please, Jessie. Just a minute.'

'I said—' Sloane hissed.

'Fine. But just a minute,' I interrupted her. I knew I had to deal with him at some point, and the hurt in his eyes was getting to me, even though I was still angry. 'Can you give us a minute?' Sloane huffed and walked off.

'Thanks,' Freddie said. He lowered his voice, took a step closer, the familiar Freddie smell hitting me. 'I wanted to say that I'm sorry for what happened to you. And I'm sorry you felt like I was on Callum's side.'

He looked sincere and open and I felt myself soften. 'Well, weren't you?'

'There aren't any sides. At least, I don't see it like that. I just wanted you to hear him out.'

My stomach dropped, all my goodwill dissolved with the fizz of an Alka-Seltzer freshly dropped in water.

'Wait,' I said, realisation dawning. 'You still believe he didn't do it, don't you?'

He ran his fingers through his hair, frustrated.

'I don't know what's going on with you at the moment,' he said. 'You're pushing us away – me, the girls. But for what it's worth, we all care about you. Libby's quite upset, you know, they all are. As am I.'

Fantastic. They'd all been talking about me behind my back.

'I've got to get to registration.'

'I really think you're overreacting,' he said, to my back – I was already out of there, needing to put distance between us.

'I really think you're a dick,' I muttered, wishing I'd never met him.

CHAPTER TWENTY-SIX

By lunchtime I was an inferno, having replayed every interaction and text with Freddie and the girls in my head a million times. I was an outsider. I would always be an outsider. I might as well embrace it.

I was steeling myself for our Feminist Society meeting later. I had considered not turning up, but figured why should I be the one to miss out when all the nastiness was down to them? I wasn't going to let them get to me – not more than they had already. Besides, I knew Sloane would back me up, no matter what, and that was absolutely what I needed – I'd brought her along for moral support.

'No magic,' I said, as we walked to the classroom.

'Oh, come on, not even a little bit? What if they're being total bitches?'

'No! None at all. Promise?'

She sighed. 'Fine! But you're no fun.'

I took a deep breath and pushed the door open, already in full defence mode. Libby was at the front of the room sorting some papers, Summer and Tabs were arranging chairs in a circle with the help of a few other students. They all looked happy and smiley and like they hadn't even registered me not being there, let alone missed me. Until they saw me that is – and Sloane. Then the smiles definitely dropped.

Libby strode over to us. 'You came then.'

She was trying to keep her face neutral, but I could see the anger writhing underneath her poised and primped features. It kind of gave me a thrill. Did she seriously think I wouldn't come? This whole meeting had been my idea.

'Of course I came.' I had my estate agent smile at the ready.

'Hey,' Tabs said, looking genuinely happy to see me. Summer nodded at me. 'What can we do?' I asked. I saw Libby blanche at the 'we', glaring at Sloane.

'You can help us with the chairs,' Tabs said, clearly trying to keep things civil.

'Great.' Sloane and I set to work, pushing desks back, arranging chairs, Libby's eyes on us the whole time. People filed through the door in a slow trickle until there were about fifteen of us – mostly the younger years, which surprised me. Maybe that was a good sign – that the next generation was determined to make a change.

'Right, let's get started then.' Libby ushered everyone to sit down. Summer and Tabs sat either side of her while Sloane and I settled on the other side of the circle. 'So, welcome to Queen Vic's first Feminist Society. Let me give you a bit of background about why we decided it was important to start this in the first place. I'm sure some of you will know already, but for those that don't know the background' – she narrowed her eyes at Sloane – 'we thought we'd explain what happened last year.'

She carried on talking and I sat there squirming, not enjoying the feeling of her taking charge of it all. This was my story too.

Please let me do something to her. Sloane's voice in my head caught me by surprise. I'd forgotten that trick.

No, I thought back as firmly as I could. Though my resolve was waning.

'So yes, that's the background,' Libby went on. 'Now we thought we'd show you the video we made that was featured in the press as it encapsulates a lot of the culture that was such a problem here. Although fortunately, things have changed quite a bit since then.'

Not if Callum Henderson's anything to go by, Sloane said.

Summer stood up and turned the lights off, Tabs loaded up the video and my face appeared on-screen.

'Our film is about the appalling way girls are treated. Still. Every day. Especially at Queen Victoria Academy. I wish we hadn't needed to make this particular film, that it was something we didn't still need to highlight or talk about, but sadly that's not the case.'

I was instantly transported back all those months. How awful the boys were – but also the amazing camaraderie between the girls. I remembered recording that piece to camera like it was yesterday, the smell in the room, the feel of my jumper against my skin, the swirling emotions. My anger dulled to sadness.

Just then the door opened and a boy walked in, looking flustered. I guessed he was Year Seven or Eight – he definitely hadn't gone through the Year Nine hormone explosion yet.

'Sorry,' he stuttered. 'I wasn't sure what time . . . am I late?'

'Wrong room, mate!' Sloane said – ostensibly to me, but loud enough that everyone heard it. I nudged her.

The boy blushed, a fierce, blotchy red. 'I'm looking for Feminist Society?' His voice was even smaller now.

'That's us. Come on in,' Summer said warmly.

'Are you joking? Guys, come on, this is Feminist Society – the clue is in the title. Letting boys in kind of defeats the object of the exercise, no?' Sloane said.

'Sloane!' I whispered, taking in the circle of gobsmacked faces staring at her.

'Outside!' Libby snapped, storming over to us, Summer and Tabs hot on her heels. 'Now.'

I followed, dutifully, annoyed with Sloane, but also with Libby for treating me like a child who needed to be reprimanded.

'That's it,' Libby said once we were all in the corridor, the door closed behind us. 'You need to go. I knew we shouldn't have let you come.'

'I was just pointing out the obvious,' Sloane said.

'You "shouldn't have let us come"?' I asked Libby, incredulous. 'It's not up to you to decide anything. Have you forgotten that this whole thing was *my* idea?'

'Well it *was*, and then you were apparently too busy hanging out with Ms *The Craft* reject over here to bother planning any of it. And then you have the nerve to turn up and be absolute bitches.'

Part of me wanted to point out that it wasn't me who had been a bitch, and that of course I didn't agree with what Sloane had said, but the other part was reeling at Libby accusing me of abandoning them. *They* had abandoned me.

'I don't know what friendless-desperado bullshit she's pulled on you, but seriously, Jessie, you need to take a minute and look at yourself. She is not a good look for you.'

'Maybe you should just leave for today and we'll get together later and talk about—' Tabs started, quietly.

Sloane interrupted her, turning to Libby. 'Maybe *you* should take a good look at yourself. Some feminist you are, turning your back on your friend.' She was up in Libby's face now, a darkness overtaking her features.

'Let's go,' I said, turning on my heel and pulling Sloane away, desperate for air. 'They're not worth it.'

'Libby? Libby?' I heard Summer fretting from behind me. 'Get her some water, Tabs, she's going bright red. Calm down Libby, breathe. You're giving yourself a stress rash.'

I smiled. I couldn't help myself. A rash – the original and the best.

Nice one! Sloane said in my head. *You are fun after all.*

CHAPTER TWENTY-SEVEN

Whenever someone is tempted in a movie, it's always shown the same way – the evil, grinning Devil sitting with his pitchfork on one shoulder; a pleasant, smiling haloed angel on the other. Light versus dark, good versus evil, right versus wrong. It's so clear that right should win.

And so we push back on the bad every day in a million different ways – by not mentioning your friend's hormonal spot or giving your sister the last slice of pizza or returning the £5 note to the person you saw drop it, instead of keeping it for yourself. Tiny daily actions of resistance, of good.

But what the films don't tell you is how *good* giving in to the bad feels. The murky, spiky, dangerous bad – the bad that's in us all.

Revision Facts – *Dr Jekyll and Mr Hyde* (English)
1. One of the main themes of *Dr Jekyll and Mr Hyde* is the duality of human nature – the idea that everyone has both good and evil within them.
2. In the book, the choices the characters make determine whether they are considered a good person or not.
3. The piousness of Victorian society meant that many people were told their feelings or thoughts were bad,

making them question whether they could be good people if they had bad thoughts.

4. Dr Jekyll and Mr Hyde are the perfect example of this war between good and evil in the Victorian era – wealthy, respected, intelligent Dr Jekyll in public vs sinister, evil, murderous and unrepentant Mr Hyde in private.

5. We are ALL a bit Jekyll and Hyde, whether we care to admit it or not. The question is, which one wins . . .

What if we stopped fighting the bad and gave in to it instead? Soaked it up, swam in it, bathed in its glory. What if we told our friend it looked it like she had Mount Vesuvius on her chin? What if we ate that last pizza slice? What if we kept the £5? That feels pretty good too. As does shutting up your bitchy, judgemental friend who has completely stabbed you in the back.

'You are such a badass!' Sloane was grinning like she'd just won the lottery. 'Bet it feels good, doesn't it?'

'It kind of does. Who died and made her Head Feminist?'

'EXACTLY!'

We had left school, sneaking out through the staff car park. I was, for the first time in my life, officially truanting – well, for the second time actually, if you count the whole escaping school to try and flee to the mainland thing last year. Sloane had assured me she could witch our way out of being in trouble (I didn't ask exactly how) and that it was only half a day. I resisted the urge to point out I had a maths test tomorrow and I could have really done with the revision session today. I knew what she'd say about that – *use your magic*. And actually, maybe she was right (as she always seemed to be). What's the point of having these powers – of being such a powerful witch – if I couldn't use them to make my life a bit easier?

We were heading to Sloane's, winding our way through the back of town, the heady mixture of freedom and fear of someone seeing us making me buzz. I felt like a cross between a warrior queen and a spy.

But something was still bothering me. 'You know you shouldn't have said that to that poor boy though, right?' I said. 'Libby totally overreacted, but he had every right to be there.'

'Well, in my opinion, he *didn't* have a right to be there,' she said. 'I know you're one of *those* feminists – the "it's all about equality" ones – but I'm here to tell you that's never going to work. Equality isn't enough. We need to have *more* power than men. Look at reproductive rights – look at what they're doing all across the world – America even. Women gained rights there in the 70s, but now it's being taken away again by *men*. And do you know why they're doing it? To let us know they still have the power – over EVERYTHING. Our lives, our work, how we dress, our rights, our bodies. Equality will come back to bite you on the arse. And not just a nibble – a Great White chomping off your whole arse until you're lying there bleeding out.' She took a breath. 'This is me.'

We'd gone to the far end of town, past the big posh houses, further along even than the estate and down a small, unkempt path. We were now standing in front of a small, one-storey building, which stood alone in an unkempt field. It was verging on a shack, only it was made of breezeblock, not wood.

'Wow,' I said, taking it in. 'I didn't even know this was here.'

'I know, cool, right? My hidden paradise.' She put the key in the door. '*Our* hidden paradise – mine and my mum's, I mean. She works so much I forget she's around sometimes.'

'Is she not in now?'

'What day is it . . . Friday? No, she's working.'

'What does she do?'

'She's a nurse. Shift work and all that.'

A thick, musty smell hit me as soon as we walked through the door.

We walked through into a dark, perfectly square room. The curtains on the one window were drawn, the small slit between them letting in only a thin sliver of sunlight.

Sloane turned the light on and the room came into view properly. There was one small sofa up against a wall, a shabby coffee table in front of it and a faded, threadbare rug which took up most of the floor. There were some stock pictures on the wall, the kind that come with the frames – flowers, a seascape – nothing personal. There didn't seem to be anything personal anywhere actually. No piles of books or clothes or mail, no photos. Maybe it was because they'd only recently moved in.

Sloane saw me looking around. 'It's not much,' she said defensively.

'It's nice,' I lied.

Then I froze. There was a dead bird hanging by the windowsill. 'Your mum doesn't mind stuff like that?'

'Nah, she's super laid-back. And besides, she's hardly ever here. Always working. PR stops for no one.'

'I thought she was a nurse?'

A minuscule pause.

'She's both. Nurse's pay these days, it's insulting. She does some PR office work in between shifts.' Her eyes flickered, the briefest of movements. 'Right then. Let's get this party started!'

I followed her into the kitchen area, desperately wanting to open all the curtains and let some air into the place but resisting the urge. She opened the fridge and pulled out two beers, opening them both and passing me one.

'Uh, I'm good thanks.' I glanced at my watch; it was just gone two.

'Suit yourself.' She shrugged. 'I would've thought you'd need one after that debacle.' She took a glug of hers and it looked satisfying. *So satisfying*, the devil on my shoulder said. Why not? I held my hand out to take the bottle, its coldness sharp against my palm.

'Callum seemed OK this morning,' I said. 'A bit pale, but still well enough to shoot me a dirty look. Did our spell work?'

'Of course! These things just take time,' Sloane said. 'You have to keep the faith. That spell was a super powerful one, but a slow burn. Get the popcorn ready and watch and wait, it'll be worth it.'

'Out of interest, why the dead bird?' I asked. 'Is that for a spell or a new interiors trend?'

'That was for something fun I was working on.' She grinned, the mischievous glint back.

'Tell me more.'

'It was just a little revenge spell – nothing major, but still fun. The landlord here has been giving me grief, so I . . . sorted it out.'

'I know you said there's no such thing as Dark Magic but . . .' I paused, unsure how to express my discomfort without making her upset.

'There isn't. Just like there's no good and evil – nothing is as clear cut and simple as that. Not black and white, but shades of grey.'

I swigged some beer, the fizz catching at the back of my throat. 'But didn't you say your sister got into Dark Magic?' Her face instantly dimmed, the lights in her eyes going out. I felt bad for bringing it up. 'Sorry, I shouldn't have asked.'

She found her smile again, though it was a weak one. 'Stick with me – I'll let you know what's OK and what's not.' She downed the rest of her beer. 'Talking of which. I have some fun planned. Wait here!'

She disappeared into the bedroom and emerged a few minutes later changed from her school uniform into her usual all black, a long trench coat completing the look. She was holding a bundle of clothes. 'Here – get changed into these. I'll be back in a minute.'

She left, leaving me to trawl through the various garments – thick jeans, dungarees, faded T-shirts, hoodies and even a dress – shades of grey indeed. I settled on a pair of slightly tighter than I'd usually go for black jeans and an old Guns N' Roses T-shirt. I scrunched my uniform into a tight ball and shoved it in my bag.

A loud honk of a car horn came from outside. 'Jessie! Let's go!' Sloane shouted.

I opened the door and looked out. Sloane was grinning, her head sticking out of the window of the driver's seat of a small pale blue car, loud pop music pumping out.

'What are you . . .?'

'It's Mum's car. Don't worry, I've driven it loads. Hop in. Let's go!'

'But you've been drinking?'

'God, only a few sips! I'm fine – I'm a pro.'

Her reasoning was good enough for my beer-tinged logic. Besides, what was one more black mark on the hexing a friend, truanting, day-drinking list? If you're going to go in, you may as well go all in.

I ran round to the passenger seat and got in, moving the pile of stuff into the footwell – a mini bag of rice cakes, carton of juice, a teddy and some scruffy toy cars. Sloane pulled off before I'd even closed my door, the tyres screeching against the gravel. I glanced back and saw a car seat – thankfully empty.

'This is your mum's car?' I asked, bewildered.

Sloane grinned. 'OK, it's a neighbour's. They won't miss it though.'

'Sloane, we can't do this,' I said. 'Not even the beer was enough to dull the rising nausea of wrongness.

'It's fine, honestly. We're friends with the neighbour. Mum borrows the car sometimes, she just wasn't in to ask. Relax.'

'Hmm.' I wasn't convinced, but I made myself push my worries to one side. 'Where are we going?' I asked, putting my seat belt on.

'On an adventure!' She took her eyes off the road for longer than I appreciated.

'What kind of adventure?'

'I don't know yet – that's part of the fun of it. I thought maybe we'd head to the sea.'

That sounded like a fine enough plan to me. I turned the music up, so loud it filled the car and tickled my ears, then settled back and looked out of the window as we sped towards the ocean.

CHAPTER TWENTY-EIGHT

'Can't I just use breadcrumbs or something?' I asked. 'Or chocolate? I've got a KitKat in my bag somewhere.'

We'd made it to the sea and were crouching in the sand, on an empty stretch right at the end of a beach on the west side of the Island – the chalky, cliff-lined side, which is way more dramatic than the rest of the coastline. Sloane was trying to teach me how to summon a bird with my powers. It was harder than she made it look and I was getting frustrated.

'It's about connection,' she explained. 'You need to zone everything else and once you do that, you'll be able to channel into their wavelength.'

'And then what? I say, "Hey, Mrs Birdie, fancy coming for chat?"'

'You just picture it coming to you. Think of yourself like a magnet, pulling it towards you.'

I sighed, looking at the waves licking the sand, darkening the shoreline and then shrinking away again, swallowed back into the sea. I shifted my weight. My knees were starting to hurt.

'Can't you just do it?'

'I want you to learn. It's important.'

'Why?'

She paused, looking mildly flustered. 'Because I feel

responsible for you. For your development. We obviously can't rely on your family to teach you anything about anything.' She pushed her hair out of her face. 'Besides, it's fun watching someone find their power. So come on, concentrate.'

I breathed out my frustration, tried to clear my head. It took me right back to when Nonna had taught us to light a candle – my first bit of purposeful magic. I got it then, I could get it now. Deep breaths.

It was quiet anyway, just the sound of seagulls and waves, the odd passing car on the road high above us. I zoned them out until there was a blanket silence, deep and flat and empty. I thought of a bird coming to me, pictured myself a magnet, like Sloane had said, and sat with that thought on repeat.

I felt a nudge and opened my eyes. A seagull was perched on the sand in front of us, its head moving in terse, curious turns. I did a double take, too scared to move in case I scared it off. Had *I* really just done that?

'Hmm, seagulls are a bit big for what I had in mind,' Sloane said. 'Release it.'

'How?'

'Sorry, I forget you're a baby witch. Just imagine it flying away and say, "I release you."' I did as she said and sure enough, the bird flew away.

'How about I get the bird this time?' Sloane said, sounding impatient now. She didn't even close her eyes, just stared ahead to the sea, and the next minute a tiny little brown bird – I had no idea what kind – hopped on to her leg, its black eyes blinking in confusion.

'You're not going to love this next bit, but trust me, OK?' She held her hand out and the bird hopped on to her palm. 'And remember it's only a bird.' She closed her hand around the bird and gently stroked its head with her other hand, then in one swift movement, she broke its neck.

'Jesus, Sloane!' I stood up, backed away, my heart pounding with sledgehammer force. 'Why the hell did you do that?'

'It's fine. We're going to do something special.'

'This is wrong.' It was so wrong, my ears were ringing with it. What was I doing missing school? That wasn't me. And missing school to kill animals? That *definitely* wasn't me. 'Can we just go home please?'

She stood up, the bird lying lifeless on the sand between us. 'I know it seems horrible, but please – trust me. You do trust me, don't you? We are Sisters, after all.' She edged towards me, her eyes sincere and soft. 'Sit down, please.'

I took a deep breath and slowly, reluctantly, sat down. 'What are you going to do with it?' I asked, in a low voice.

'The ultimate!' She grinned, flashing her teeth. 'Resurrection!'

The word rang in my ears, bouncing around my head, comical but also thrilling. 'You're kidding, right? We can't do that!'

'We most definitely can. For most witches it involves a lot of elements – hard-to-find ingredients, cauldron, the right moon – Yawnsville. But for us – Sisters of Endor – we don't need that stuff. We just need each other and our kickass, badass, mega-special power.'

'But . . . that's definitely Dark Magic, isn't it?'

'Why would *creating* life be bad? That's a patriarchal mindset.'

'I don't know, Sloane . . .'

'Bitch, you're a WITCH. This is your birthright. Your magic is such a massive part of you and what are you doing with it? Clearing up friends' spots and making coffee hot?' *Uh, yes, that was about right.* 'It's time to do something bigger. Besides, you want to bring that bird back to life, don't you?'

Well there was a point I couldn't really argue with. 'Fine,' I relented. 'What do we do?'

She placed the bird in the sand between us. We sat cross-legged, facing each other. 'So, first we need to create some energy. Lay your palms facing up and pump your hands like this.' She tucked her fingers into her palms to make fists, then released them and repeated. I copied her, feeling slightly silly, like I was doing some kind of universal hand gesture for boobs. 'For this next bit, you're going to have to concentrate like you did before and then some. We're going to zone out of all other sounds, tune into each other and imagine this bird flying. Picture it really clearly. We'll cup our hands over the bird and repeat a spell, OK?'

'Got it,' I said, thinking how I really didn't have it at all.

We did a few more minutes of fist-clenching until my fingers were sore, I had nail marks in my palm and Sloane deemed that a suitable amount of energy had been generated, then we placed our hands over each other and over the dead bird – like a dead bird one potato, two potato.

As soon as our hands touched, I felt it – a surge of power, electricity. That buzz that starts in my fingers and spreads like a current through my whole body. I'd had it when Nonna had first taken us up to Tennyson Monument, and when I'd done a spell with Mum and Bella to make Nonna better, and I was having it now. It felt reassuringly exciting. Sloane closed her eyes and cleared her throat.

'Mother Nature, hear our cry, make this dead bird once more fly.'

I joined in, repeating the words, clearing my head of everything but visions of our bird flying off into the afternoon sky. Again, and again, and again we recited the words, my hands getting hotter with each repetition, my back aching.

Finally, I felt something. The slightest flutter, the tiniest movement brushing against my palm. I snatched my hand away, opening my eyes. And there it was – the tiny black eyes of the bird were blinking, confused, its wings twitching tentatively.

'WE DID IT!' Sloane practically screamed, reaching across and pulling me in for a hug, nearly killing the bird for a second time. 'Oh my God we actually did it! This is amazing – this is—'

'You always said we could …' I was confused at her enthusiasm.

'I *thought* we could – I *hoped* we could – but I didn't know for sure! This is massive. Massive.' Her eyes were shining, practically glowing fluorescent, her cheeks flushed and pink, like a porcelain doll turned rogue. The bird took a dazed, cautious step, then another one, and another one – walking in a full circle, like it didn't know what it was doing or where to go. It flapped its wings, like it had just remembered they were there, and then, after a moment's hesitation, it launched itself into the air. It flew away in slow, effortful flutters, heading in a worryingly straight line towards the wall of the cliff face. I turned away, knowing something wasn't right.

Sloane hadn't even noticed, she was too excited. 'You are one powerful witch, bitch!' she shrieked. 'Full respect!'

'I don't understand. I mean, thanks but—'

'I've tried that with other people, other Sisters even, and we haven't even got close. You are something else. And together – holy crap – together, we're the bloody dream team!' She was practically jumping on the spot, a ball of energy. She held her hand out to me and helped me up, the link between us still fizzing, tangible. 'Now let's go have some goddamn fun!'

CHAPTER TWENTY-NINE

The banging about, stair traffic and general morning noise woke me up the next morning. My head was thick and sore. Not hangover type sore – no mouth like a badger's arse this time – just heavy and dense, like a boulder was resting on my shoulders. Various parts of my body were aching and something was digging into my side – my phone, I realised, as I groped around. My totally dead phone that must've been in my pocket when I crashed into bed, fully dressed still in Sloane's clothes.

My bed had a layer of sand in it, damp and grainy, and, I realised with horror, my hands were stained with something dark. Something that looked worryingly like it might be blood. I squeezed my eyes shut, trying to summon memories of how it might have got there. Nothing.

I felt on my side table for the alarm clock Mum had got for me when she had tried to implement a no-phones-in-the-bedroom-after-10 p.m. rule that had lasted a grand total of three days.

8:10. Arse! I was running late.

I jumped out of bed, retrieved my crumpled uniform from my rucksack and stuck it on, attempting to ironing out the creases with a licked palm. It would have to do, as would a quick wipe with a hot washcloth rather than a shower.

I ran the water until it was almost scalding hot, lathering my hands with soap and scrubbing at the marks on them, an image of Lady Macbeth springing to mind.

Revision Facts – *Macbeth*, Act 5, Scene 1 – 'Out, damned spot. Out, I say!' (English)

1. Shakespeare's use of the imperative verb 'out' emphasises Lady Macbeth's familiar desire to be powerful – she is commanding the spot to be gone.
2. However, in this case, she is sleepwalking, and therefore not in control, thus showing how it is nature that has ultimate power.
3. In this scene she is speaking in prose instead of iambic pentameter or blank verse, which represents her mental disorientation and how her noblewoman façade is slipping.
4. The scene demonstrates her eternal guilt at having committed murder, which persists no matter how hard she tries to push it down.
5. You can scrub as hard as you want, but you can never scrub away your guilt.

I wiped off the caked mascara that Sloane had insisted on putting on me, tugged back my knotted hair and thoroughly brushed my teeth. I grabbed a piece of toast on my way out, though after one bite I couldn't quite stomach the rest. Something was gnawing at me, twisting my insides, but I couldn't work out what. Maybe I'd eaten a dodgy prawn I didn't remember? I really couldn't remember much about last night – including getting home, though I was pretty sure that I hadn't done a repeat of last time and drank twice my bodyweight in spirits. Other than that first beer at Sloane's house and a homemade revival drink she'd given me, I didn't remember drinking anything at all. Maybe that was it – maybe the pounding head and general heaviness was down to dehydration.

I met Sloane at our usual place, the corner by the '*Slow Cats*' sign (the lack of a comma always made me laugh). She was perched on the wall, as usual, drinking a Red Bull, as usual – but looking pale and red-eyed, which was not usual.

'Hey, sleepyhead,' she said, handing me a can and hopping off the wall. I went to put it in my bag for later, my twisty guts telling me they weren't ready for a chemical onslaught just yet. 'You should really have that, you know,' she said, gesturing to the can. 'You need to replenish – we did some serious magic yesterday.'

Ah yes, the magic hangover. That explained it.

'What time did we get home by the way?' I asked. 'I literally don't remember anything.'

'I'm sure it will come back to you.' There was something in the way she said it that set me on edge – sneaky, sarcastic, amused. 'Especially once we get to school,' she went on.

OK, *definitely* something.

Before I could press her on what she meant, we had reached the school. And it became very obvious there was . . . something going on. A frenzy. That's the only way I could describe it – groups of students huddled round phones, loud squeals, quiet mutterings, dashing between groups – and the staring. As I got closer an uproar from a group of boys on the steps greeted me. 'Oi Oi! Here she comes, mate,' I heard a voice say. Harry was patting Marcus, a delighted grin on his face. Marcus smirked at me – and winked. My stomach lurched. Just as the cold sweat of dread was threatening to envelop me, I spotted the one person I least wanted to see.

Callum.

And this time he really didn't look well. He was no longer pale; his skin was now waxy, dull. His eyes were dark and so deep-set they had a touch of the skeletal about them. I had to look away. But not before I caught a look of sheer hatred and . . . that whiff of fear again?

'See, I told you it would get worse,' Sloane whispered, grinning. 'Who's laughing now, hey?'

This was what I'd wanted, I reminded myself. To make him suffer. And it really looked like he was. So why did it feel so gross? I forced myself to remember my uniform covered in blood, his sneering face . . .

'WHAT HAVE YOU DONE?' Libby was stomping full force towards us from the other end of the corridor, Tabs and Summer either side of her. I did a double take, trying to work out who she was talking to – but it was definitely us. My stomach lurched.

Sloane stopped, crossed her arms and jutted a hip out, her face wearing a textbook 'bring it on' expression. Libby was flushed and furious, and wearing a baseball cap and no make-up, which was not like her at all. She got close to Sloane and raised a fist in her face. I thought that she might be about to hit her – but then, at the last minute, she opened her hand, a fistful of hair cascading out in sad, lifeless flutters.

'Oh no, having a bad hair day?' Sloane asked, barely restraining a smirk. Libby sprang forward, but Summer and Tabs held her back.

'A bad hair day? It's falling out by the handful!'

'I'm sorry for your loss,' Sloane sneered, 'but I had nothing to do with it. You've said yourself I'm just a wannabe witch, right? So I couldn't have, even if I wanted to.'

'I don't for one minute think you're capable of magicking up anything other than a freakily bad outfit, but I do know you're deranged enough to find a way to poison me or some other dark shit and I swear to God I'm going to—'

'Libby, leave it. They're not worth it,' Summer said, pulling her away.

I felt dizzy, sick, like the air was suddenly too thin. Sloane was smiling – a cold, hard, victorious smile.

'And YOU!' Libby hissed, pointing at me. 'Who even *are* you any more? What has happened to you?'

'Seriously, Libby, let's go,' Summer said, avoiding my eyes, pulling at Libby more forcefully. They backed away.

'You could have at least dumped him first,' Libby shouted back, just as the bell rang.

'What was she . . . what just . . .' I couldn't find the words. All kinds of thoughts and feelings were tugging at me from the corners of my mind, but I couldn't make sense of them, couldn't articulate them. I felt like a computer that someone had spilled coffee on, the liquid flowing through my system, overloading me, frying my circuit board. 'Did you do that? To Libby's hair? Did you make it fall out?' I managed, the words catching like shards of glass in my throat.

'Oh, it was nothing, just a light thinning spell. It will grow back. And I mean, it was kind of your idea – genius one. You were right about what you said last night, she really does care about her hair.'

I thought I might vomit. Right there, on her thick, chunky shoes.

'Ladies!' Mr Williams shouted, striding down the corridor. 'Bell went five minutes ago, to class please.'

'See you at break!' Sloane said, sauntering away like she'd just revealed nothing more dramatic than her preference for cornflakes over Rice Krispies.

***

By the time I got to registration, I was a mess – and late. I walked in while Ms Simmons was in the middle of taking the register. She shot me a carefully curated, disapproving teacher look and carried on. I sank into my seat, trying to ignore the fact that I could feel twenty-nine pairs of eyes on me.

'I've just got to nip next door to ask Ms Jawad about assembly – be sensible please, I'll be back in a minute.' Ms Simmons left and the class went nuclear.

'How's Freddie, Jessie?' Jenna Simms called across at me, much to everyone's amusement. 'I noticed he's not in today. Is he ill? Or just heartbroken?'

'What are you talking about?' I asked, uneasily.

'Oh, come on. You know.'

'I really don't.' I felt the frustration rise.

'Ohhh,' Jenna said, elongated and dramatic, addressing the class rather than me. 'She didn't know she was being filmed. Oops.'

'Here.' Lucy Fielding passed me her phone, a video playing on it. A video of me, wearing Sloane's jeans and Sloane's Guns N' Roses top, up against the wall on the beach, snogging the face off Marcus.

CHAPTER THIRTY

I blinked, trying to compute what I was seeing. It didn't make any sense.

'Bring back any memories?' Jenna asked, laughing.

No, it didn't, I wanted to scream.

How could that be me? I mean, I knew it was me – of all my problems right now, I hadn't gone blind – but I didn't remember it. At all. I didn't even remember *seeing* Marcus last night, let alone kissing him. My stomach heaved, I felt dizzy, liquid – all the worst feelings from last year, from before, were returning full force.

'Right.' Ms Simmons reappeared. 'Assembly is on, so let's go.'

The class stood up, scraping chairs, the thrill of fresh gossip still lighting up the air. I was on a mission – I had to find Sloane and try and work out what the hell had happened last night.

'Jessie.' Ms Simmons stopped me as I was nearing the door. 'Can I have a quick word?'

No thank you. 'Sure.' I was itching to escape, and really didn't want a teacher probing right now, as much as I loved Ms Simmons.

'Is everything OK with you at the moment?'

'Yeah, fine,' I said, aware that things were completely, one hundred per cent the exact opposite of fine, but also knowing that there was no way I could even begin to explain them to Ms Simmons.

'You seem a bit ... out of sorts. I've heard that your concentration has been off in lessons and I saw you were absent yesterday afternoon. I wanted to check everything is all right. I know you had some ... issues last year.'

Issues was certainly one way of putting it. 'I've been feeling a bit unwell actually,' I muttered, unable to meet her kind and genuine eyes. 'I'm still not quite right ... I should probably go.'

'Of course,' she said. 'I'm here if you need me.'

I pegged it, in the most controlled manner I could manage.

Sloane was waiting for me outside the classroom, as I knew she would be. There were clusters of girls all excitedly chatting in the hallway, running through the drama of the day, and a handful of teachers trying to move people along.

'What have you done?' I hissed, checking no one was close enough to hear.

'What do you mean?' Her smile didn't falter. 'Ah, you've seen the video. Great get-out clause, hey?'

'What do you mean?'

'With Freddie.'

'I didn't want a get-out clause, I wanted—'

'Well, you did actually. You said you wanted to break up with him. That was your wish – remember? The thing you said you wanted. I told you – I'm your Fairy Witchmother. Marcus just so happened to be a convenient fix – and my god, his mind is like an empty shell. So easy to hex!'

Sloane was right. I had said those words at the cove. But I hadn't for one minute thought that she would do anything about it. I'd thought I was just having a deep and meaningful with a friend. This was all wrong. Back-to-front and twisted and tight like a knotted necklace I couldn't even begin to untangle.

She slung her arm around me and led me down the corridor. I was too stunned to resist.

'I'm really sorry if it's made you angry.' Her voice was gentle but it set me on edge. 'I was trying to be a good friend. Trying to do what you wanted. Besides, you're better off without him. He chose Callum over you, remember? Plus, he's just plain dull – nice to look at, but dull. A dead weight, pulling you down. And now you're free to fly.'

The word 'dead' rang in my ears. I shivered. She could have done worse. I had a horrible, sudden, dawning realisation that, with Sloane, it could always be worse. Her arm felt heavy across my shoulder.

'Why can't I remember anything about last night?' I asked.

'It's probably a magic blackout.' She was breezy, matter of fact.

'I woke up with blood on my hands,' I said.

'Ah.' She dropped her arm now, looked around us to check the coast was clear, and pulled me into an empty classroom. 'That must've been from the cat.'

'What cat?' I asked, fear clawing at my chest.

'Oh, Jessie, you must remember *that*?' Her eyes bore into me, questioning, sympathetic.

'Remember what? I told you, I don't remember anything!'

'Look in the front pocket of your rucksack.'

My hands, shaking, swung my rucksack round and unzipped the front pocket, terror biting at my insides. I had no idea where this was going, no idea what to expect, though I knew for a fact that whatever it was, it wasn't good. I fished around gingerly inside the pocket, my fingers moving between the pens and packets of gum and loose change. They fixed on something alien, a fabric strap, something metal – and I took it out slowly.

A pink cat collar, spattered with blood, a small silver-coloured plate with the name '*Puffball*' engraved on it. I dropped it instantly.

'What is this?' I could feel sweat forming on my lip. The room felt like it was getting smaller, its walls bearing down on me.

'You wanted to do more magic. Said you never get the chance at home, that you could only be your real self around me, that resurrecting that bird was the most alive you've ever felt and you wanted to try something bigger.'

'So Puffball is a cat we . . .' I couldn't force the word out. 'And then . . . brought back to life?'

She shook her head. 'Oh, dude, it wasn't *we* – it was just you. And Puffball . . . didn't make it.'

My throat closed up. Where was the air? WHERE WAS THE AIR?! I leaned against a desk, head bowed, trying to stop the spinning. Sloane rubbed my back, her touch sending icicles through me, setting my teeth on edge.

'I would remember that.' I managed to force out the words. 'Surely I would.'

'We did do a lot of magic. You must have a really bad blackout. I wouldn't worry though – it's just a cat, at the end of the day. And you didn't mean to do it – well, I mean, you did – but you didn't mean for it to *stay* dead.'

Vomit rushed into my mouth at the word *dead*.

Had I done something so terrible? Could I have? I risked looking at Sloane, trying to work out if she was telling me the truth, if she'd *ever* been telling me the truth. This time, when my eyes met her pools of darkness, an alarm went off full-blast in my head. I *very* suddenly felt *very* not safe. I needed to get out of there, but I knew I had to keep the extent of my freaking out to myself until I had processed what the holy hell was happening. All I knew for now was that I couldn't trust Sloane, and I wasn't sure I could trust myself.

'You shouldn't tell anyone,' she said kindly. 'There's no need. I won't either – it can be our little secret. Other people wouldn't understand, not like me. I've got your back. Witch Sisters for ever.'

'Thanks,' I said. The words seemed now to hold a threat. 'We're so late for lessons. We'd better go – don't want to draw attention to ourselves.'

'Good point,' Sloane said. She looked at me for a fraction too long, like she was assessing whether I really was fine or not. I silently thanked past Sloane for teaching me how to block people reading my thoughts. 'Hang out after school?'

'Sure,' I said, trying to keep the screaming doubt and fear from my voice. 'I'd love to.'

CHAPTER THIRTY-ONE

As soon as Sloane and I had parted ways, I practically ran out of school, needing to put as much distance between me and her as was humanly possible.

My head was thick with thoughts, too many thoughts to pin down, like I was carrying a full bucket of water that kept sloshing over the sides, no matter how slowly I went. Thought Whac-A-Mole – just when you think you've got to grips with one, another one pops up. What we'd done to Callum, what Sloane had done to Libby, what I'd done to Freddie. And, hanging over it all like a thick, black, furry, threatening cloud, was Puffball. How could I ever look at Dave again?

I'd gone from shy, painful loner to evil cat murderer with only a brief stint as a normal(ish) girl with friends in between.

I strode out of the school gates, not knowing where I was headed, only that I needed air. And distance. I could still feel the fabric of the cat collar against my skin; the images of the blood spots clung to the inside of my eyelids. The thought of a dead cat turned and turned inside my head, a Ferris wheel of fear. Or a rollercoaster that only went down, one I couldn't get off. I scraped the corners of my mind, desperate to find some recollection of last night, when I had done those awful things—

I stopped. No. I couldn't just accept what Sloane had told me. I needed to remember for myself – that was the only way to know the truth. What Sloane had told me – it was a jigsaw with pieces that didn't fit together. That wasn't me.

Only ... maybe it *was* me – the me that I seemed to have grown into. The me who put animal blood on my face, the me who skipped school, the me who cheated on a test, the me who made Callum sick, the me who hurt Libby. *That* me could well have done something like this. Maybe Sloane wasn't the problem. Maybe I was.

Because the harsh truth of it was that it wasn't Sloane's fault – not all of it, anyway. It had been my idea to make Callum sick, me who had hurt Libby first.

What's the saying? *You can lead a horse to water but you can't make it drink.* Sloane may have led me to the water, but I had lapped that water up like I had been lost in the desert for months.

And now it was me who had to work out how to get myself out of this mess. To make things right. I adjusted myself – wiped my face with the back of my sleeve – and then began to sort my thoughts, stacking them slowly one by one until they made some kind of sense.

I needed to come up with a plan.

CHAPTER THIRTY-TWO

I walked for hours. Up along the coast path, looking down at the tiny coves and ant-like people, down along the seafront, feeling the spray of the sea on my cheeks, and back up to the Downs, revelling in the wide-open space. I was trying to walk off my thoughts, walk off my guilt, walk off my deep, dark sadness. But it followed me, like it was my shadow, every step of the way.

All Nonna's speeches about power and responsibility were repeating themselves in my head. *Two sides of a coin*, she'd always said. *Power without responsibility is dangerous.* I'd failed her. She'd hate me when she found out – I'd become the black sheep of the family, it would be all over the witch grapevine and she'd definitely never take me to any coven meets to show me off again. The embarrassing family secret – The One Who Turned Bad. I'd have to make myself a bedroom in the cupboard under the stairs with an old duvet and some bags of flour for pillows and I'd lie in there and Think About What I'd Done for the rest of my miserable life.

I walked and walked and thought and thought, desperately trying to work out a way to fix everything, to make everything right again. I couldn't bring Puffball back to life and I didn't know how to undo the spell on Callum without asking Nonna for help, but by the time I stopped walking, I knew my next steps. One, stay as far away from Sloane as I possibly could. Two, apologise to the girls. And three, find a way to somehow get them back.

I shuddered, took a deep breath, and headed home, desperate for the safe and familiar, for the smell of Mum's slightly burnt food, the sound of her sewing machine whirring, for the clank of Nonna's bangles and the waft of lavender and patchouli, for Bella's constant stack of parcels and the glow of her ring light.

***

'Ah, that must be her now,' I heard Mum say from the living room as I walked in the front door.

'Sorry, I went to a café and did some revision,' I called out, the lie falling easily out of my mouth.

I walked through to the living room. Someone was in with Mum – I could see the back of their head. Mousy-brown hair tied up into a neat bun.

'Oh sorry, I didn't realise you had a gue—'

The mousy bun turned around.

'We were wondering where you'd got to,' Sloane said. 'We were worried.'

My legs nearly gave way at the sight of her.

Here.

In my house.

In my space. Talking to my mother. Penetrating my safety net.

I did a double take, making myself close my gaping mouth. Sloane looked like a different person – gone was the black hair, the black eyeliner, the black clothes. The jewellery was pared down, all skulls removed, and she had colour on her cheeks, emphasised by the light pink sweater she was wearing. She looked like a reimagining of Sloane. Sloane the Good.

'Sloane's been filling me in on a few things, Jessie.' Mum's voice was cold. I felt sick – the bile rising, the acid burning at the back of my mouth. 'You'd better sit down.'

'I'm sorry,' Sloane said. She looked worried, concerned – and, to me, utterly fake. 'I know you didn't want me to tell anyone, but I came to drop your homework in and ... well, we got chatting. It just came out. I felt like your mum should know. I'm worried about you. All your friends are.'

The white heat of utter panic spread through me, tingling and hot. I realised that Sloane, who had never seemed scary to me before because she had always been on my side, now truly held all the cards. She could play me like a puppet.

'I ... I ...' No words came. I didn't even know where to start.

'I thought we'd brought you up better than that, Jessie,' Mum said.

I felt the tears forming, tried to blink them away. I focused on breathing. In, out, in, out. She knew. Sloane had told Mum what I'd done.

'Oh, sweetheart.' She came and sat next to me on the sofa, putting her arm around me. It was almost too much to bear. 'You know that if you're struggling with school – with anything – we're here for you. Playing truant is not the way to go, no matter how hard it feels. There is always help. You can always come to us.'

I blinked. Mum's face was all genuine, gentle concern.

Nothing else.

Nothing more.

She gave me a hug. Over her shoulder, I sought out Sloane,

looking to her for answers. She was grinning – a dark, satisfied grin that made my spine freeze over.

'Well, I'd better be going.' Sloane stood up, placed her mug on a coaster. 'Lots of revision to do.'

'Of course,' Mum said, untangling herself from me. 'Thank you so much for dropping Jessie's work round. And ... well, it was lovely to meet you. You're welcome here any time.'

'That's so kind, thank you. It was lovely to meet you too.' Sloane looked the picture of perfect – neat, tidy, friendly. 'I'll see you again soon, I'm sure of it.'

My skin prickled.

'I'll see you out,' I said, barely managing to conceal the anger in my voice.

'And then back here immediately please,' Mum said. 'We need to talk.'

I waited until we were in the hallway, and then turned on Sloane. 'What the hell are you playing at?' I hissed. 'What was that?'

'I don't know what you mean,' she said. She was playing innocent, gaslighting me. 'I just brought over some work you missed after you disappeared this afternoon. Tut, tut, truanting, again. What's that, twice in one week? I thought you'd have been a bit more grateful, Jessie. Someone obviously has to keep you on the straight and narrow.'

I gasped, trying to find the words. 'Was it supposed to be a warning of some kind?'

'A warning about what?'

'A warning not to tell anyone about the cat – about last night.'

'You were the one who did those things, Jessie, not me. You

can tell anyone you want.' She was confusing me, with her mind games and trickery. 'I told you, your secret is safe with me.'

'Get out. Just get out and leave me alone.'

'Well that's not very friendly,' she said, as I practically shoved her out of the door.

'I don't want to be your friend.' As I said it, I realised how achingly true it was.

I knew this was my fault, not hers, but I didn't like who I had become around her. I didn't like that I was truanting and drinking and kissing boys I hated and not trusting the people who loved and supported me. Sloane was a dark whisper in my ear – she was bad energy, with a rotten heart at the core, and I wanted nothing to do with her. I needed her out of my head, out of my life and out of my house.

Her mask had finally fallen, the fake smile giving way to what looked like a genuine sadness beneath. 'That's too bad,' she said, staring at me intently, her eyes wide and unblinking. 'I think we made a great team. But I'm pretty sure you'll see the light and come back to me. And besides, I make a much better friend than I do an enemy. As I think I've proved.'

Revision Facts – Cunning and Deceit and its Place in Evolution (Biology)

In the animal kingdom, there are many examples of animals who use cunning and deceit to further their species:

1. The cantil, a snake belonging to the pit viper subfamily, can move its tail so that it resembles a wriggling worm to lure prey close. Then the cantil strikes and injects its prey with deadly venom.

2. The margay, a small feline from Central and South America, has the ability to mimic the calls of baby monkeys in distress. This attracts concerned adult monkeys, who the margay then attacks and devours.

3. The Photuris firefly spies on other species of firefly, mimics their flashing pattern to attract an unsuspecting male wanting to mate, and then attacks and eats them.

4. The cunning and deceit exhibited by the cuckoo in its breeding behaviour is one of the wonders of the natural world. The cuckoo never raises its own young. It lays an egg in another bird's nest. Once hatched, the cuckoo chick balances the host's eggs, one by one, on its back and throws them out of the nest, leaving the host parents tricked into raising the cuckoo chick as their own.

5. The cunning and deceit exhibited by Sloane Smith was even more of a wonder of the natural world than if the cantil, margay, Photuris firefly and cuckoo were to all band together and form a superhero cunning club. And that was not good news.

I slammed the door behind Sloane and leaned back against it, taking a minute before I went back to Mum. Now that Sloane was out of the house and out of my personal space, I felt lighter. I wasn't naïve enough to think for one minute that it would be plain sailing ahead – I had a lot of fixing and making up to do – but I knew in my gut I'd made the right decision by cutting ties with her.

'Ah there you are, petal,' Nonna said, jangling her way through from the kitchen. 'I was just finishing up with a client—' She stopped abruptly, then rushed over to me, grasping me by the shoulders and looking me up and down.

'What's happened?' she asked.

'I'm fine,' I replied. Though fine wasn't quite the right word for it.

'No you're not. I can sense it.' She stared into my eyes, searching, probing. 'Was someone just here? I'm sensing darkness.'

'Uh, yeah, my ... someone from school. They were just dropping my bag off.'

'Hmmm.' Nonna wrinkled her nose, as though she could smell something bad. 'Well, whoever it was, you'd be wise to stay away,' she said.

She wasn't wrong.

CHAPTER THIRTY-THREE

My chat with Mum was as painful as predicted and involved a lot of me nodding dutifully, quietly crying and promising to do better. Afterwards, I'd escaped to my room to revise. And I really had revised – quadratic equations, particles, Elizabethan England, representation of women in John Ford's westerns and bloody *Macbeth* – Shakespeare's witches cackling out at me from the earmarked pages.

I studied for hours. Partly to make up for my absences – in body and mind – and partly because I needed a safe place to lose myself. While my brain was soaking in all this information and rolling it around and reforming it, it couldn't focus on anything else. It was my safe harbour.

Mum came up on her way to bed to deliver me a hot chocolate and tell me that she'd called school and covered for me but informed them I would definitely be back tomorrow, which made me feel slightly terrified. I knew I had a lot of facing up and making up to do with the girls – and Freddie. The thought of having those conversations and rehashing the last week made me feel nauseous. How would I even approach it? 'I'm really sorry about my behaviour but I had my mind taken over by a powerful witch who wanted to destroy me and everything nice I had built in my life. And by the way, I'm a witch too.'

Hmmm. Not sure that would do the trick.

'I'm really sorry about my behaviour but I hung out with a powerful witch (I'm a witch BTW) and got drunk on a cocktail of power and anger. And rum.'

I might just keep it simple. 'I'm sorry I was a dick.' That was about all I could say – without revealing the one thing that would put the final nail in my friendship coffin.

***

The next morning was bright and crisp, the edges of autumn definitely creeping in now, like long, knobbly fingers tickling the earth. A change was coming, and that felt good. God knows, I needed a change.

I pushed gnarly thoughts of the Sloane Problem to one side, trying to concentrate on the positive, determined, redemptive vibe I'd cultivated last night. Stage One of my plan was to make things right with the girls. With them on my side I could do anything. The question was – was it too late?

There they were, waiting at our usual meeting place: Summer's bright-blonde hair easy to spot, Libby's booming laugh carrying through the air.

I took a deep breath.

'Hi,' I said, the word coming out as a squeak.

Libby snapped her head round, saw it was me and rolled her eyes. 'No thanks.'

'Can we talk – please?'

'We don't want to talk to you.'

Summer looked at the floor, the wind whipping her hair in front of her face so I couldn't make out her expression.

'I know you're angry at me,' I said. 'I know I've been an idiot, but I really want to explain.' Though *how* exactly I was going to explain anything, I didn't know.

'Go away, Jessie.' The hatred in Libby's eyes was killing me. Pure and unadulterated and all for me.

'Summer?' I said, knowing she was more likely to listen to me. When she looked up, it smacked even more – there wasn't hatred there, just a gut-wrenching double whammy of hurt and disappointment. 'I want to explain,' I said again, more urgently.

Tabs looked from Libby to me to Summer, assessing the situation, avoiding my eyes.

'You've done things you can't explain, Jessie – things you can't take back,' Libby said. I flinched – she didn't know the half of it. 'I think the phrase is, "you've made your bed, now lie in it". So go and do that – lie in the big double bed of bad with your freakshow BFF and leave us alone.'

'Let's go,' Summer said. They started walking away from me.

'I'm not even friends with her any more!' I shouted.

'Too late!' Libby shouted back.

I watched them as they walked away, out of sight. My plan wasn't going so well. I had been thoroughly, decisively ousted – cast aside like an odd sock. A dirty, smelly, riddled-with-holes odd sock that had never fitted properly in the first place. It hurt.

My overwhelming urge was to run home and seek shelter. To skip school and avoid this Hunger Games of a day. But I was trying to Do the Right Thing, and sadly I knew that in this case it meant facing up to the mess I'd caused, whatever that entailed.

The next person I had to talk to was Freddie. I was dreading it. Which meant it was the right thing to do. I took a deep breath and set my sights towards school.

I didn't see anyone I knew on the rest of the walk, or in the general milling about before tutor group, or in the five minutes moving between tutor and first period – which was History, without anyone I knew. My thoughts were like a tangle of Christmas lights in my head – too intricately intertwined to pick apart. It wasn't helped by Mr Hargreaves droning on about the Nazi regime and Goebbels and propaganda and war, war, war.

I asked to be excused, faking the period pose (clutching my abdomen while pulling a pain-face) and escaped. I needed air and quiet – I headed to the quad toilets in the hope that they could deliver on at least the latter of those.

As I rounded the corner out of the Humanities block, I bumped into Summer – literally – she was carrying a bundle of papers which all fell on to the floor in a very scene-from-a-movie type way.

'Watch it!' she said, before realising it was me. Her face changed – she looked startled and then angry.

'I . . . toilet,' I said, flustered, answering a question she hadn't even asked, waving my pass around like a fool. I crouched down to help her pick up the pile of papers.

'I can do it myself,' she snapped, not making eye contact.

'I want to help.' I worked slowly, knowing I needed to make the most of the opportunity.

'About earlier . . .' I started.

'Don't.'

'Please, Summer, I really want to sort this out.'

We stood up now, having collected all the papers, facing each other awkwardly. The distance between us was short – but it felt like a giant gaping chasm.

'I don't know if *I* want to, Jessie,' she said. 'I'm confused about everything. I don't know if you're who I thought you were.'

I forced a sob back down my throat. 'Well, for the record, I'm sorry about deserting you for Sloane. And for what I did to Freddie, and – well, for everything. I miss you. I miss you all and I really want to make it up to you. I supped at the cup of darkness but now I'm back to normal. Goofy Jessie, good at maths and Kardashians trivia.'

Supped at the cup . . . the thought stirred something inside me, some recognition, but I didn't have time to work out what.

Summer half-smiled, unable to resist, and in that moment I felt a strand of the Christmas lights come loose from the snarled tangle in my head. 'You do know a lot of Kardashians trivia, it's true.' She paused. 'Look, I can't speak for the others, but I think if you want us all to be friends again then we need to know you're . . . back to being you.'

'Actions not words?' I asked.

'I guess, yeah. Look, I've got to get these photocopies back to Mrs Matthews,' she said, walking away from me.

'Actions not words,' I shouted after her, allowing the hope to creep in. Because if I hadn't lost Summer, then I still had a chance at making things OK.

CHAPTER THIRTY-FOUR

My encounter with Summer gave me the boost I needed to keep me going – and get me back to Goebbels. Though he didn't get much of a look-in actually – all I did for the rest of the lesson was think about how I could show the others I really was back to my old self.

Actions not words. Summer wasn't asking me to stand up in the canteen and sing Justin Bieber's *Sorry* or to organise a flash mob. She meant making my loyalties clear. Being there for them, going back to being the friend I was before, who turned up for sleepovers and Feminist Society meetings and everything in between. That I could do. Even if I had to sit and eat my humble pie – which may be the one thing in life that tastes worse than the school's cottage pie – I would do it. I would prove to them I was sorry and, more importantly, that I was myself again.

***

I strode into lunch with my heart pounding but hopeful. They were all already at our table, laughing and chatting and being themselves. I watched them for a moment. Tabs gave Libby a playful slap on the arm, probably in response to some crude comment about her love life, or lack thereof. Summer, as always, gave Tabs her juice box to open – we always took the mick out of her for her fear that the pointy end of the straw would somehow pierce her hand if she did it herself. I felt my absence so keenly it was like a poker in my ribs. I got into the queue for a panini, willing myself to stay calm.

'Well hello,' a low voice said into my ear, sending a current of despair ripping through me. 'I've been looking for you.'

I didn't turn around to look at her. I didn't want Sloane anywhere near me and I especially didn't want the girls to see her anywhere near me. I took a step forwards, getting as close to the person in front of me as I could get without mounting them.

'I don't want to talk to you, Sloane.'

'That's not very nice.' She sighed, lowered her voice. 'Look, I'm not exactly sure what's happened here – one minute we were having fun and doing some amazing magic and generally putting the world to rights and the next you're telling me you don't want to be friends. What have I done wrong? I've been a good friend to you. *You're* the one who murdered poor Puffball—'

'Stop!' I snapped, unable to help myself. I forced myself to keep my voice calm. 'I've learned a lot from our time together but I . . . I don't feel comfortable with the type of magic you do. When I'm around you, I'm not the person I want to be.'

I was trying to stay neutral. Trying to not piss her off or tip her over the edge. I knew her power and it scared me.

'Well that's a load of bullshit, Jessie. *Not the person you want to be?* I'm sorry to be the one to tell you, but it *is* the person you are, at your core. The Sisters of Endor aren't just known for being powerful, they're known for being *bad*. Dark as the night.

And that's what you are, whether you want to be it or not – ask your precious Nonna. If she'll actually witch up and tell you the truth for once.'

My throat tightened; my ears started ringing. 'No,' I whispered. 'That can't be right.'

'And those bitches.' She looked over to the girls, who were all looking right at us. 'They were never your friends. Not really. They don't even know who you are – *what* you are. Do you think they'd still want to hang around with you if they knew who you really were? And what you've done?' She took a step closer. 'Why don't I tell them and we'll see?'

'No!' I shouted, then lowered my voice, conscious of the people around us. 'Please, don't do that.'

Her expression softened. 'Look, I get it. You're freaking out – you want to go back to the old you because the new, powerful you is so scary. But trust me – you just need some time to adjust and then you'll never look back. I'm doing this for your own good.'

'Why would you even want to be friends with someone you have to force to be friends with you, Sloane?'

She sighed. 'I like you – you're a kindred spirit. Plus, I need you. I came all the way here just for you.'

I stared at her. She'd come here *for me*?

We'd got to the front of the line. My appetite had completely shrivelled up and died but I took a panini anyway. I was trapped. Cornered. If I told her to bugger off, which I was desperate to do, she'd tell everyone all about me and hex my friends and then even more damage would be done. I had no way out of this.

'Come on then,' she said, with a bright smile. 'Let's sit.'

She led the way, taking the route straight past the table the girls were on. I angled my head down, trying to keep the tears at bay and walked past them without daring to make eye contact.

A hostage.

CHAPTER THIRTY-FIVE

The rest of the day trudged by in a blur of shame and fury and utter despondency, my hope withering like a salted slug. I would be Sloane's prisoner for the rest of my days – forced to eat with her every lunch as I watched the girls laughing and bonding over their mutual hatred of me until graduation. I considered that maybe I should try harder to get her to move on, to go back to the rest of her coven, or to try and stop her from harming more people, but how? By staying friends with her – as far as she was concerned – I was protecting my friends as best I could. That was all I could do for now.

There was one thing I promised myself, though. I wouldn't do any more Dark Magic with Sloane. She might be able to blackmail me into being friends with her – but that's where it ended.

Five minutes before the end of Biology I was packed and ready to go and eyeing the clock. I knew Sloane had German so she'd be in the language block, which made me a few minutes closer to the gates than her. I was poised. When the bell finally rang, I sprang from my chair, totally ignoring Ms Fairlawn's calls about homework, and sprinted out of the door straight for the main gate. I shoved people out of the way, picked up the pace and, not looking back, felt lighter with every step I took.

My phone beeped as I rounded the top road (I'd avoided the seafront route home just in case). My heart jumped at the thought it might be a text from one of the girls – I pulled it out from my bag, hopefully.

It was from Freddie.

> I think we need to talk.

My heart sank right down to my shoes. Yes, we did need to talk, but I wasn't sure I could take any more today. And holy crap I was not looking forward to that conversation. There's taking responsibility for your actions in theory, and there's taking responsibility in actual real life to someone's actual real face which felt waaaaaay less appealing. There was no escaping it though. I had to, as Nonna would say, put my big girl knickers on and woman up.

> That would be great.

> I've left school already tho. Bus stop at the top of Gull Lane in 5?

> Sure

It occurred to me as I waited, fidgeting, at the bus stop, that yet again I had no idea what I was going to say – no explanation to give. I mean, I couldn't remember it even happening, so I *literally* had no explanation. At last, I saw him approach. I tried to think brave thoughts, but I would have rather sat all my exams three times over than have the conversation we were about to have.

'Hi,' I said, tentatively.

'Hi.' He looked different – hard and drawn. He felt separate and unreachable, not mine to touch and breathe in – and it hurt. An actual, physical pain, a tiny little knife jabbed in right below my ribs. We moved to a wall just behind the bus stop.

'I'm sorry,' I said, at the same time as he went to speak. I carried on though – if I didn't, I might buckle and lose my nerve. 'It was a terrible thing for me to do, to kiss Marcus,' I cringed as I said it, 'and to not tell you and for you to find out the way you did. I've got no excuses, no explanation, I'm just really sorry. For all of it. You deserve better than that.'

I stared at the pavement, waiting for him to reply.

'You're right,' he said. 'I do deserve better. It was a supremely shitty thing to do.' I nodded, still not making eye contact. 'Why did you even do it? I thought you hated Marcus?'

'I do!' I shouted.

'Well, I don't understand then. Were you not happy with me? We could've talked about it. It's so not like you. At least, I *thought* it wasn't like you. I thought we were . . . I dunno. Better than that. I guess I was wrong.'

His words had all the soul-destroying weight of your parents telling you they're not angry with you, they're disappointed.

'It wasn't like me,' I said. 'Not deep down. I had a . . . blip. I'm working on it. But it was wrong, I treated you badly and I'm sorry.'

239

We both sighed. The distance between us was so big he may as well have been in Australia. I had run out of words. What else could I possibly say? I hated the idea that he wouldn't be in my life any more. Just someone I would see across the canteen, the classroom, the hall.

'I know it might take a long time,' I said. 'But I'd really like it if we could be friends at some point.'

'Uh, yeah, that won't be for a while. Plus I'm friends with Callum and you don't seem to be able to handle that.' I stayed quiet. 'About that,' he went on, 'the reason why we've been getting closer again is that he's confiding in me about some really horrible stuff that's been going on at home. I didn't tell you, because it's not mine to share, but I thought you deserved an explanation.'

I swallowed. I had an idea what Callum's problems at home might be and it made me feel sick to my stomach.

'How is he?' I asked quietly. Freddie shook his head. 'Really bad, actually. Last I heard he was in hospital – some sickness thing, but they don't know what it is and—'

'I've gotta go,' I said, already walking away. 'I just remembered something. Thanks. Sorry. SORRY!'

I didn't glance back to see what I imagined would've been a confused, possibly pissed-off expression. I didn't have time.

I had more important things to worry about.

CHAPTER THIRTY-SIX

'NONNA!' I called, slamming the front door behind me, out of breath from running home. 'Nonna!'

I raced through to the empty kitchen, went to Nonna's annexe – no sign of her.

'Nonna!' I shouted again, running to the back of the garden, out to her potting shed.

'Jessie,' she said, appearing at the door to the shed in her usual gardening attire – apron on, hair tied in a turban, hands covered in soil. My shoulders relaxed at the sight of her. 'What's the matter? Why aren't you at school?'

'There's something really important I need your help with, but I can't tell you everything, I just need you to trust me.'

'I think we'd better sit down,' she said, taking me in, like a wise, all-seeing owl. 'Let's go inside.'

Nonna moved with tortoise-like speed. So slow I had to restrain myself from pushing her along. She untied her apron (slowly), closed up her shed (slowly), walked to her annexe (slowly), washed her hands (slowly), boiled the kettle (slowly) and poured the tea (slowly). It was like she didn't know my nemesis could well be dying and it was down to me to stop it. Eventually she sat down next to me on her yellow sofa, the familiar smell of lavender and patchouli encompassing me.

'So tell me all about it,' she said, sipping her tea and placing it on the side table (slowly).

I had to force the words out of my mouth, like skydivers being pushed out of a plane. 'So ... I've got myself into a bit of ... I've done something which I'm not proud of ... I ...'

'Spit it out.'

My eyes caught on the smiling photo of Nonna and Gramps. I was about to let her down, so badly. Nonna was my favourite person in the whole world and I couldn't bear seeing the disappointment in her face.

I took a deep breath. 'OK, I've got in over my head with something – magic related – and I need to fix it.'

Her eyes were on mine, interrogating my soul, but full of love and kindness too. 'You've been lost,' she said, nodding. 'But I can see you're coming through. And do you know why that is, Jessie?' I shook my head. 'Because you're strong. I don't mean just strong with your powers – I mean inside. You're strong inside. And no matter what you may think, I've always known it.' She patted my leg, her bangles jangling. It took everything to hold it together and not collapse into her, sobbing.

'I don't feel very strong right now,' I said, my voice cracking. 'But I need your help and it's urgent.'

'Well, why didn't you say – I've been strolling around like a sloth on Nytol! You should've given me a kick up the arse. Come on then, let's be having you.'

***

The cove was hard to find. In fact, it was near impossible to find. I'd only been there twice, each time going a different route, and

242

the fact that its entrance was a relatively indistinct rock – of which there were many – made it like finding a needle in a haystack.

I cast my mind back to that first day Sloane had taken me there, trying to retrace the section of coast path we'd walked down. Eventually I found the sidetrack we'd eased on to, recognised the big, twisted tree, but couldn't see the rock – the mystical rock that gave way to reveal the cove. I found a couple that didn't feel quite right and didn't have the mark on them, but tried them anyway, following the instructions Nonna had given me before I left her. I laid my hands on them, sitting there for a few minutes like a total lemon, waiting for something miraculous to happen. Nothing.

My urgency turned to fear, which turned to frustration. I dropped my head and groaned. My eyes fixed on a line of ants, uniform and determined, marching past the rock, into the bushes. I watched as they went along the side of the rock face, into the bushes, further along and then made a sharp turn left – disappearing under ... another rock. Loosely hidden, but very much a rock.

It didn't look like I remembered it, I was sure it hadn't been behind bushes before, but then I saw the mark – the three straight lines with the star – and knew it was the right place.

I scrambled through the thick gorse on my hands and knees, sharp stones digging into my knees, low-hanging twigs catching in my hair. I placed my palms on the rock. This time it was going to work – it had to, because if it didn't I was screwed. I did exactly what Nonna said, channelled my power, pictured the rock moving aside, pictured the cove. The rock turned hot beneath my hands, and sure enough, started moving, the lapping water and sandy bay coming into view, the familiar smell instantly hitting me.

It had been easier than I'd expected and the thrill of succeeding pushed me on. I ran through, the sand getting darker and firmer as I neared the water, the sudden thought that Sloane might be there occurring to me only at the last minute. I looked around, holding my breath – it seemed clear. The tide was just going out. It took me a minute to get my bearings, to remember where we'd buried the jar – but I used the remnants of the fire pit, the driftwood seats and stone circle to guide me and soon I was on my hands and knees, digging frantically.

I cupped my hands and dug, and dug, and dug, my fingertips numb and throbbing from the grainy sand, my back aching, channelling a dog desperate for its long-buried bone. But there was nothing below the sand except more sand. I widened my search area and dug some more, stopping every now and again to look around and reassure myself I was in the right place. I was – I must be – we'd definitely been to the right of the fire and far enough back from the shoreline that it wouldn't get washed away.

I thought back to that night, remembered how exciting it had all seemed – how free and light and happy I'd felt, Kate Winslet on the bow of the *Titanic* being dry-humped from behind by Leonardo DiCaprio level happy. It seemed like a lifetime ago and a completely different me – gullible and foolish and trusting. I remembered leaning on a rock after we'd buried the jar, relishing the prospect of Callum suffering because of me and thinking how good witnessing his downfall was going to feel.

Leaning on a rock! Of course. I'd leaned on a rock that was right next to where we'd buried the jar. I looked around. I was too far towards the centre, too far from the rocks. I moved closer and began my frantic digging again but with more conviction this time.

Finally, my hand struck gold – or glass, to be more precise. I prised the object out and shook off the sand. There it was in all its glory, the Callum curse jar. I felt a wave of relief rush over me – part of me had worried Sloane was on to me and would have come here herself already. Obviously she was more naïve than I took her for. Though *naïve* and *Sloane* weren't really two words you'd put together. Maybe she had just underestimated me.

Either way, I was ecstatic that I had it. I unscrewed the lid and knelt down, emptying the contents on to the sand. Blocking the wind, I lit the candle, taking a deep breath and centring myself, hoping, wishing, with everything I had that this would work. Finding a suitably sharp rock, I did as Nonna had instructed and scraped Callum's name off the candle, the red wax splintering and curling with each gouge – the whole time repeating the spell:

'Undo what was done, hear my plea,
Undo what was done, so let it be.'

It was therapeutic – scraping and digging and seeing his name disappear bit by bit, seeing the bad I'd done begin to be undone. When it was completely gone, I gathered the remaining contents – the remnants of the burnt sage and hair and the nails, put them back in the jar and went straight to the water.

I waded in until the water was lapping over my feet, seeping through my school shoes and tights, the cold making me gasp. I held the jar in the water, watching as a wave ran into it, filled it, then rushed back with the contents, carrying them out with a satisfying strength and noise. I held the jar there, still repeating the spell, for a few more minutes, needing to be sure that every last piece of it was gone, erased, feeling the waves bring me something like hope each time they washed in. I could do this. It would all be OK. I'd made mistakes – big ones – but I could fix it. I *would* fix it.

I didn't let myself think of Sloane and the menu of retribution that might lie ahead. I just focused on the hope.

CHAPTER THIRTY-SEVEN

I took the long way home, via a café and along the path up to the Downs, even though my wet tights and shoes were starting to chafe. There was something about the pain that I liked. I took in big gulps of sea air and coffee, hoping they would reinvigorate me in their respective ways. At least I'd done something useful, one small thing in the long list of things I had to do to make right all that I'd made wrong.

And then I saw him. It took me a minute and a few squints to know for sure, because he appeared to be almost half the size of Before Callum, but it was definitely him. He was sat on a bench staring out to sea. I sped up, but he saw me approaching, stood up and started walking away.

'Callum!' I called after him, beginning to jog. 'Wait up.'

He walked faster, not even turning round to glance at me. I jogged faster too, really hoping this wasn't going to turn into an actual race as I was pretty sure I wouldn't come out on top in that scenario, even given his deteriorated state. 'Callum!' Eventually I levelled up to him, panting and feeling light-headed. 'Did you not hear me?' I puffed.

'I heard you,' he said, staring ahead and still striding. 'But I don't want anything to do with you. Leave me alone.'

'How are you feeling?' I asked anxiously, hoping he would say, 'Weirdly, much better in the last five minutes.'

'How the fuck do you think I'm feeling?' he snapped, suddenly turning round to me. His eyes were sunken and hollow but glaring all the same. I jumped, shocked by the venom in his voice. 'I've been lying in bed in pain like I've never felt before, thinking I might be dying and sometimes wishing I would so the pain would stop.'

I cowered away from him, disgusted with myself. 'That sounds terrible,' I said, my voice tiny and fragile. 'Do they know what it—'

He laughed then, a horrible, strangled chuckle. 'Of course *they* don't know what it is. But *we* know, don't we, Jessie?'

I swear my heart stopped beating – full on froze, paralysed. 'W-what do you mean?'

He leaned in. 'Oh come on now, are you going to play innocent with me? Tell me you haven't got your cauldron out lately.'

I dropped my coffee, the cup rebounding and splashing liquid all over my shoes and up my tights. He stared at me, enjoying watching me squirm, taking my shock as his proof.

'I thought you were joking, back in March – that bullshit at the party with Freddie – telling him you were a witch and then trying to prove it. I thought you were just being a weirdo, wanting attention.' He ran his fingers through his hair. 'But then when that video you made got out and everyone watched it, he told me. He *told* me you weren't kidding.'

I stared at him. *Freddie* had told him I was a witch? But Freddie didn't know.

'But – but Freddie didn't believe me,' I said.

'I'm not talking about Freddie. I'm talking about my dad. *He knew*. He told me that you were a witch, like you said – that your whole family are witches. Said to get you to the event, take some pictures, then steer clear of you until he'd got things in place. And I didn't believe him. Which turned out to be a bad move because look what happened.' He shook his head at me, like I was a naughty puppy that had chewed a shoe. 'I'm interested, Jessie – how long have you been plotting this? Was it the reason why you were with Freddie in the first place – to get to me?'

'Don't flatter yourself!' I snapped. 'I was with Freddie because I liked him. And as for you, you've been completely innocent in all of this, I suppose? Never done one single thing wrong?' My anger was bubbling up. 'You didn't try it on with me when you were with Libby? You didn't lie about it when I rejected you, you didn't spread rumours about me all over school? You didn't mastermind a scoring system for all the girls—'

He snorted. 'I mean, I like the word *mastermind* but—'

I was fully angry now. 'I admit it. I had the tiniest, tiniest, seed of hope when we spoke at that newspaper event – hope that you'd changed. But then you ruined my uniform, as some sort of sick humiliation and I realised I'd been right all along. You haven't changed a bit.'

'I didn't put that blood on your uniform!' He was practically shouting in my face. I looked around, checking no one was around to witness this. 'I'll own everything else – which, by the way, happened a lifetime ago—'

'Six months. It was six months ago.'

'Fine. Six months ago. But I did not put that blood on your

uniform. Like I said at the time – believe me or not, I don't care any more, but I didn't do it.'

'As if. You're a bully, Callum. A weak, pathetic little boy who's scared no one will like him if they knew the real him, so he terrorises people into liking him.' Even as I was saying it, it occurred to me that perhaps that wasn't true – at least, not any more. But if it hadn't been Callum who put the blood on my uniform ... Then I'd been wrong about everything and had pushed my friends away for no reason. I shook the thought out of my head. 'You're just like your dad,' I finished, spitefully.

His face dropped instantly, a thundercloud setting in. I'd gone too far. He stepped closer to me, his face so close to mine I could see the tiny red veins in his bloodshot eyes.

'Don't ever compare me to him.' His breath was hot and sour. 'And I hardly think you're one to talk. Your friends know the real you, do they?' I swallowed hard, my anger giving way to fear. 'Maybe we should give that theory a go, *witch*.'

He turned sharply and walked away from me without another word.

CHAPTER THIRTY-EIGHT

Callum knows.

Callum knows.

Callum knows.

That was all I could think the whole way home. I tripped over tree roots, I bumped into people, I took a wrong turn because all I could focus on was the fact that Callum Henderson knew I was a witch and was going to tell everyone. I was officially done for.

Maybe I could persuade Mum that we should move away, with Nonna this time, start afresh somewhere completely new, as we were so used to doing. I mean, what did she really have here – other than family and a house and a new business and a boyfriend and roots and . . . argh.

It was a lost cause. There was no way over it and no way under it. I was totally going to have to go through it. Swishy-bloody-swashy.

***

I walked in the door a mess – freezing, red-faced, blotched eyes and nerves on fire. The wet-footed walk home combined with the adrenaline surge and mounting panic had taken their toll and all I wanted to do was jump into bed with a hot water bottle.

'Jessie!' Nonna shouted from the kitchen. 'We've got some news.'

'We?' I asked, squelching through to her.

'We,' Mum said, looking up from one of the many thick, dusty leatherbound books scattered all over the table.

'No need for the gaping fish mouth,' Bella added, from behind her laptop. 'We can be helpful when needed. Even though I should be revising and Mum should be sewing. Families, hey.'

'I . . . I mean, thanks. Did Nonna—'

'Yep, she's filled us in. As much as you've filled her in – which isn't all that much, obviously; Sloane's an evil witch who has been doing bad stuff and has turned your friends against you and you think she's been lying about her mum being here *and* you're worried about what she's likely to do next. Oh, and you've done bad stuff you're trying to find a way to fix. Is that about right?'

I nodded, not knowing how else to reply and not enjoying all the mentions of 'bad stuff'.

Mum stood up and wrapped me in a big, tight hug. 'How are you doing?'

How was I doing? How *was* I doing? Well . . .

'I don't know how to begin,' I said weakly.

'How did it go at the cove?' Nonna asked, all business.

'Fine. Well, I did what you told me. How do I know if it's worked?'

'You wait and see.'

'Great, helpful.' I flopped myself in the armchair in the corner and took my shoes off, small pools of sea water collecting

252

on the floor. It felt good to sit, to be home, to feel safe in some small way – even if it was only temporary. *Callum knows.* 'So, what's this news?'

'Well,' Bella said, eyes wide with excitement. 'We've made progress here! You were right to think that Smith isn't Sloane's real surname. And you were also right about the Scottish connection – Sloane is actually a Gaelic name, first used in an ancient Scottish tribe and get this – it means *warrior*. And you mentioned something about an accident with her sister. I've found an article about it, which you'll definitely want to read, and Nonna—'

'I found her mum!' Nonna jumped in, grinning like a Cheshire cat. 'Your hunch about her not living with Sloane was right. She's on her way now.'

'Oh, that's great,' I said, trying to force some enthusiasm into my voice.

'She was actually nearby, in Sussex, following up a lead on Sloane. She'd been looking for Sloane for a while – since Sloane was cast out from the coven and ran away. Sloane had cast a masking spell on herself so she couldn't be found. Quite advanced magic, really. Anyway, her mum was very pleased to hear from us. She sounds like quite a decent one, which makes a change for that coven.'

'What do you mean?' I asked.

Mum put a steaming cup of tea and a pint glass of iced water on the side table for me, giving me a little back rub as she did.

'The witch community isn't all unity and light,' Nonna continued. 'There are factions and divisions and many, many differences. Down here, we've always been on the … lighter side of the conversation, but in other places, including Scotland, they've traditionally taken a much harder stance. Scotland suffered hideously with the witch hunts – thousands were tortured in the worst ways imaginable and burned at the stake. It was outright butchery and organised mass murder.'

My skin prickled, standing to attention. 'Wow. That's … terrible.'

'Exactly,' Nonna said, sadness pooling in her eyes. 'So you can see how we've ended up on different paths with our craft. Sloane's coven in particular have a reputation for being very anti-men, going out of their way to cause suffering and seek revenge on any who they feel have wronged women. In the nastiest of ways. Though maybe they're trying to change their ways, if they cast Sloane out for what she did.'

'Here.' Bella thrust a sheet of A4 into my hand. 'The article about Sloane and her sister.'

I ran my eyes over the printout. It was an article in *The Berwick Bugle*.

Local Twins in Catastrophic Cliff Fall.

I scanned the article. The incident was exactly as Sloane had described – with one very important difference. My head span, thoughts exploding like fireworks.

'Your mum and I need to have a word with you, petal,' Nonna said to me, as I looked up from the article. 'Let's go next door.'

'Uh, OK,' I said, starting to feel nervous.

Nonna grabbed one of the dusty books from the table and went through to the living room. Mum and I followed, settling ourselves on the sofa opposite the armchair Nonna sat in. I perched on the edge, bracing myself.

Mum put her hand over mine, giving it a gentle squeeze. 'There's something we need to talk openly with you about. I'm sorry it's taken us so long.'

'Go on . . .' I said, suspicious.

'I'm guessing you found out you're a Sister of Endor not from the internet like you said, but from Sloane, who is also a Sister.' I nodded. 'There's a reason why we wanted to wait a while before we told you.'

'The Sisters have ... a history.' Nonna said. 'Their exact origins aren't documented. The magic is hereditary, but no one knows why some are chosen. What we do know about them, is that they often veer towards the darker side of magic.'

I sat statue-still, letting the words sink in, remembering what Sloane had said about Sisters of Endor being 'dark as the night'. I'd hoped she had been lying about that, like so much else, but no; she'd been telling me the truth. Darkness, badness, wrongness – I couldn't escape it. It was in my nature. The panic caught in my throat.

'Essentially,' Mum carried on, gently, 'they are more powerful than other witches. That power is often used for bad.'

'Like what?' I whispered, not sure I wanted the answer, but knowing I had to ask.

'Oh, you know,' Nonna said. 'Revenge, retribution, reprisal—'

'But that's not all of them, Jessie,' Mum interjected. 'There are many cases of Sisters who do good, who are healing and nurturing. The reason we didn't tell you this in the first place is that we didn't want you to feel like you were predisposed to Dark Magic. We wanted to give you time to learn the foundations of our magic – the healing, the positive role witches can play in nature.'

I swallowed. I hadn't been wrong, then. The Dark witch who had made Callum sick, killed a cat, punished Libby – it had been me, all along. I couldn't blame Sloane for it. 'Don't for one minute think this is your lot,' Nonna said, fierce and forceful. 'You are strong enough now to stay away from the darker side of magic.'

I flinched thinking back to everything I'd already done. 'But how do I know what's OK and what's not?'

'You'll know,' Nonna said. 'You'll know deep down.'

I gulped down a big fat ball of fear and guilt and shame and more fear. Mum and Nonna were both staring at me, and I could only pray they couldn't see the truth.

Nonna sighed. 'It's easy to get carried away with the thrill of power, Jessie. We've all been there. When I talk to you about power and responsibility, I'm talking from experience. We have the power to heal, but we also have the power to hurt, and that's not something to be taken lightly.'

I could feel tears pinching at the back of my eyes, a tightness in my throat. Why had I thought that Nonna was being anything other than protective and loving? Why had I not trusted her?

'Having said that,' she carried on, putting her hand over mine, the warmth of it comforting me, 'we believe in you, despite what you may think. And we believe you are strong enough to do the right thing.'

'We do, darling,' Mum said. 'And, more importantly, we're here to help you, no matter what. We hope you know that.'

'I do,' I whispered. And I really did.

'You might find this useful,' Nonna said, handing me the book she'd been holding.

The leather on its cover was so smooth it felt like silk, worn down by decades and decades. Its musty old book smell caught in my nose instantly. On the cover was the symbol from the cove – three straight lines and a star. As soon as I touched it, I got a shock, a thrill, a wave of electricity. A deep, well-like, ancient connection.

'This symbol!' I said, the excitement surging. 'I recognise it! It's on the rock at the cove! What is it? What is this?'

'That's Molly's symbol – your great-great-great-great-grandmother,' Nonna looked wistful. 'That cove you've been going to must be the one she used to use. I remember hearing about it, but I've never been.'

I opened up the thick cover, and there, in faint, spidery writing, it said:

THE JOURNAL OF MOLLY DOWNER

'It's her journal,' Nonna continued. 'Like you, she was a Sister of Endor, the only other documented one in our family, besides you, of course. Your mum and I can help you with a lot when it comes to your magic, but there's a lot you're going through that we don't understand. We thought reading this might help you.'

I took it all in, gently stroking the soft, aged pages, my eyes following the curls and flicks of the handwriting. This ancient book was from one of my ancestors, one who had been a Sister. It was in my blood. It was coursing through me, this deep, deep, ancient connection that made me who I am.

'But before you get stuck into that,' Nonna changed her tone, back to business, 'you'd better check your phone – my senses tell me you've just had an important message come through.'

I got my phone out to check and saw that my screen was lit up with notifications. I had a text from Libby, with a forwarded voice note.

> Hey, got this weird message from Callum – think it's meant for you? Guess he doesn't have your number. Does it make sense to you?

I listened to the voice note. It was muffled and distant and hard to understand, but two phrases were very clear: 'Jessie' and 'make her stop'.

I shot up from the sofa so fast I felt dizzy. 'I've got to go!'

CHAPTER THIRTY-NINE

I rang the doorbell of Callum's house, breathing hard and waiting impatiently for the sound of footsteps.

'Can I help you?' A lady answered the door. Someone I'd never seen before, though judging by the duster in her hand, I guessed she was the cleaner. I was relieved that it wasn't Callum's dad.

'Hi, I'm a friend of Callum's,' I said, the word 'friend' catching in my throat. 'Is he in in?'

'He's out. He left with a friend of his.' My stomach rolled. *A friend.*

'Ah, thanks. I was meant to be meeting them. Did you happen to see the, um, friend?'

'Black hair. Black clothes. She had—'

I felt cold as ice. I didn't know why or what she was planning but I was one hundred per cent sure it wouldn't be good.

'Did they happen to say where they were going?' I asked, my mouth sandpit-dry.

'No, sorry.' She went to close the door. 'Oh, are you Jessie?'

'Yes!' I said, too enthusiastically.

'I've just seen there's a note here for you.' She handed me the envelope and closed the door.

My name was in bubble writing on the front, a heart in place of the dot above the 'i'. I ripped it open.

It was on a small piece of paper – grey, with a border of stars; scrawled childish handwriting. The paper and the handwriting. I had seen a note like this before.

A sudden pressure pushed at my temples.

The note Callum had shown me, the day my uniform was ruined, summoning him to the girls' changing room – it had been written on the same paper.

Sloane.

Revision Facts – *An Inspector Calls* (English)

1. One of the main themes of *An Inspector Calls* is social responsibility: how do we look after one another within society?

2. Priestley looks at social responsibility through other lenses, including gender, class and age. Priestley's message around gender was that traditional stereotypes are damaging and stop society from progressing.

3. Dramatic devices are used throughout the play – for example, the photograph which the Inspector shows the characters. He only shows it to one person at a time, so none are sure whether they have seen the same photograph as the others.

4. Each character has an immediate response to the photograph.

5. Priestley also employs the use of a cliffhanger. A cliffhanger is when the audience has to wait to see what happens.

It had been Sloane all along. How had I missed what was right under my nose?

I didn't have the luxury of time to look back on all the events that led us here and work out each time I'd gone wrong. I had no idea what Sloane wanted with Callum now, what she was planning on doing with him – *to* him – but at least I knew where they were. And that I had to stop her, somehow.

***

The cove was easier to find this time, thankfully. It was late afternoon by the time I arrived, the sun hidden behind a wall of grey clouds – the type of clouds that are neither here nor there, not about to clear, not about to burst. Just grey and flat. They cast a shadow over the whole cove, making it feel ominous and cold – far from the warm, inviting picturesque cove I'd first encountered. The sea was rough and angry, the tide swollen, big waves crashing into the narrow channel and spraying over the sand like it was shouting.

I didn't need to search for Sloane; she was sitting on one of the driftwood benches in front of a roaring fire, her dark hair blowing in the wind. She stood up as soon as I'd stepped through the rock.

'Yay! You made it!' She was smiling, eyes wide.

'Where's Callum?' I asked lightly. I couldn't gauge the mood she was in and knew I had to tread carefully if I wanted him back in one piece.

'Come and sit, come and sit,' she said, beckoning me over. 'We need to have a chat.'

'Sloane, where's Callum?' I asked again, trying to stay calm.

261

'Good present, hey?' She rubbed her hands together in glee. 'Especially now.'

'What do you mean?'

'*You know.*' She looked at me, expectant. 'Now that he knows about you. About *us*, I suppose, except I don't really care. Whereas you kind of seem to.' I tried to hide my shock. And my panic. She couldn't possibly know he'd found out. 'I mean, it was a bonus really, I was just getting him for you as a make-up present, but when I looked in his mind and saw the conversation you'd had – well, that was the icing on the cake. It was meant to be!'

'What do you mean, you got him as a make-up present?' I asked, trying desperately to make my voice as even as it could be, though my insides were screaming.

'I wanted you to know I was still here for you – after we had that little misunderstanding and you told me you didn't want to be my friend. I know why it was – you feel guilty about Puffball and about the other stuff, and you're sad that your shitty friends don't want to be friends with you any more. But we'll always have each other. So Callum is my make-up present to you – to prove to you once and for all that I have your back, that my loyalty is with you. That I will do anything – *anything* – for you.'

'But what would I want Callum for?' I asked.

'I'm your Fairy Witchmother, remember?' I nodded. 'We sat right here and I asked you what you wanted and what you were afraid of. You said you wanted to break up with Freddie – which I sorted. And you said you were afraid of another round of Callum Henderson torturing you. Here you go! Now we can make sure, once and for all, that he never gives you problems again.'

I eyed her cautiously. Was she putting on a show? More worryingly, was she being deadly serious – had she actually taken Callum for *me*?

'I never break my promises, Jessie. Best friends don't do that.' She poked a stick into the fire, the tip of it catching. 'But I thought we could have some fun with him first – it will be even better doing it in person. That last curse was a slow burn, so to speak. Not as satisfying.'

I cleared my throat. 'Sloane, I don't want to hurt Callum any more.'

She narrowed her eyes at me. 'Come on, you don't mean that.'

'I really do.'

She shook her head, stared at the fire, took a deep breath. 'It's a shame, Jessie. I thought you'd turned a corner, when we did that resurrection – which, I might add, you were BRILLIANT at – I thought you were getting it, finally. Feeling the rush, enjoying the power. You're a Sister of Endor – darkness is in your blood, it's not something you can hide from. You've been so sheltered for so long, Jessie. It was great seeing you discover all the possibilities we have available to us. We have fun together – don't we have fun?'

I looked into the fire, focusing on the flames, the stacked wood being slowly charred, turning black, then white. I thought back to the fire the first time we'd come here – how she'd taught me to control it. It had felt amazing.

'We did have fun, Sloane,' I said slowly. I would do whatever it took to get Callum back, and if that meant playing along, I would play along. 'We *do* have fun.'

'Exactly!' she said, invigorated, jumping down from the rock. 'We're the same – you and I. We're sisters – literally. Witch Sisters. Practically superheroes.' I nodded, even though I was pretty sure Wonder Woman wouldn't resort to making another girl's hair fall out because she had annoyed her.

'And everything we did to people, they one hundred per cent deserved.' Sloane was animated now, waving the lit stick around like she was conducting an orchestra, the sea behind her the perfect, powerful backdrop. 'What Callum did to you was hideous – unforgivable – and that was on top of everything he did to you last year. He was never going to learn – he would have been terrorising girls for the rest of his life if we hadn't done something about it.'

I'd heard the speech before, except this time I wasn't buying it. Still, I nodded again, turning my head ever so slightly, still trying to work out where Callum might be. Jagged cliff edges perched out on either side of the cove, gulls squawking and circling around them, I noticed a cave in the far corner – its entrance dark and ominous. But no sign of Callum.

'I just feel so guilty, about Puffball,' I said, stalling for time.

'You're still worrying about that?' She shrugged the thought off. 'Really, don't. I mean to be honest, you didn't even do anything. You were asleep in the car.'

My ears rang, the hair on my skin standing on end. I took a second, almost hoping that maybe the crash of the waves had meant I'd misheard. My gut told me I hadn't. '*What?*'

'It wasn't you, it was me. You were actually asleep in the car.' Sloane smiled, like she was serving me up a treat. 'I lied because I needed to make sure you wouldn't tell anyone about

264

all the other stuff. So you see, you don't need to feel bad. We're all cool.'

Cool was not the word for what we were. Inside, I was raging, exploding. Everything came crashing back to me as if I was seeing it for the first time, under a lens of clarity, the cling-film filter ripped away. Things started slotting into place. I had been right all along, but Sloane had made me doubt myself. I hadn't done that to Puffball, I couldn't remember that night, but not because I'd drunk too much – because of *what* I had drunk. I truly had supped from the cup of Darkness.

'The drink!' That drink you gave me that night – the remedy – you drugged me!'

'"Drugged" is a harsh word for it . . . it was some strong herbs.'

'You put the blood on my uniform.' I said it flatly and evenly like the cold, hard fact I knew it to be.

'Actually that *was* Callum. But yes, I hexed him to do it.'

'And the note was you.' I was reeling, everything stacking on top of one another, a tower of truth. 'But why bother when you could've just hexed him?'

'Just an added little extra – my idea was to find the note and use it as evidence in case you needed persuading it was him, but as it happened you didn't, and he showed you the note himself. Which I actually thought was a pretty bold move.'

I took a deep breath, letting the realisations sink in.

'The blood on your uniform was a bit extreme, but totally for the greater good though – you needed to be forced into action. I needed you to get angry.'

I forced a smile. 'You're right. You needed me angry and now I am. Where *is* Callum?'

'That's my girl! You want to get started! Follow me.'

She bounded up the rocks, taking big steps, using her hands to pull herself up, balancing on uneven ones. I followed, my arms shaking, trying to keep my focus, the stone cold and unrelenting beneath my hands. We climbed our way almost to the top of one of the cliffs that jutted out over the cove. And there he was, sat on a flat rock, leaning precariously up against the side of the cliff wall, his hands bound behind him, his eyes looking utterly terrified.

'Ta da!' Sloane waved her hands in a flourish. 'Now, I know the whole thing about witches being drowned is a bit of a myth – they were actually mostly burned or tortured – but I quite liked the symbolism of it, so I thought drowning would be a good way to go.' I looked at him, trying to work out why he wasn't speaking or screaming or running. 'Oh he can only do what I tell him,' she said. 'That's fun too! Watch this.' She turned to face him. 'Callum, stand up.'

With difficulty, he stood up, his legs shaking and unsteady, the wind whipping his hair across his tear-tracked face.

'Take two steps forward,' she said. I watched with a building sense of horror as Callum obeyed, the two steps taking him right up to the edge.

I needed to get him away from here – fast. My heart leaped as a gull screeched above us. 'Why don't we take him back down, Sloane?' I suggested. 'I'm not good with heights. I'd rather have some fun back in the cove.'

'I can make him jump now if you want? Straight into the sea. Call—'

'STOP!' It came out before I could stop it, all my false calm and false ease gone.

Sloane's eyes widened in recognition. Recognition and disappointment. 'Oh. You don't like your present? You don't want to play with your present?'

'It's not that.' I was choosing my words carefully, walking on a tightrope. 'I'm very grateful, but—'

'UGH!' she roared. 'It's always the same with you people! I step in, do something nice for you, and what do I get in return? You're all ungrateful bitches. Do you know how many witches from our coven were burned in the trials? ALL BUT TWO. And only because those two fled. Boys, men – they're against us – always have been and always will be. They may not tie us to the stake any more but they torture us in different ways. Why can't you people see that? Open your eyes!'

'I know what happened to your sister, Sloane.' I spoke quietly, aware that the tiniest misplaced word or movement could have horrific consequences. 'I know she's not in a wheelchair.' A pause. 'I know she's dead.'

The smallest glare of recognition, of doubt crossed her face before she laughed, her eyes wide. 'Slow clap for Jessie, well done. Think yourself a regular little Sherlock, do you? You remind me of Isla actually. She was fun and into testing our powers and seeking revenge on those who deserved it at one point, like you. And then, funnily enough, she turned into a coward, like you. She started drifting away from me, not liking the magic I was doing, listening to other people. She didn't like the gift I got for her either. I brought Dylan Morris to her on a plate, thought we could teach him a lesson. But she lunged at me, made me stop. That's when – when she fell.' She looked to the floor, scraping her boot against the loose stones. 'I miss her.

So much. Even though she was a coward. Now Dylan is walking the streets probably causing more damage and Isla is dead. And that's not fair, is it?'

She blinked away tears. I didn't say anything.

'IS IT?' she asked again, anger coming back.

'No, Sloane, it's not fair. It was a terrible accident – a tragedy. But you can't do anything for her now.'

'Well – that's where you're wrong! See, that's where *you* come into it,' she said, her face lighting up. 'After the incident with my sister, my coven kicked me out – they said I'd gone too dark, that I wasn't adhering to the coven's path. So I made it my life's mission to fix things. I'd heard the gossip about you on the witch grapevine, saw the video you made. I knew you were not just a Sister, but a super-powerful one. And you were doing good things – avenging, teaching those pigs a lesson, making the world a better place. I knew you could help me.'

I glanced at Callum; he was shaking, the fear in his eyes making him almost unrecognisable.

'Help you how?' I asked, intrigued and scared at once.

'To bring her back.'

My stomach lurched. 'W-what do you mean, Sloane?'

'Resurrection, Jessie! When we did it on that bird so easily, I just knew we could work our way up to bigger things. That's why I killed Puffball – so we could try on her – but I'd made the brew I gave you a bit strong and you'd passed out.' She stepped closer, eyes gleaming in the encroaching dusk. 'We can do it, Jessie. I know we can. Together. We're a good team. We can bring Isla back and then everything will be fixed.'

'Sloane.' I spoke very clearly, raising my voice over the sound of the waves. 'I'm not doing that again. Ever. That is not the kind of magic I am going to practise.'

She stared at me, as though working out whether I meant it or not. Then she nodded.

'We'll see about that, shall we?'

Then she reached her hand out, and, in one swift, smooth movement, pushed Callum off the edge of the cliff.

CHAPTER FORTY

'Sloane!' I cried, rushing to the edge, looking over and seeing nothing but a splurge of white where Callum's body must have entered the water. 'What have you done?'

'What are you going to do now, Jessie? Let him die because *that's not the kind of magic you are going to practise?*'

I didn't have time to think. I just dived.

The water was cold and hard, a sudden thump that shocked my body, taking my breath away. I surfaced, looking around, taking a breath and diving back under, my eyes stinging against the salt water, the waves forcing me sideways. The water was relatively shallow, even for high tide, but it was hard to get enough impetus to reach the bottom with the waves battering me.

I came up for another breath, glancing around again. I used a rock that was jutting into the water as leverage to push myself deeper, down to the bottom. It was only a few feet down but it was dark. I reached wide with my arms, legs, trying to feel something other than water and sand.

And then finally, finally, I felt him. I gripped his shoulder, put the full weight of my arm under it and started to push up to the surface.

I wasn't strong enough. He sank back down. Once more I

went to the surface and took a gulp of air, the hope beginning to drain out of me. I wanted to cry. To let myself sink into the waves that were so violently pushing me around, to let them have their way. It was useless. This was more than I could manage. I closed my eyes and let the tears come, my salt water mixing with the sea's.

And that's when I heard it. A voice. Not mine, not Sloane's or Callum's. A voice I didn't know, soft and soothing, yet powerful, coming from somewhere outside of myself. *You can do it. You are strong.*

It wasn't me, but it was somehow connected to me, deeply, intrinsically. Molly. I just knew it. She was here, protecting me, guiding me. And it was all I needed.

Taking a deep breath, I placed myself, centred myself. I wasn't a normal teenage girl trying to drag a boy out of the ocean. I was a witch. A strong, powerful, capable one. I was nature and moons and oceans and waves, I was unity and force. The sea was part of me and I was part of the sea. I closed my eyes, becoming as still as I possibly could, and summoned every bit of magic I could find from within me.

This time, when I dove back down, it was with ease and speed, almost as if the water was parting for me. I found Callum instantly, hooked my arm under his shoulder again, and pushed up from the sea bed, the sea helping me on my way, urging me on to the shore, the water eerily calm now, apart from the friendly surge pushing me forwards.

I managed to drag him on to the sand, the sea ebbing away to give us land. He was still and white and bloated, his lips a horrible blue, his limbs heavy and solid.

I put my ear to his mouth, listening for breath, even though I knew there was none.

'Callum!' I shouted. 'Callum, don't do this to me!'

'I think it's better he's dead, don't you?' Sloane was standing on a rock just above us, her hair splaying out behind her like some angel of death. 'If he's alive, he'll just tell everyone that you're a witch.'

'I DON'T CARE, SLOANE!' I shouted, my words echoing around the cove, filling the space, becoming real. I meant it. At last, I meant it. I didn't care who knew. I *wanted* people to know the real me. The person I truly was.

I started pumping Callum's chest, to the tune of *Staying Alive* – I remembered it from a first aid course. Shit, or was it *Happy Birthday*? No, that was washing your hands. It was definitely *Staying Alive*.

Nothing was happening; his body stayed limp beneath my hands.

'Sloane! Help me! Please.' This time there was no echo. This time my voice got swallowed up by the rocks and the sand and the sea that was now crashing violently once more against the shore. 'SLOANE! I need you!'

'If you want him to live, you know what you have to do,' she said.

No. I wouldn't do that. I couldn't do that. It was wrong. I wouldn't open the gate to my darkness. I kept going, frantic, aching, cold, desperate. *Pump, pump, pump,* on his chest – I kept going, kept going – then my mouth on his, *blow, blow. Pump, pump, pump* again and again on his chest, my mouth on his, *blow, blow.*

272

Still nothing.

I crumpled beside him, crying, my head on the sand, giving in. *What had I done?*

It was wrong to bring someone back from the dead ... but was it right to let someone die when I might be able to save them? When it was my fault they were dead in the first place? Is this where black and white becomes grey? Doing the wrong thing for the right reason? Was that what Nonna had meant about knowing I would make the right choice?

I felt like I didn't *have* a choice. Magic was the only thing that might, just might, work. But I remembered the bird – how it had flailed and walked round in circles and had flown into a rock – it had been wrong, unnatural, and I shouldn't do that to Callum. I knew in my soul it was a Bad Thing, but, looking at Callum, at his blue lips, his white skin – I knew I had to.

I was running out of time. I pushed myself up from the sand, sat back on my knees and started making fists and releasing. I did it over and over, until my hands were hot and my palms were tingling. I closed my eyes and hovered my hands over Callum:

'Mother Nature, hear our—'

Callum spluttered. My eyes shot open, fixing on him as he coughed. A guttural, deep cough. I moved him on to his side, letting him convulse all the sea water out, rubbing his back, shaking. His eyes stuttered open with effort, filling with a whole new terror when he saw me. His lips parted in an effort to speak, but he ended up clutching at his throat in pain.

'Please,' he rasped, his voice raw. 'I won't tell anyone ... I promise.'

I almost laughed, the thought of worrying about that now seemed ridiculous. 'I'm not going to hurt you,' I said. 'I was helping you. And you can tell whoever you want – I honestly don't care. That's not what this was about. Anyway, you're OK now, I've got you.' Although I looked around the cove as I said it, aware that I had no idea where Sloane was.

I collapsed into the sand, sobbing and sorry and sore, allowing myself a moment to fall apart. We stayed like that for a while, me curled up in a ball, him laid out on the sand, coming around. When I thought I'd exorcised it all, I lifted my head and sat up, offering my hand to Callum. He hesitated a moment, then took it.

We shuffled towards a rock we could lean our backs against, not having the strength to stand up yet. We were both shivering, the wetness and shock sinking in. The sky was clearing now, the grey clouds turning white, the sun peeping out from behind them. The cove looked nice again. Welcoming and warm and wholesome – so different from half an hour ago. Like Sloane had brought the darkness and now she was gone we could all breathe again.

'Where is she?' Callum asked, his eyes wide with terror, his voice barely a whisper.

'I don't know.' I surveyed the cove, my skin goosebumping. I had a sense she'd gone, though with Sloane nothing was ever certain.

'Thanks,' he rasped. 'You didn't have to help me.'

'You're welcome,' I said. Meaning it.

'That was pretty ... wild. It's real, that whole life flashing before your eyes thing. It was scary.'

'I bet.'

'It was weird though. I saw everything. Like, everything, from every point of view – it was 3D almost. And not pleasant.' His voice caught and he reached his hand to his throat. 'I'm sorry.'

'For what?'

'For everything.'

'Me too.'

'I don't think you ever need to apologise again now – you're definitely in credit.' He winced in pain.

'Don't speak any more. We need to get you to a hospital, get you checked out. Do you think you can walk yet? We should call your dad too.'

His face darkened. 'No. Not yet.' He paused. 'I'll call my mum.'

I smiled. That was good.

He managed a smile back. His hair still had a thick layer of sand wound through it but the colour was starting to creep back on to his face, the blue morphing into mottled pink patches. I had saved Callum Henderson's life. I took him in, thinking back through our history together – that first encounter with the notes in Maths, him kissing me in the post office doorway, and everything that had happened since. We had a knotted, stormy history entwined with a lot of hatred and darkness. But we were both people. People who had flaws, who were fallible, who hurt and had been hurt. And people who had maybe just saved each other.

*⁣**

'Jessie!' Mum cried, running over to us. Handy Andy was next to her, and, behind them both, a woman with mouse-brown hair and dark eyes who must have been Sloane's mother. 'Are you all right? What happened?'

The relief at seeing her made the sobs worse. She fell on to the sand next to me and wrapped me in a hug. 'It's OK, it's OK. You're OK.'

I nestled against her chest, breathing her in, not wanting to leave, to break the spell. Andy knelt down to help Callum, his other arm protectively around the bundle that was me and Mum.

I looked at Mum, questioningly.

'It's OK, he knows everything,' she said, smiling through the tears.

'Yes I do,' Andy said, his face open and honest and loving. 'And I don't care. I mean, I'm all for it. Witch solidarity!'

'Where's Sloane?' her mum asked, frantic. 'SLOANE!' she cried out, her voice broken and haunting.

'She's ... gone,' was all I could manage.

CHAPTER FORTY-ONE

'I'm a witch,' I said, forcing the words out. They attempted to jump right back in my throat.

I'd eventually managed to persuade everyone to meet with me – after many, many apologies, which had got progressively more heartfelt and needy and wretched. I wasn't worried Callum was going to tell anyone; I knew he wouldn't. And not because he was scared, but because we now seemed to have reached an agreement – maybe that's what saving someone's life does to a relationship. Either way, he wasn't around to tell – his mum had whisked him off in the dead of night and no one had heard from him since.

I only knew this because when I went round to deliver one of Nonna's restorative concoctions, the cleaner had told me in an urgent, scared whisper. Bob Henderson had stepped down as MP, citing 'personal reasons', which I hoped meant he was being investigated for his abusive parenting and would receive appropriate consequences, though I feared, knowing the world, it probably wouldn't happen like that.

Sloane had gone too, disappearing from my life as suddenly as she had appeared in it. And while no one knew where she was, the general consensus among the all-knowing adults was that she had left the Island.

I felt a few different ways about that, not least slightly uneasy, like we had unfinished business. I'd wanted to see her reunited with her mum (who turned out to be lovely) and I'd wanted to see her happy – or happier, at least. I had to hope that would come. And in the meantime, her not being around was a helpful start for getting back on track with the girls. The rest was down to me. Mum had made her big revelation to Handy Andy, which – aside from him briefly fainting – had turned out fine. Now it was my turn.

***

'Oh God, what has that freak done to you?' Libby groaned, standing up from the log she had been sitting on. 'I'm not having this conversation again. I'm so witched out – stick a fork in me, I'm done.'

Summer and Tabs stayed silent, wide-eyed, staring.

'Please, please, just listen. There's so much I need to explain. And she's not a freak, for the record.' Libby tutted and shook her head, her whole body stiffening. Panic clawed at me, this was not how it was supposed to go – not at all. The atmosphere was charged and dirty and mean all over again. 'Agh, that's not even what I wanted to . . . I just . . . need you to know . . . I . . . yes, I'm a witch.'

'And I'm Beyoncé, nice to meet you,' Libby scoffed.

'Hear her out,' Summer said. Calm, even, open.

'Forget about the Sloane stuff for a minute, if you can,' I said, knowing that 'the Sloane stuff' was over-the-top flippant for all that had occurred. 'The truth is, my family are all witches and we have been for generations. I didn't know I was – didn't know anything about it at all – until we came to the Island. Being

278

here sparked off my powers. I couldn't control them at first, but I'm getting to grips with them now.'

'And what powers would these be?' Libby asked, her voice full of scorn. 'The power to make some really bad friend choices? The power to completely mug off your perfectly nice boyfriend?'

Ouch.

I pushed on. 'Do you remember last year, when Callum broke out in that sudden rash in class?'

Libby frowned. 'I remember him having that allergic reaction, yes.'

'And when Marcus's nose grew, that time in the canteen?'

'*Seemed* to grow. No one saw it properly.'

'And when Dave Pearce's nipples leaked milk? When a ball came from nowhere and hit Coach on the head? When your dad lost his voice that day after we'd been in detention? When the video we made suddenly started playing again, even though it had been switched off?'

'I knew something was weird about that!' Tabs shouted. 'That was you?'

'That was me. That was all me. Some of it accidental, some of it on purpose.'

'My spots getting better?' Tabs asked.

I nodded.

Libby's face was contorting, her cogs whirring, working through everything I'd just said, trying to make sense of it all. If it wasn't all so tense, her expression would have made me laugh.

'That's bullshit. There must be other explanations for those things.' She stood up again, pacing. 'Has Sloane brainwashed

279

you? Drugged you? What has she done to make you believe this crap?'

'This started before Sloane. I know it's really hard to get your head around – trust me, I've been there – but it is true. And honestly, you don't even have to believe me. I just needed you to know. I needed to be honest with you. I love you guys so much and I really value your friendship, but it could never be totally real when I was hiding such a big part of me from you.'

There was quiet. I felt like it was a Moment. Like this was a crossroads of my life. One path led to no friends and misery, and one led to finally being my real self with real friends. It was a lot. My life felt like a film.

'It's true,' Summer said. Out of the blue. 'She's telling the truth.'

Now it was my turn to stare, wide-eyed. She smiled at me, those piercing, all-knowing blue eyes shining on me.

'You knew?' I asked.

'I suspected,' she said. 'I didn't know anything for sure, but my mum said some things, left some books around … I was confused about certain things that had happened and I think she was trying to point me in the right direction. And it makes sense. So much makes sense. Though, also, so much still doesn't.'

I nodded. I had so much explaining to do.

'How do your powers work?' Tabs asked. 'What else can you use them for? Do you have a coven? Do you go to—'

'WHAT IS WRONG WITH YOU ALL?' Libby shouted. 'Have you lost your minds? You're crazy, all of you. She isn't a witch, she's a confused girl who got caught up with a psychopath and has now, apparently, been brainwashed!'

I had no choice. I could have sat there a
Libby getting angrier and angrier and tried to
but I felt like that would have gone on for ever.
lit the fire.

Just lifted my hand and, all of a sudden, flame
licking at the sky, dancing.

'What the—' Libby jumped back.

I figured I was all in now. I waved my hands around
the flames follow my movements, pushing them down
them up, moving them side to side.

'That's amazing!' Tabs said.

'Wow!' Summer was mesmerised.

'I ... you're ...' Libby, perhaps for the first time in her
was lost for words.

'I'm a witch,' I said. 'Like I've been trying to tell you. And
hope that's OK, because I really want to still be friends.'

There was a long pause. So long I could've done any number
of things in it – fried an egg, made a cup of tea, had a quick
shower. It was painful. We all stared at Libby, watching, waiting.
Her eyes were fixed on the fire, her expression going through a
series of emotions – anger, confusion, intrigue, anger again,
bewilderment.

Eventually, she looked back up at me, as if taking me in for
the first time, which, I guess, in some ways she was. I must have
seemed like a different person to her all of a sudden – not the
hapless Jessie who was freakishly good at maths, freakishly bad
at sport and had a penchant for the Kardashians, but a two-
faced, conniving Jessie who had been lying about something so
massively massive it couldn't even be fathomed.

wanted to tell her I was all of those things. Still hapless, still
ᴅd at maths and freakishly bad at sport and still with an
ᴇxplicable soft spot for the Kardashians. My heart was
ᴜmping so hard in my chest it felt like it was trying to break
ee.

'Well, holy shit!' she said eventually, her lips curling into a
mile. 'Aren't you the dark horse!'

My whole body relaxed, the tension instantly dissipating,
tears springing to my eyes.

'What are you crying for, you fool?' Libby said, walking
towards me and wrapping me in a hug.

The big button of her jacket caught on my nose but I didn't
care as I breathed in her familiar perfume and hair-spray
scent and let myself sob. Soon I felt more arms around me as
Summer and Tabs joined, all of us forming a tight, intricate
ball.

'I wasn't sure if . . . I was worried you . . .' I snivelled into the
centre of the ball.

'Jessie, we love you,' Tabs said.

'No matter what type of weird you are,' Summer added.

'Don't get carried away,' Libby said. 'We draw a line
somewhere. I mean, goblins and axe murderers are a type of
weird too far.'

'Vampires?' Tabs asked.

'Ugh, don't even!' Summer said.

'So, these powers of yours,' Libby said. 'Can they magic me
up a hot boyfriend?'

We all laughed, tight in our little unit, holding on to each
other.

Revision Facts – Social Constructs in Sitcoms (Media Studies)

1. In the pilot episode of *Friends*, we see Rachel run out of a potential domestic set-up that would have seen her trapped in a loveless marriage.

2. Later in that episode, her new friends help her cut up her credit cards that her father paid for – this is symbolic of cutting ties with her family and their expectations of her and being embraced by her new family – her friends.

3. Throughout the series, it becomes clear that the friends get love and support from each other in a way they don't get from their biological families.

4. The people these characters rely on are each other.

5. No matter what you go through – failed marriages, unplanned pregnancies, fertility issues, job losses, evil witches coming to town and threatening your whole existence – you can always depend on your friends.

NINE MONTHS LATER

'We did it!' I squealed, grabbing Tabs for a hug as we left the hall after our Media Studies exam – we were the last of the exam foot soldiers, all the others having finished earlier in the week.

Our last ever GCSE.

I felt the relief wash over me as I blinked in the bright sunshine. My whole body seemed lighter, my head as clear as that crystalline water you only ever see in tourist photos of places like the Maldives – no murky facts to remember or constant worry clouding it. It had been a full-on year and we were out the other side of it – free and light and bright, with absolutely nothing pressing to do other than work out holiday plans. And worry about results, but I pushed that thought firmly away.

'How did you find it?' Tabs asked, her face still tight with tension.

'OK, I think. Nothing I wasn't expecting. I went off on a tangent a bit about friends as family in the question on themes in a popular sitcom – and also managed to sneak in a bit about what a shit, controlling boyfriend Ross was.'

'Of course you put in your Ross theory,' Freddie said, coming up next to us as we walked. 'I'd be disappointed if you didn't shoehorn it in somehow.'

'I couldn't resist,' I said. 'Are you coming to the party tonight?

I'd be more than happy to elaborate further on why a man making his so-called one true love give up her dream job is not in any way a romantic ideal that we should be rooting for.'

'I was going to come, but I'm now having second thoughts.'

I elbowed him. 'Oi!'

'I'm kidding. But I have heard it all before and totally agree so can we skip the repeat? I'll see you guys there – you have a pre-party to attend by the looks of it.'

Freddie and I were on good terms. Good-ish, anyway. We'd had some big, hard, honest conversations after everything happened. We'd talked about Callum and how difficult it had been for Freddie, trying to be there for his friend but not wanting to upset his girlfriend – "a rose between two thorns" was how he put it, until I gave him a glare for calling me a thorn. I got it though. And I felt like I got both Freddie and Callum a lot more too.

I'd told him about the whole being a mega-powerful witch thing and he'd been surprisingly OK, after he got over the shock of it. He said he always knew there was something different about me, and it wasn't just my views on the best Kardashian, but he'd never worked out what. He'd thanked me for saving Callum's life.

We also did a full-on relationship dissection, which, it turns out, is easier to do when you're both being totally honest and not hiding strange superpowers. We'd reached the conclusion that our giant Great Wall of China sized barrier had been down to secrets on *both* sides and each of us pushing the other away. I wasn't sure we'd ever be girlfriend and boyfriend again, and I wasn't sure if I wanted to, though maaaaan, I missed the kissing, but it was amazing to have him back in my life, especially as he was the only one who truly understood my love of reality TV.

'There they are!' I heard Libby yell.

She ran over to us, closely followed by Summer, Bella, Mum, Andy, Neve and Nonna, who all pounced on us enthusiastically, gathering us into a massive, rugby-scrum hug. Their excited screeching was so high-pitched my ears started ringing.

'We've finished, we've finished, we've finished!' Summer sang, jumping up and down and taking us all with her, before grabbing Neve for a separate side-hug. The two of them had struck up quite the surfing-and-then-some relationship – to the point where neither of them could help grinning like lunatics every time they were in each other's presence.

'Guys, you'll wear Nonna out,' I said, managing to break free and take a breath.

Nonna looked offended. 'Give over. I'm fine, thank you very much.'

'You didn't need to come, you know,' I said. 'I don't think it's standard practice to have a celebration committee at the gates. I wouldn't have felt hard done by.'

'We wouldn't have missed it for the world,' Mum said.

'They made me come,' Bella added. 'Kidding – of course we all wanted to come.'

'Well done, guys!' Andy said, beaming with pride at all of us. He really was kind of sweet. And he was wearing a half-decent, pun-free T-shirt too.

'So, back to ours for pre-party partying?' Nonna asked.

Libby's eyes lit up and she linked arms with Nonna. 'Can we get the cauldron out again, pleeeeease?'

'Damn right we can,' Nonna said, with a huge grin and a glint in her eye.

It was one of Nonna's many party tricks – getting the cauldron out when my friends came round. When she was on her best behaviour, she used it to cook up a vat of hot chocolate. But when she was being mischievous (which was often) she liked using it to perform some wow-factor magic – even when the cauldron wasn't strictly necessary. Last time we'd had a horror movie sleepover we ended up having to sleep with all the lights on as she scared everyone so much with floating candles, talking paintings and a flock of birds circling the house (we were watching *The Birds*). She liked showing off – and she liked that she could now. And so did I.

'Oooh, and Jessie, can you do that thing where you change our hair colour again?' Summer asked, linking her arm in mine. 'That was awesome.'

'I don't care what else you do as long as you keep my skin clear,' Tabs said, linking my other arm.

'The summoning the animals thing was cool too,' Libby said.

I smiled at Nonna. My lessons had stepped up a gear and we had begun to test my powers. She trusted me fully now – and it showed.

'Let's just start with some food, shall we,' I said. 'I mean, like, normal, everyday, home-cooked food. I'm starving.'

'Maybe not cooked by me, though, hey?' Mum laughed.

'Man, for witches, you can be pretty boring sometimes,' Libby said.

Everyone laughed.

***

The fact that my friends knew about me – *everything* about me – and they still loved and accepted me had completely changed my life. For the first time in for ever I felt myself – a version of myself I hadn't even known existed. Secure, confident, loved and accepted . . . jaunty angles, supernatural powers and all. In a weird way, despite all the pain in the process, I knew I had Sloane to thank for that. Without her, half of me would still be lurking in the shadows.

I silently thanked her, wondering where she was and how she was doing, hoping she'd found some peace herself, somehow. I had a feeling we would meet again . . . but I knew that this time I'd be ready for her.

My mind flicked to Callum. He would've finished his exams two days ago, if he'd still been here. I could see his face from that day clearly, the sand in his hair, his lips tinged blue, I could still taste the salt water in the back of my throat, feel the burn of it in my sinuses. As with Sloane, I silently thanked him too and hoped that wherever he was, he was OK. I was less certain I would see him again.

'What's the serious face for, Jessie?' Summer asked, nudging me out of my reverie. 'We have some celebrating to do.'

'We definitely do,' I said. And she was right – there was a lot to celebrate. Exams were over, I'd come to my senses, Callum wasn't dead, and I had great family and great friends who knew the real me – warts and all – and loved me anyway.

Not literal warts though – please witch gods, don't give me those to deal with.

ACKNOWLEDGEMENTS

By some miracle, here I am again – another book down. Yay!

I am so lucky that my book two experience was as enjoyable as it was and not, as I was expecting, the hell-fest that writing a second book can be. The biggest thanks have to go to my amazing, talented, generous editor, Lena McCauley – for your encouragement, ideas and patience, for getting my jokes and for believing in me and Jessie enough to let me write another book in the first place! Massive thanks to everyone else at Hachette on Team *Hexed* – my PR and marketing megababes Lucy Clayton and Beth McWilliams for doing such an amazing job getting *Hexed* out there, my copy-editor Gen Herr for having the keenest eye for detail, Ruth Girmatsion for overseeing those final stages when I've read the book so many times the words blur into one, to my proofreader Cat Phipps for having a forensic spy level eye for detail and to my designer Alice Duggan for the gorgeously striking cover of both books. I've always felt super supported at Hachette and I appreciate how no one has ever complained (to me) about how much I email and all the silly questions I ask.

A whole stadium of thank yous to my wonderful agent Helen Boyle at Pickled Ink who has the patience of a saint and gives pep talks better than the pope. If the pope gives pep talks – I'm assuming he does? My point is, she's brilliant.

This last year and a bit has been an absolute blast for so many reasons, one of the biggest being getting to know other debut authors through the GoodShip Twitter group I had the good fortune to fall in with. They're an extremely talented, kind, generous, funny motley crew and if I'm ever confused, nervous, pissed off, excited or scared about something, I know someone there will help me in whatever way is needed – advice, empathy, resources, celebratory pineapple gifs or just some bad jokes. I am LOVING seeing the second wave (and third and fourth for some people) of your books coming out and you genuinely inspire me every day.

Talking of extremely talented, kind and generous authors – I'd also like to thank the lovely lot at UKYA – in particular Kat Ellis, Holly Race and Naomi Gibson for being so supportive and generally lovely. And a special shout-out to the dark and twisty horror YA peeps who have let me slip in on some of their events by virtue of the fact I have witches and despite the fact I am the biggest scaredy-cat going – thank you, Kat, Amy McCaw, Cynthia Murphy, Andreina Cordani, to name but a few – I have never read so much murder and bloodshed as I have in the past year! I blame my nightmares on you.

Continued, never-ending thanks to my Flugels – Claire Wetton and Catherine Coe – you guys rock and I adore you, but you already know that. To my 66% published crew – Becca Langton and Alice Ross – Alice, you're next, Becca you'll be soon – can't wait! To Kate Weston and Lucy Cuthew for your lovely quotes on book one – I admire you both hugely and was so, so pleased to have your support.

I promised myself I wouldn't write a thesis this time round so some final ones – big thank you to my Isle of Wight family and friends for all your encouragement and support – special thanks to Nola for driving me around to drop off proofs and for the general cheerleading and to Annie for being my unofficial Island PR and doing such a great job shouting about *Hexed*.

Thank you wholeheartedly, never-endingly and always to Will – for the time and the space to write, for the belief and the motivation and the tea and/or gin depending on what was needed! And to Hux and Coop – thank you for calming down on the wrestling outside my office door when it was needed – I appreciate it.

Lastly, and perhaps the absolute most mahoosive of thanks to everyone who read, reviewed, bought, sold (booksellers – I LOVE YOU), talked about and engaged with *Hexed*. I thought the biggest thrill would be seeing my name on a book in a bookshop, but it turns out it's actually hearing from people who have enjoyed and connected with the book. I so hope – am praying to all the awesome witches – that you enjoy this one too.

ADVOCACY, RESOURCES AND FURTHER READING

WEBSITES

everydaysexism.com
The Everyday Sexism Project was set up by Laura Bates as a place where women could record instances of the everyday sexism they experience no matter how big or small, knowing that it helps to feel heard and that we're in this together.

ukfeminista.org.uk
UK Feminista supports students and teachers to promote gender equality across education. Their website has lots of great resources for schools and individuals, and they also provide training and campaign for gender equality.

thefword.org.uk
An online magazine that covers all aspects of contemporary feminism including books, film and TV, politics, music and more. Run by volunteers and open to submissions.

fawcettsociety.org.uk
One of the OGs of feminist organisations, the Fawcett Society is a membership charity that campaigns for equal rights for women in all areas of life.

bloodygoodperiod.com

Brilliant charity who give period products for those
who can't afford them and provide menstrual education.
They're full on, fun and straight-talking, and are encouraging
us all to talk about periods more.

heygirls.co.uk

Hey Girls make chlorine and bleach free ethical
and environmentally friendly tampons and pads, AND
every time you buy a product, they donate one to girls
and women in need – what's not to love? Great products
and lots of period information on their site.

ohne.com

A brand that does great 100% organic tampons
and research-based period products to help you through
your cycle. Brilliant care bundles, a thriving community
and great period information too.

BOOKS

Girl Up by Laura Bates
You Got This by Bryony Gordon
Feminists Don't Wear Pink curated by Scarlett Curtis
Moxie by Jennifer Mathieu
Blood Moon by Lucy Cuthew
The Poet X by Elizabeth Acevedo
Bad Feminist by Roxane Gay
Diary of a Confused Feminist by Kate Weston
Instructions for a Teenage Armageddon by Rosie Day

After a brief (but fun) stint working in television and as a
primary school teacher, Julia Tuffs decided to take her writing
dreams more seriously. She lives in South West London with
her family and ragdoll cats (Billy and Nora) and spends her
time writing, reading, dreaming of holidays and watching too
much reality TV. She aims to write the kinds of books that
shaped and inspired her as a teenager.

The HEXED series (HEXED and TWICE HEXED) are
her first books for teens.

Find her on Twitter @JuliaTuffs